An Invitation to Port Berry

# An Invitation to Port Berry

## K.T. DADY

*Port Berry Book 2*

Choc Lit
A JOFFE BOOKS COMPANY

Choc Lit
*A Joffe Books company*
www.choc-lit.com

First published in Great Britain in 2024

© K.T. Dady 2024

Cover art by Dee Dee Book Covers

ISBN: 978-1781897393

*Acceptance changes the world.*

# CHAPTER 1

*Samuel*

Samuel Powell was on a video call, listening politely to Sophie Moore go on about salmon paste.

'People still eat it. What do you think, Mr Powell? My grandad loves a corned beef sarnie from time to time but much prefers fish paste. Ooh, should we get some sandwich spreads? I'm thinking costs will be low, and I'll be the one who . . .'

Her voice faded into the breeze coming through the open window of Samuel's home office. She really didn't need to pitch to him again. He'd already said yes more times than he'd cared to, and yet, there she was, on his computer screen, still going on about the food bank she was keen to start in the small fishing village where she lived, Port Berry.

Samuel had plans of his own, and she was pinching minutes that weren't allocated to her. He kept his sigh to himself, silently hurrying her along. A word with his PA would be in order if meetings weren't staying within their allocated slots.

He hated sloppiness and inefficiency, deeming that kind of behaviour a complete waste of time. Well, it certainly wasted his time anyway. 'Miss Moore, I'll see to it someone sends over a box of sandwich spreads. Now, if that's all, I—'

'Ooh, would you like to pop over yourself one day? You can—'

Never one for interruptions, Samuel gave her a taste of her own medicine, not that it seemed to bother her. 'Look at the time, Miss Moore. It really does run away with you, doesn't it? I'll have to go. Got another meeting in five.' He hoped that would do the trick.

Sophie's hand swirled around the tip of her dark ponytail. All very unprofessional in his opinion, and why on earth she was slouching over a commercial freezer was a question he couldn't be bothered to ask.

'You can call me Sophie,' she told him, sounding quite sweet, but not enough to lighten his bleak mood. She started rambling again, causing him to tap his foot beneath his shiny white desk.

'Sorry, got a call coming through.' He waggled his mobile, making sure she couldn't see the blank screen. 'Client is waiting.' She went to speak, but he cut off their video chat and took a much-needed calming breath.

He checked his online calendar, the contents of which he made it his business to know inside out, and was pleased to see his PA hadn't squeezed in any face-to-face meet-and-greets with Sophie Moore or anyone else at the Happy to Help Hub. He shut down his computer and headed out to the hallway.

Glass walls either side of the front door ensured sunrays swept over the large white floor tiles of the wide, open space.

Samuel opened a cupboard door, pressed a few numbers on a pad, and retrieved his car keys from the bunches in the key box as soon as it pinged open. Closing everything up and setting the alarm, he stepped outside into the warm daylight and jumped into his dark four-by-four.

As soon as he reached the closed gates at the end of the driveway, he remembered he didn't have his bottle of water. Chastising himself, still irritated because he was running late, he quickly headed back to retrieve the water from the fridge, before heading off once more.

*I am not feeling this today.*

The drive from his home in Penzance to Looe was proving his least favourite out of his recent trips, but needs must. He just hoped traffic was light.

At least his car was comfy, and he had his water, notebook, and pen. His little sister, Hannah, was out for the day with her art club, so he didn't have to worry about getting back for her, not that she needed him around fussing, as she often told him.

He flexed and unflexed his hands around the steering wheel and took some deep breaths. He knew why he was particularly twitchy right now. The ten-year anniversary of the death of their parents was fast approaching. He hated that day more than any other. He could still see the lorry . . .

Concentrating on the road ahead, Samuel hummed along to the soft instrumental jazz playing in the car. He needed to relax. It was all getting too much lately.

*Perhaps I should skip the drives for this month.*

Any excuse. June, October, December. It didn't matter when. If he wanted the result he was after, he couldn't put it off.

Before that fateful day he'd had a good life. University was fun, his circle small and friendly, and his part-time bar job close to his rented uni digs was a laugh a minute. He had no idea how everything could change so drastically within seconds.

Taking another deep breath he brought himself back to the task in hand and the drive. He reflected that being midweek, the roads weren't too bad.

\* \* \*

Samuel had reached his destination. An old white sign staked to the ground many moons ago was pointing right, telling all, Looe was in that direction, but his car purred away upon the grassy verge, unmoving through lack of instruction.

Samuel swallowed hard, then reached for his notebook and pen on the seat to his side. He scribbled down how he was feeling, how long the feeling lasted, and on a scale on one to ten how high his fear was.

*Four. Not bad.*

Even though his fear level wasn't that high, was it low enough to get him to cross the invisible line? That annoying road sign had been tormenting him all week, beckoning him closer. All he had to do was drive forward.

*Come on, Sam.*

He returned his hands to the steering wheel and forced his tight grip to relax. He put his foot on the accelerator, gently guiding his vehicle to the crossroads, then he indicated right, drove past the road sign and stopped on the grassy verge the other side, pleasantly surprised at himself.

*Bloody hell! I did it.*

Drawing in a huge gulp of air, he wrote down how he was feeling, put the notebook and pen back on the seat, turned the car around, and headed home. His mission for today was complete. Next time, he'd try for the next road, and one day, he'd make it all the way into Looe and perhaps stop for a coffee. Yes, that would be nice. Once he got used to travelling to that place, he would move on to the next, but for now, he had a win. Small but helpful.

Samuel drove home trying for elation and victory, but all he felt was fed up and useless. He was doing something positive to beat his condition, but it never seemed to spark joy. His frustration and lack of patience interfered on every level. The only ones to praise him were his sister, and his former therapist, who had now moved away. He missed having an expert to talk to about the matter, but at least he knew what he had to do to help tackle the issue. All he wanted was a normal life. One that didn't have him take stupid, boring journeys to places he didn't actually want to visit.

He told himself to stop being so miserable and to smile, but his grimace in the rear-view mirror didn't help matters.

'Enough!' he yelled, then counted to ten, controlling his breathing.

There were things in his life that were blessings, and it was time to focus on them instead. It often helped relieve the anxiety and anger. Sophie Moore talking about salmon paste came to mind, making him crinkle his brow. He shook it off, not allowing the slight twitch in the corner of his mouth to spread.

*Oh, what a morning.*

Perhaps he would take a trip next door to Port Berry and check out their drop-in hub. At least then he might get fish paste out of his head. Although, it was better than wallowing in his agoraphobia.

He huffed out his frustration as he thought about that stupid sign to Looe that he was sure he would knock seven bells out of one day. It even entered his dream the other night, chasing him down the road, leaving him waking in a pool of sweat. Seriously, that sign had to go, or perhaps it wouldn't bother him so much if he could just get a mile or two past its existence.

Samuel's shoulders sagged. Exposure therapy was starting to give him the right hump. Why couldn't the healing journey be as pleasant as it sounded? Thoughts of quitting filled him, as it did every time he attempted to fight his irritation.

It was decided. He'd go check out the Hub, then go home. After all, it was only a matter of time before he was sipping a hot beverage along the coast of Looe. He'd made it everywhere else he'd attempted so far, so he'd make it there as well. Then he'd find a new spot until the whole of Cornwall had been completed.

'Bloody nightmare,' he mumbled, giving the cream steering wheel a thump with his right hand.

It was all well and good having these big ideas, but he knew when it came down to the practice part of his therapy, it wasn't as easy as it seemed.

'Argh!' Samuel yelled through gritted teeth. Perhaps an hour in the gym would be best before work. Being a bear with a sore head never went down well with clients, and the way he was feeling, he could happily chew someone's head clean off.

*Breathe. Just breathe. Everything will be . . . What the hell . . .*

To his astonishment, a woman in a racing wheelchair was powering along in the middle of the narrow lane in front of him, seemingly without a care in the world.

Samuel swore under his breath at what he deemed reckless and stupid. Could she not see how dangerous her actions were? She was low to the ground, and the big vehicle he was driving could squish her in seconds, then what? Roadkill, that's what. Well, not on his watch. He had enough on his plate as it was without her causing him more mental health issues.

As the road widened, she stopped and looked down at her left wheel. Samuel wondered if she was all right. He pulled up and jumped out to ask, holding his hand up as though on lollipop duty as he approached.

Rosy cheeks, sea-blue eyes, and an aggravated frown met him head on. 'What are you doing?' she snapped before he could speak.

Samuel almost choked on his scoff of a laugh as he slapped his chest. 'What am I doing? What about you?' He watched her glare at her left wheel before scowling his way again.

'I'm exercising. This is a racing wheelchair. It can go on roads and terrain and—'

'How about you take it off-road before you get yourself killed.'

'I'm perfectly safe, thank you very much. You're the only road hog causing problems around here.'

Samuel splayed his arms. 'Road hog? Are you kidding me right now?'

'Entitled much!' she yelled.

'Are you insane? Look around you. You're in the middle of the bloody road. Look at the size of my car. Had I not been paying attention, I could have run straight into you. Think about those kinds of consequences for a moment.'

'I know all about those kinds of consequences, thank you. How do you think I ended up in this thing in the first place.'

Samuel lowered his voice. 'I'm sorry.'

'It's okay,' she replied in the same tone.

He watched in silence as she settled back in her chair, taking deep breaths and loosening her grip on the push rims. If it were Hannah exercising, he'd want her to be on a safer road. 'Look,' he said, keeping his voice low in an attempt to reason with her.

'Look nothing,' she snapped. 'Just get out of my way. You have no business stopping women going about their day.'

Just for a moment, she rendered him speechless. Part of him wanted to leave her to it. Why should he care? Because he would want someone to care if it were his sister, that's why.

His heartbeat calmed. 'I'm just concerned,' he said softly.

She seemed to stare at him for a moment before getting ready to leave. 'I'm fine.'

Samuel stepped closer, blocking her path. 'You're being inconsiderate.'

'Me?'

He nodded. 'Yes, you. What if I had run you over, hmm? Then what? I would have to live with that.'

She gestured to the road. 'It's broad daylight, and I'm clearly visible.'

'You're low to the ground and this road is quite narrow in places. You get idiot drivers racing around here.'

'I do know,' she mumbled, but he heard.

'Why don't you just exercise somewhere safer?'

She pointed forward. 'I'm heading for the coastal path.'

'You can get to that without being on this road.'

'Yes, I know, but I'm here for a reason.' She grabbed her rims and set off around him.

He huffed, then sprinted to her side, but she carried on ignoring him, which was way more irritating than when she was defending herself. He moved in front of her — foolishly — causing both an emergency stop and a whack in the shins for his own stupidity.

*Ow!*

He took another calming breath and pursed his lips into a tight smile. 'This road is known to be dangerous for cyclists, and they're up higher than you. I'm just trying to help.'

'Thank you, but I don't need your help.' Her words were soft but firm, giving him no alternative but to back off.

However, Samuel Powell was no pushover. Being a businessman gave him transferrable skills, and making deals was something he could do in his sleep. Only, she wasn't a client, and by the look in those beautiful eyes of hers, she wasn't about to listen to anything more he had to say, but he still had to try. 'Would you let me drive behind you until you get to the turn off? My car can be your shield.'

She gave the smallest shrug with one shoulder. 'If it makes you feel better.'

He tipped his head her way, smiled, not allowing it to hit his eyes, then clambered back into his vehicle and waited until she was ready.

She glanced over her shoulder, looking unsure about his motives, then set off.

Samuel hummed to himself as he guarded her with his four-by-four all the way to the coastal path. There was no way her death was going to be on his mind all night.

The sporty wheelchair took off along the hard terrain, and he could see her arm muscles flexing, no doubt burning frustrated energy — exactly what he needed to do.

Winding up his side window, he headed home, happy she was safe, fed up he had bothered to stop in the first place, and completely annoyed on every level that the stranger had somehow managed to get under his skin, make him curse, and, worst of all, cause a tiny flutter to hit his heart.

*Nope! Just nope, nope, nope.*

# CHAPTER 2

*Lottie*

As soon as Lottie was sure the man with the gorgeous amber eyes had driven off, she brought her wheelchair to a halt. Her body was shaking from the adrenaline rush, and her arms ached from adding a sprint into her efforts.

'Argh!' she quietly vented. No one was around, but it didn't matter. She still wasn't up for a massive scream.

For months, Lottie had planned today's trip. Not even her brother, Spencer, knew her plan. He'd be just as infuriating as the road bloke, all huff and puff and no understanding. It had to be done. It was the only way.

There was a young man back in hospital who had a fear about being in the sea again after he'd hurt his back from a dive. She'd heard someone tell him he had to get straight back out there else he would always have that fear, and the longer it went on, the harder it would be to get over. Right there and then, she was determined to get back on the same stretch of road she had been run down on. Being stopped by a tall stranger with a swoon-worthy smile fit for any romance film wasn't part of the plan.

Lottie stared out at the view of the sea. 'Flipping heck!' she mumbled, biting her lip so as not to laugh.

The trip over had been relatively easy. Her new sporty wheelchair took some getting used to, but all in all, she was fine. Gratitude filled her, causing tears to blur her eyes for a moment as she touched on her achievement. She was so lucky she didn't have the fear the man in hospital had. Sure, there were a few nerves, but nothing she couldn't handle.

Relief hit her next, swiftly followed by happiness. She blew a kiss to the sky, believing her deceased aunt helped get her to the coastal path in one piece.

'Yes, I know I shouldn't have been on that road, and I promise I'll take the safer route back,' she said, looking up at the clear blue sky.

The man with the neat dark hair was back in her thoughts, not that he went too far since they went separate ways. It was kind of sweet the way he shielded her along the road. She so wanted to report back to her friends but that would mean full disclosure, then they'd all tell her off for going about her quest alone, and Spencer would flip his lid.

'I think we'll keep this between you and me, Auntie Rebecca.' She winked at the sky, then bent to pat a golden spaniel that had trotted over to say hello.

The dog ran off, and Lottie waved to the owners ambling in the near distance. It was time for her to head home.

She was happy about her completed task and surprised the big vehicle that had followed her didn't trigger anything negative, seeing how it was the same sort of car that had knocked her off her bicycle and put her in a wheelchair. She had come a long way since that day, and it was a wonderful feeling to know she was doing so well.

After the morning she'd had, she fancied a moment relaxing, and seeing as Spencer was busy training a teenager at their flower shop who wanted some work experience, she knew she could go straight home, get out of the racing wheelchair, and hang out in the garden for a bit before getting changed to head off for her lunch date.

Thoughts of her small greenhouse kept her company on the shortcut to her home on Berry Hill. The lettuce in particular was coming along nicely. With small batches of salad growing, Lottie's plan to hand out fresh food to her neighbours who lived alone, like her, was looking good.

Her neighbour and friend George was out in his back garden enjoying the warm June sunshine when she got back.

Having replaced a few of the six-foot fences with a low two-foot border, George was now able to help Lottie there if needed.

From the moment they came to live with their aunt when Lottie was two and Spencer eight, George Watson had been like family, even more so when their aunt passed away, and Lottie appreciated him so much. He was the dad she never had, and she figured he enjoyed making a fuss because he lived alone with no family to visit. Plus, he was Rebecca's best friend, so he took it upon himself to carry on where she left off.

'What you up to today, little miss?' asked George, stepping over a shrub to help open the door to the greenhouse so she could enter with ease in her new day-to-day electric wheelchair that the residents of Port Berry had bought her as a surprise through a recent fundraising event.

'I'm going to make a list of everyone local who might like some of my veg from time to time. Small portions for one.' She beamed his way, happy he held an approving smile.

'Well, it suits us, doesn't it? So, why not others. Good plan. I'll come out with you on some of your rounds.'

Lottie looked over the small spring onions growing. 'So much can go to waste when you live alone and the only option is to buy more than you need because the packaging contains a lot.'

'Ooh, yeah. I've been down that road. You can buy a small pack of mixed veg for stews, but they don't seem to do much like that when it comes to salad around here. Only those bags that go soggy after being opened for two days. Well, that's no good for anyone, is it?'

'No. That's why I thought I could add some to the food bank every so often. It's important to get your five a day in, right, George?'

His cheery face looked happier than normal, and Lottie wondered why.

'What are you grinning about, George? You look as chuffed as a cat with a ball of wool.'

George chuckled. 'I wasn't going to say till tonight, but I might as well spit it out now.'

Lottie laughed at his obvious excitement about something, and, yes, he was right to spit it out, as there was no way she would be able to hang on till their scheduled games night. 'Come on, George, you're killing me.'

He leaned closer, glancing around as though a nosey neighbour might be earwigging from behind the fence. 'I won some money on the lottery. Didn't want to say till it was in my bank, in case I jinxed it or something. Anyway, that's the last of my mortgage paid off now.' He pointed back at his house. 'I'm officially the full owner.'

Tugging him low so she could throw her arms around his shoulders, Lottie cheered. 'That's brilliant, George. I'm so happy for you.' She felt his sigh and pulled back to meet his warm eyes.

When Rebecca died, her life insurance had covered her home and shop, so Lottie and Spencer never had to worry about those bills. It was nice to witness someone else feeling relieved to pay off a debt.

'We should celebrate tonight with pizza and your favourite cider.' Lottie gestured to his home. 'I'll get Spencer to join in with games night as well.'

'Oh, I don't mind him off on his dates.'

Lottie raised her eyebrows. 'I think we both know he doesn't date. Hook-ups are more his style, and anyway, he doesn't go out as much as he used to since my accident. He seems content living alone in our little flat above our shop.' The glow in her face faded as she stared at one of the wheels on her chair.

'He's growing up, Lottie. Nothing to do with you, so don't you start with the blaming again. Probably reached a stage in his life where he wants a bit more peace. Now, tell me, why aren't you at work today?'

'I wanted to try out my new racing chair to see how I got on exercising that way.'

'And did you conquer that road where you got knocked down?' He gave her a knowing look.

'How did you . . . I didn't tell . . .' She grinned while shaking her head. 'I swear, there's no one on this planet who knows me better than you.'

George indicated towards the back door of the house. 'I remember you going down Berry Hill on your skateboard and falling off and spraining your wrist. Before it was better, you were off on that thing again. It's a steep hill, and one that scared many a kid, but not you, little miss. You've been up and down that road on roller skates and bikes, never one to let fear stand in your way.'

It was true. Lottie never did let the hill get the better of her, even in her manual wheelchair.

'I had to do it, George. And I knew I was being reckless using that road, but no one would understand that I needed to face where I was hit. It's hard to explain, but it made sense to me.'

'And that's all that matters. And look, here you are, back in one piece.' His eyes narrowed. 'Did it go smoothly?'

Lottie immediately saw amber eyes scowling. 'Yes,' she decided, as talking about the four-by-four tailing her would only worry George — leading him to call the police, no doubt. No harm came to her, so it was best to just forget the whole thing ever happened. The stranger was just a busybody on his high horse, thinking he knew best.

It was really annoying having the tall man with the stern voice at the front of her mind. She promptly brushed him off. She'd lived in Port Berry all her life and had never seen him before, so the chances of bumping into him again were slim to none. There was therefore zero point to thinking about him even if he did intrigue her. Anyway, she had a lunch date to get ready for.

* * *

The ride down Berry Hill in her new electric wheelchair was so much better than using her manual one. And going back up would forever be a breeze.

Lottie had never paid too much attention before to the steep road on which her lemon-washed harbour house sat. She'd lived there since she was a nipper and had been up and down that hill more times than she could count, even messing about in a pram with her big brother chasing her, wanting his turn.

Her first attempt of wheeling her manual chair up the slope had been a nightmare. She was flushed, sweating, had pains shooting up her arms, and was sure she would roll back to the bottom and tip, but after a while, she grew fitter and stronger, and the hill wasn't as tough. The fancy-schmancy electric wheelchair she was comfortably snuggled into made navigating the hill so much easier.

The sun was shining high in the sky, warming her body and soul. Oh, how Lottie Jordan loved summer. It was her favourite season, and June her favourite month. She had a feeling something good was close by. Anything after being knocked off her bicycle in January the previous year and ending up with a spinal cord injury that took away the use of her legs was an improvement.

Lottie happily purred along Harbour End Road, where her flower shop was, but she wasn't going to pop into Berry Blooms.

For the past couple of weeks, she'd been chatting to men on an online dating site, and so far a few of them had asked to meet her in person.

Russ, her ex, had left her, stating he couldn't cope with her no longer being able to walk, and she quickly realized he only ever adored the beauty queen side to her. A trophy girlfriend on his arm. She still had her looks, but it didn't matter to Russ.

There was no way Lottie was going to cry over him anymore. No, sir! It was time to find someone else she could happily spend the rest of her life with, and the dating site was a good start. She hoped.

Andrew seemed nice online and was happy to drive to her neck of the woods for a coffee at Harbour Light Café, which Lottie suggested, as it belonged to her good friend Ginny. If she was going to meet strangers, it was best she did it in a safe environment close to home.

Because the weather was so nice, tables and chairs were placed outside the café, and Lottie secured herself one furthest from the door.

Ginny came out with a food order for another table, then smiled at Lottie as she approached. 'You all right, chick?'

Lottie nodded, glancing over her friend's red tea dress. She so wished she had Ginny's confidence to wear clothes that weren't the latest fashion. In Ginny's case, anything 1940s.

Ginny perused the harbour. 'He not here yet?'

'No. I'm a bit early.'

'Okay. I'll bring you out a tea. Won't be a sec.'

Lottie straightened her pink floral top, pleased with her choice of outfit, and waited patiently for her date to arrive.

*I should have told him about the wheelchair.*

The worry was creeping up on her. What would he say? And would he listen to her explanation of why she kept that part of her life hidden? She felt so deceitful, but she had her reasons. After Russ, she wanted to make sure someone could love her just for herself and not because she was pretty, as people always mentioned on first seeing her. Surely the wheelchair wouldn't be too much of a problem.

A young man around her age approached, smiling and holding a bunch of pink roses. His dark eyes dropped to her side, and his cheerfulness turned to a frown of confusion, then annoyance.

'Hello,' said Lottie, swallowing hard. 'Andrew, right?' They'd spoken via video chat before, so she knew what he looked like but still felt the need for confirmation. Especially because she hadn't seen him angry before and that certainly seemed to be the look he was sporting now.

Andrew nodded, eyes still on her wheel poking out from the table. 'Why are you in a wheelchair? What happened?' He spoke quickly and remained standing.

With her chin raised and tensed shoulders, Lottie went all in. 'I was knocked off my bike last year and now I can't walk.'

'Is it temporary?'

'No.'

Andrew's flower-holding hand dropped to his side, taking the blooms with it. 'And you didn't think to mention this?'

'You seem angry.'

'That's because I am. I came all the way here to meet you, only to find out you're in a wheelchair.'

'Does it matter?'

'Yes. It flaming-well does. You kept it hidden, which means you're a liar.' Andrew turned sharply, tossed the flowers into the mesh bin along the pavement, and stomped off.

Lottie took a breath, ignoring the couple at the next table whispering while peering her way. There was no way she would allow her trembling lip to take control of the situation. She'd known there was a real chance the news of her legs wouldn't go down well, so it didn't come as a total shock.

Ginny came out with a pot of tea for one. 'Still no sign?' she asked, placing down the tray.

'He took one look at my wheels and scarpered. I don't blame him. I wasn't exactly honest.' Perhaps she deserved it for not telling him beforehand. She'd decided when arranging the dates that she wasn't going to tell any of the other men lined up for dates either. The hope had been that one of them would surely like her for who she was and not see the chair.

Ginny pointed at the roses stuffed into the bin. 'He never did that, did he?'

Lottie shrugged as she nodded, then watched Ginny retrieve the blooms.

'Here, Lott, you can sell these in your shop later.' Ginny reached over and lightly tapped her hand. 'His loss, eh, chick?'

'I didn't tell him about the chair, Gin. I haven't told any of them. I know it might make me out to be some sort of fraud, but I just want someone to like me and not care about anything else. Is that too much to ask?' Ooh, that stupid lip was quivering again.

'Hey, don't you stress,' said Ginny. 'You're beautiful inside and out, and you're in your prime!'

Lottie scoffed. 'In my prime?'

'Twenty-nine, Lott. That's prime, right there. Wait till you're thirty-four like me — then you can have a sulk about being on your lonesome.'

'You can sign up for online dating too, Gin,' Lottie said with a grin.

Ginny laughed. 'No, thanks. Anyway, when have I got time? I'm always busy with Mum and this place.' She lightly touched Lottie's shoulder. 'In all seriousness, are you okay?'

Lottie raised her chin. 'You know what, I've had a great day today, and I'm not about to let this get me down. I'm on a mission to get on with my life, so onwards and upwards.'

'Good for you.'

Lottie sighed. 'I might as well head to work, seeing how I've not got a date now.'

'Nah, you stay here, chick. Spencer can cope. Sit and have your lunch in the sun. I'll bring you something out. What do you fancy?'

'Not Andrew, that's for sure.' Lottie shared a laugh with her friend before ordering fish fingers, chips, and beans. Whenever she felt down as a child, her aunt would serve up that dish and all would be right in the world again.

Ginny headed back inside, and the couple at the next table went back to their own business.

Lottie gazed out to sea, wondering if her aunt was looking down on her now.

*Oh, Rebecca, what would you say?*

A light warm breeze blew her strawberry-blonde hair away from her face. She quickly repositioned her fringe, then sipped her tea.

Never mind her aunt, Spencer wouldn't be best pleased when he found out she was out and about meeting men from a dating site. Not that she was going to tell him just yet. That was one conversation that could wait. He was only six years older but acted as though he were her dad at times. Nope, her brother making a fuss could definitely wait.

Lottie's thoughts turned back to her date who had dumped her before he'd even sat down. Was that some sort of record? It occurred to her to cancel the rest of the week, but she didn't want to judge all men by Andrew. And Russ.

She twiddled with her teacup while watching the boats in the harbour. Port Berry had a way of making her feel calm. The quaintness, the tranquillity, the community. When the weather was on side, she really could simply sit there for hours and just watch the world go by.

Ginny plonking a plate full of hot food on the table made Lottie jump out of her daydream of frolicking in the waves with a man who loved her.

Lottie reached for her purse. 'How much do I owe you, Gin?'

Ginny's hazel eyes glistened more than the tips of the sea. 'You'll never guess what. Some bloke only went and paid for your meal before he left.'

'What? Who? Why?' Lottie's head was darting left and right.

'Not seen him before, but he had that suave sexy CEO vibe, without the tie. Anyway, I asked him what his game was, and he said he saw what that Andrew idiot did to you outside.'

'Oh.'

'Yeah, big oh.' Ginny scanned the harbour. 'Did he not come say hi?'

'I've not seen anyone.' She sighed, wishing she'd noticed Mr CEO. Perhaps he would have been a better date.

# CHAPTER 3

*Samuel*

Samuel looked around the small back room of the Happy to Help Hub in Port Berry. He was sure the area couldn't store much, and the front wasn't much bigger. He figured the place must have once belonged to one of the adjoining shops, unless some of the premises along Harbour End Road were that small.

A couple of years ago when he came up with the idea for the Food Bank Café, he knew straight away it had to be in a new building in Penzance, and he was so pleased when it opened. He didn't want an old café feel like the one a few doors down, where he'd just had lunch. Not that there was anything wrong with Harbour Light Café. He found it had a warm and friendly feel about the place, and he thought the nautical theme was fitting.

Sophie was standing in front of him, all animated arms and non-stop talking. She sounded desperate for help and guidance on the food bank matter, and in all honesty, he couldn't blame her. The state the country was in, with the cost of living seeming to rise every five minutes, was it any wonder someone knocked on his door for help?

There were four brown boxes on the side, overloaded with food donations already, which Sophie proudly announced. But what more could be done with such a tiny space?

Samuel missed half of what Sophie jabbered on about, focusing only on the business side of things. The Hub was there as a go-to for those in need, and he'd heard about the recent homeless man its existence had helped. The food side would have to stay small. There was no way they could offer what his place did, unless they put their local café to good use. He decided to leave that up to them. For now, Sophie seemed keen to start finding out who in her own community needed feeding.

'I think you're right to check on the housebound first, Miss Moore.'

'Sophie.' She smiled as she turned.

The twenty-seven-year-old fishmonger intrigued him. He'd worked with executive business people with less enthusiasm. It was energizing to see someone so upbeat and determined.

Her green eyes were boring into him as though waiting for a response, so he figured he must have zoned out again.

'Hmm,' was his non-committal sound.

'I've put word out all over Port Berry, and the local supermarket are placing a crate out by their front door for donations, thanks to you speaking to them.'

'You're welcome.'

'I tried, but they ignored me. Anyway, there's a flower shop along here, Berry Blooms, and they have a delivery van we can use for getting about. Once we've got more supplies, we can start making up the food parcels. When I say we, I mean the volunteers here, not you.'

He flashed her one of his work smiles.

'Oh, and thanks for lending us Kaz to help out. She came in handy, advising us on shopping lists. I have those printed out now.'

'It's best to keep to non-perishable goods here. At the café, we can use fresh food because our cooks make use of it straight away.'

'I wish we could ask the local farms for their produce, but I can see how that might be a bit much for us right now.'

'Baby steps, Miss Moore.'

'Sophie. Yes, definitely no running before walking.' She let out a hushed squeal while clutching her hands together in front of her chest. 'It's exciting, isn't it, Samuel? I mean helping people, not them starving.'

He stepped out into the main area of the Hub, giving the impression he was checking out the framed affirmations on the wall, but his mind was elsewhere, thinking about the time charity workers helped feed him when his world went to pot and his sister was in a recovery centre after the accident. He hadn't told Hannah about Port Berry yet.

While he was thinking about the conversation he would have at dinner that night with his little sister, Sophie was still chatting merrily away about who knows what. He needed to get his head in the game before he came across as rude, which he was sure he already had, not that it seemed to faze the woman. She was definitely on a mission. He knew all about that adrenaline rush. Starting the Food Bank Café was probably the last time he truly felt pumped.

'I'll have some fruit brought over. Apples and oranges last a good few days. If you know of any older residents who need help, check what they can eat. They—'

'Might have dietary requirements due to their medication and stuff.'

He really did hate being interrupted, and she certainly had a habit of doing exactly that. Letting it slide, because her excitement was clear, he made his way to the door. 'I'll visit another time if you—'

'Oh yes. Please do.'

*Right!*

'See you soon, Miss Moore.' He ignored her saying her first name again as he stepped out into the sunshine. When it came to anything linked to business, he didn't like lines to become blurred. In his work circle, everyone knew their place and it made life simple.

* * *

The lady in the wheelchair was still sitting outside the café. He stared at the back of her frame for a moment before heading to his car, shaking off the memory of the man with the roses dumping her on the spot. Had someone done that to his sister, they would have got a right hook.

Starting the engine, he smiled to himself, hoping she at least enjoyed the meal he'd paid for. The least he could do after arguing with her in the road that morning.

The drive along the country lanes back to his home in the neighbouring town was peaceful, and the tension in his neck eased.

A minibus sporting large colourful flowers on its sides was just pulling out of his gates as he arrived. He waved to the driver, then headed inside, pleased his sister was home earlier than expected. Schedules didn't matter when it came to her. Hannah was top priority, always.

The large door to his house was wide open, revealing Hannah sitting on the bottom steps of the swirl of a staircase, removing both her prosthetic legs.

'Ooh, I'll be glad to get in my chair.' She indicted to the electric wheelchair to her side.

'Are you sore, Hannah? I'll get your cream.'

'No, it's okay. I'm just a bit achy. Help me up, and I'll tell you all about my day.'

Samuel helped his sister into the wheelchair and placed her prosthetic limbs in the cupboard in the hallway. 'I wasn't expecting you back so soon.'

'Someone got sick, so we agreed to call it a day.'

'Did you get much painting done?'

Hannah's state-of-the-art wheelchair glided with ease across the shiny floor, entering the kitchen. 'I did, but I left them back at the centre. I might finish the ones I have here tomorrow.' She yawned and stretched her arms. 'Not sure yet. Might have a pool day.' She beamed a smile, which always made her nose crinkle and her whole face come alive. Something they did not share.

Samuel ran a hand through his dark locks, joining in her second yawn. 'Seems as though we're both having an early night.'

'I'll have an early dinner, if that's all right with you.'

'Haven't you eaten?'

'We only had a light lunch, and I forgot to take snacks.'

'How many times do I have to tell you to make a list?'

Hannah opened the fridge, leaning closer inside. 'I do in my head.'

'I should get you a PA.'

'Goodness, no.' She yawned again and closed the fridge door, without taking anything out.

'There's pizza in the freezer. Do you want that with some salad?'

'Ooh, lovely.'

'Get out the way then. Let the master chef through.'

Hannah laughed. 'Hey, I cook better than you. Even got a certificate that says so.' She pointed to the wall where it was mounted in a silver frame that matched the white and chrome oversized room.

'How can I ever compete with that?'

'You can't.' Hannah went over to the large white table. 'Give me a sec and I'll help with the food.'

'Speaking of food,' said Samuel, getting on with his task. 'I'm helping to open a small food bank over in Port Berry. They don't have much room. Just a walk-in hub, but it all helps.'

'That's great. I'll pop over one day.' She twiddled with a grey placemat on the table. 'Sam, I want to talk to you about something.'

He stopped unpacking the pizza from its box and turned immediately. 'What's wrong?'

'Nothing to worry about. It's just, well, I've been thinking about moving out.'

He didn't see that one coming and had no idea what to say. It was the first time she'd brought the subject to the table, and he wasn't sure what brought it on.

Hannah dropped her shoulders. 'Don't look like that. I'm twenty-five now, and I can take care of myself, and, well, I, well . . .' Her voice trailed off, making him paranoid.

'Spit it out, Hannah. You obviously have something more to say.'

Her light-brown eyes lowered to her lap as she cleared her throat. 'You're thirty, Sam.'

He tightened his brow at the strange comment. What that had to do with anything was beyond him. He waited for her to elaborate, but she remained silent. 'And . . .' he urged.

'And you've been my guardian since Mum and Dad died.'

Samuel switched the oven on. 'Get to the point, Hannah.'

'I feel I might be in your way now.'

'Why would you suddenly feel that?'

'It was just a conversation I had today with some of the others from the centre. Somebody was talking about their situation, and it got me thinking about you.'

Samuel prepared the pizza and opened a packet of cheese crackers for her to pick at while she waited for her dinner to cook. He tipped them into a bowl and handed them over, with raised eyebrows and a glint of humour in his amber eyes.

'I don't know why you find this funny,' she said, slapping his hand away from the bowl of snacks.

'All I want to know is, do you actually want to move out?' The moment of silence answered that question. 'You don't have to go anywhere until you're ready, Hannah. Or,' he added, waving her way, 'I could move out, and you can keep this place. It makes no odds. This house belongs to us both.'

'You bought this.'

'With *our* money.'

'Your money. You made it. Not me.'

'For us. It's ours.' He scuffed her hair, just as he did when she was a kid, as it still made her laugh.

'Be serious, Sam.'

He sat by her side, giving her his full attention, even though he was grinning to lighten the conversation. 'Talk to me.'

'You might want a partner one day. A proper one, you know, to live with.'

'And?'

'Well, you won't want me here.'

'Says who?'

'Okay, well, she might not want me here.'

'Then she can bugger off. This is your house not hers.'

Hannah sighed. 'Sam—'

'No, Hannah. We're a team, and this is our home. I'm not going anywhere without you, and when the time comes when you want to live alone or with someone else, that will be fine. But, only when you want, not think you should. Got it?'

She nodded and smiled. 'At the rate you're going, I probably will be the one to get a partner first.'

'Good. I hope you'll be very happy together . . . Wait, are you trying to tell me something?' The blush in her cheeks told a story. 'Hannah?'

'No. I mean, I have met someone, but it's early days, and I'm not thinking about living with him yet.'

Samuel wanted to act normal, so he went over to the work-top to continue with dinner, passing her a knife and cucumber so she could join in with preparing the salad. He had always hoped his sister would one day find a partner and live a happy life, but there was no way in a million years he wouldn't worry about her. The questions about the man she was seeing burned his brain, but he remained calm and started to chop lettuce.

Hannah burst out laughing. 'I so know you have questions.'

Samuel wasn't biting. He carried on chopping.

'He's from the Sunshine Centre. He likes art too,' she added.

*I bet he does.*

'You'll like him, Sam, but I'm not ready for you to interrogate him yet. So, another time, yeah?'

'Okay.'

'I mean it, Sam. No PI stuff. I don't want you checking him out.'

He turned, raising his sharp knife. 'I did that one time, and rightly so. He was after your money, Hannah. You have to be careful. Please try to remember you're a millionaire.'

'Well, Felix isn't after my money.' She quickly slapped her hand over her mouth.

'Felix, eh?'

Hannah tossed a cracker at him, making him laugh.

'Will he be at the Port Berry Craft Fayre? That's coming up soon.'

'Oh, flipping heck!' Hannah's laugh was muffled as she shoved a piece of cucumber into her mouth. 'Leave him alone.'

'I'll just say a polite hello and be on my way.'

'At least you'll get to meet my friends if you come along.'

Samuel scoffed. 'I always come to the centre's events and art shows.'

'Yes, but you never mingle like a normal person.'

'No one is there to chat to me. They want to see the art or whatever. Anyway, I know some of your friends.'

'Oh yeah, name one.'

Samuel chewed on some cucumber, stalling for time. He was sure he knew some names, after all, he had spoken to people at her centre. Hadn't he?

Hannah huffed. 'See!'

'Rosie.'

'Poppy, you mean.'

He raised a finger. 'Huh!'

'I would be able to name all your mates, if you had any.'

Samuel clutched his chest, mocking hurt, then straightened. 'Ooh, wasn't there a Charlotte?'

'Nooo, but there is a newbie called Lottie. She doesn't come often, due to work, but she's nice. You'll meet her at the fayre, as she'll be there selling her pictures too, which reminds me. I really need to get my list of paintings sorted so I know what I'm showcasing. See, I can do lists.'

'Good to know. I'll help. Unless of course Felix is now your right-hand man.'

Hannah rolled her eyes as she laughed. 'We really need to get you a proper girlfriend. You haven't had one since your uni days.'

'I'm happy on my own, thanks.'

'But then you'll have someone else to annoy.'

'I have Felix now.'

Hannah tossed another cracker his way, which Samuel caught and shoved in his mouth.

There was no room for anyone else in his life. The last thing he needed was someone else to worry about, even though it would be nice to have a hand to hold at times. He shrugged off the thought, swapping it for his concerns about Felix.

# CHAPTER 4

*Lottie*

'Oh, George, it's brilliant. I can't thank you enough.' Lottie beamed at the cart he'd made to attach to the front of her electric wheelchair so she could collect and deliver food donations locally; she was determined to play a part that didn't confine her to the Hub. With George's marvellous invention, she could whizz about, going door to door spreading the word and visiting those who had called with offers and requests.

'Well, you said the other day you wanted to deliver some food. I figured this would make life easier.'

As soon as the cart was in place, Lottie set off on her quest. Bay View would be her first port of call, as she pretty much knew everyone along that road.

Not all the homes were accessible, she came to realize. It would have been hard to knock on some of the doors anyway, but with the cart stuck out in front of the chair, it was near on impossible.

She petted Trixie the cat outside number four, hoping her owner would peer out of her nets and dash out for a chat. Mrs Hopkin normally did.

Lottie's shoulders slumped. 'I'm not having much luck today, Trixie.' She went to head off to the next house when her name was called.

'Coo-ee, Lottie.'

She turned her head to see Mrs Hopkin walking down her pathway, then noticed Luna behind her. 'Hello, ladies. I'm collecting for the food bank. Got any tins?'

Mrs Hopkin pointed back at her house. 'Ooh, I've got a little tin of tuna. Trixie won't mind donating one of her treats, will you, Trixie-wixie?'

The ginger cat meowed, and Lottie suspected old Trixie minded very much.

Mrs Hopkin headed back inside as Luna stepped closer to nose in Lottie's cart.

'That's a fancy contraption you've got there, love.'

Lottie grinned at the cuddly old lady who was the grandmother of her friend Alice. 'George made it. It's great, isn't it?'

'Hmm, well, it's something. You be careful. You're not a train.'

Lottie laughed. 'Is that one of your psychic warnings?'

Luna's midnight-blue eyes narrowed. 'The only warning I'm giving you is about those men you keep meeting.'

It wasn't a surprise she knew about the dates outside Ginny's café. Port Berry had the smallest grapevine, plus the dates were out in the open for all to see.

'I've only been on three dates this week.'

A light breeze blew, and Luna brushed back her wispy white hair escaping her bun. 'Why so many?'

Lottie shrugged. 'They keep turning me down, so I just move on to the next one. I made the decision when I started that I'd book all the dates in one go, and I'm determined to see it through to the end, no matter what. I've got another one in a couple of days.'

'Well, you're popular.'

'Only until they see this thing.' Lottie tapped her right wheel, really wanting to smack it hard. She steadied her frustration and smiled.

The seventy-year-old woman smiled back, revealing her perfect teeth. 'Not all will see your legs, Lottie Jordan. One might just look elsewhere.'

Unsure what to do with that snippet of info, Lottie remained smiling. Conversations with Luna weren't always easy to understand, as she often spoke in riddles. Seeing Mrs Hopkin coming back down the pathway was a relief.

'There you go, lovely,' said the elderly woman, placing a small tin of tuna into the cart. 'Ooh, not much else going on in there.'

'I've just started,' said Lottie, feeling as hopeful as she looked. 'Another hour or so at this, then I'll be full up and heading off to the Hub with my loot. I'm also seeing who would like some of my home-grown salad.'

Mrs Hopkin turned to Luna. 'We're lucky we don't need help.'

Luna nodded.

'But if you ever do, please ask,' said Lottie.

The women wished her well before heading back into Mrs Hopkin's whitewashed house.

Lottie avoided a few homes, knowing her luck wouldn't be in with certain residents, and had herself a productive morning. Her cart was full, and her throat quite dry from so much nattering. Those donating who lived alone especially liked a chat, and Lottie could do little else but oblige, knowing they were lonely. She loved a good catch-up with the locals anyway and had no problem talking to anyone.

A decision was made. As soon as she had five minutes, she'd make a list of all the locals who hardly had company, and she'd invite them to talk for the videos she was making. Some of their stories would be welcomed on the Hub's website, she was sure. Plus, it would give them something to do.

With the sun shining on her rosy cheeks, and fulfilment in her heart, she headed to the Hub. She knew her brother was there on duty for a couple of hours.

Spencer took one look at his sister and laughed. 'What on earth . . .'

Lottie splayed her arms out in front. 'Do you like it? I wanted to surprise you. George made it.'

'Did he fill it up as well?'

Lottie moved towards the back door, ready for unloading. 'No. I've been knocking on doors and talking up the food bank.'

'Looks like it worked.' Spencer rubbed a hand through his mop of ginger hair, showcasing lighter streaks of golden copper-brown.

She bit her lip and nodded. 'Yep.'

'I'll put the kettle on and then unload, then you can tell me all about this dating malarkey.'

Lottie's mouth gaped for a moment. 'Who told you?'

'You're having dates outside Ginny's. Small town, Lott.'

She thought about lying but decided she couldn't be bothered. 'So what, I'm dating. Sort of.' Considering not one man so far had made it into their seat, she wasn't sure calling them dates was the right choice of word. 'I assumed you'd have a moan about it. Give me online safety talks or something.'

Spencer turned, holding two blue mugs. 'No. I know you're not stupid. What I want to know is, why you're doing it?'

'What kind of a question is that? Why wouldn't I want to have a relationship? I had one before Russ left me, and I miss the interaction. It's quiet indoors since you moved back to the flat, and anyway, I just feel it's time for me to get back out there. I'm not crying over Russ anymore, so why not?'

'I'm worried you might be rushing things.'

Lottie scoffed. 'Rushing things, Spence?'

He shrugged and went back to making the tea.

'There's no point mumbling over there,' she snapped. 'If you've got something to say, say it. And before you do, just remember I don't judge your choices.'

Spencer's blue eyes quickly scowled her way. 'What choices? When have you known me to have a partner?'

'Exactly!'

'What's that mean?'

'It wouldn't hurt you to find someone you could settle down with. You're thirty-five now, Spence. You're the one who should be rushing.' She pulled her bottom lip into her mouth to stop herself from laughing.

Spencer made the tea and sat by her side in a comfy blue chair. 'I shall die alone and in peace, sis.'

She slapped his elbow. 'Oi, don't say that.'

'Look, we both know I'm not in the market for a missus, but you don't have to put yourself out there either. When the time's right, you'll find someone. The universe will sort it.'

Lottie scoffed, glancing at the ceiling. 'Since when have you been guided by the universe? More like whoever's up for it down the pub.'

'Thanks for that. Make me sound like a right sleaze.'

'You just don't take relationships seriously.' She knew why but wasn't about to poke the bear. Spencer had been eight when their parents, smashed out their heads on heroin, killed their baby brother. Being that much younger, she didn't have the memories of a dysfunctional family the way he did. She knew it affected the decisions he made as an adult. Family. Love. Commitment. Mostly, she knew when to leave him alone.

*I hope you find someone lovely one day, Spencer.*

She sipped her tea, ignoring his silence, and gestured at her collection of food. 'We've got enough out back now to start making up full parcels. I've got some door numbers as well today, so I know who is in need. Maybe I can drop some off later. Ooh, wait till I tell Sophie.' She glanced at the front door. 'I thought she might have popped in today.'

'She's not rostered on, but no doubt will be in at some point. Hey, did you know, she even managed to get that Mr Powell to come in. You know, the reclusive rich bloke. Not sure how she did that, but she did. Probably nagged him till he caved, knowing her.'

Lottie giggled into her mug. 'Poor man.'

'Good to have him onside though, eh?'

'I suppose, but to be fair, we do all right by ourselves down here. I reckon our little food bank will be just as successful as his big café one.'

Spencer shook his head. 'Shouldn't be successful at all, should it, Lott? It's not fair people are going hungry. We shouldn't have to do any of this.'

'I know. Goodness, it makes you feel grateful for what you've got, doesn't it?'

'Makes me grateful for Rebecca. She set us up nicely with the flower shop.'

Every inch of Lottie warmed. Her aunt was more than the best. She was everything. Without her taking them out of care and adopting them, who knows where they would be. She wondered from time to time and knew Spencer did too. They were so lucky to have had her raise them.

'We've got a few big flower orders in next week, so no more time off for dating.' Spencer started to faff about with her cart so didn't see her poke her tongue out at him. 'And anyway, aren't you supposed to be doing something at the Sunshine Centre for the Port Berry Craft Fayre.'

Lottie frowned. 'I do have time for more than one thing in my life, Spence. Anyway, I'm in front with that. I'm only showcasing two paintings, seeing as I'm the newbie there.'

'I'll buy one.'

'You will not. If anyone purchases one of my pictures, it won't be a pity sale.'

Spencer laughed, getting up to fetch some boxes. He leaned over and kissed the top of her head. 'Whatever makes you happy, sis.'

'Ooh, I'll tell you what makes me happy.' She squealed quietly, lightly clapping. 'My racing wheelchair. It's going to help me be even fitter, strengthen my arms some more, and make me feel free again.'

Spencer frowned at the tin of chickpeas in his hand. 'Feel free?'

'Yeah, that's how I used to feel on my bike.' She sighed and sank into her seat. 'I miss riding, which sounds weird being stuck in this thing, but you know what I mean.'

'Yeah, I know. Come on, let's get you back out there. You call out the shopping list, and I'll pack, then we can load you back up, and you can go be the food fairy.'

Lottie muffled her laugh with one hand. 'Meals on wheels.'

'We'll have to get you a bell.'

'Or a foghorn. I couldn't get down some pathways in this contraption.'

'Best not to annoy any potential donors, Lott. We'll get complaints. And you know how some around here would love to shut down the Hub.'

Lottie wrinkled her nose. 'Yeah, because they don't need help, so they don't care. Well, I'm not going to worry about that lot. Port Berry has loads of lovely people, and our little food bank will feed all in need.'

# CHAPTER 5

*Samuel*

Why Mrs Stepshine felt the need to blare out rock songs while he was trying to work was beyond him. Did cleaning a house even warrant such noise?

Samuel left his office chair to stand at the large glass windows, staring out at the sea in the near distance. Who was he kidding? He hadn't been working at all. All week, he'd hardly concentrated on much, all thoughts diverting to the woman in the wheelchair. The fact it was still bugging him bugged him even more.

'Enough!' he scorned himself, steaming the glass with his breath. A nice walk along the beach would wash away the cobwebs and the music rattling his eardrums.

He quickly changed into a light-grey tracksuit and slipped out the back door to take the private route to the beach, leaving his housekeeper to her party for one.

A narrow pathway, lined with colourful flowers and a wooden handrail on one side, held the most amazing view of a small cove covered in golden sand with clear blue water lapping at the shore. It was one of Samuel's favourite places.

He slowly made his way down the wide steps, not feeling the need to rush, and flicked off his sliders as soon as he reached the warm grains. The sensation of sand filling the spaces in between his toes sent his body into relaxation mode, and the soothing lapping sound of the gentle waves caused him to stop and close his eyes for a moment.

Sometimes Samuel needed respite from his life. Having money made certain things easier, but his stress levels hadn't changed much since his parents died. Everything was simpler when they were around. His perfect cereal advert family. No thought of money worries, a lively home filled with laughter, and his sister had legs.

Pulling his sunglasses down from his head to shade his eyes, Samuel stared out at the horizon, having one of his moments where he wished he could just step into the water and swim away.

He sighed and sat on the soft sand, lost and alone once more.

*I miss you.*

Samuel wasn't one for talking to the sky. He rarely enjoyed speaking to the living let alone thinking the dead were listening. And what if his parents could hear him? Then what? What would they have him do now he'd secured a home and business for what was left of their family?

He whipped out his phone to take another look at the info he'd paid for about Hannah's new boyfriend. All seemed legit, which was good. Annoying, but okay, as the young man had nothing negative on his report, so Hannah was safe, which was the only reason he snooped in the first place, not that he told her.

Making him jump, his phone rang, and Hannah's name popped up.

'What's up, sis?'

'Can you do me the biggest favour, please? I need two of my paintings brought to the centre, as we're doing a practice set-up for the fayre. You don't have to take them back, as I'm leaving everything here till the day to make life easier. They're the two in my art room on the table, ta.'

Samuel smiled as he stood. 'Sure. I'll be there soon.'

'Thank you. Love you.' And with that, she was gone.

He smiled to himself at how bouncy and carefree his little sister was and wondered if the roles were reversed would he be the same. After all, he never used to be so uptight.

Doing things for his sister sparked more joy than work, and it wasn't until he'd loaded the car he realized that fact.

'I need to do more charity work,' he told the steering wheel as he started the engine. The Food Bank Café was his biggest thrill, so maybe he could open a few more around Cornwall. He already had the small hub over in Port Berry added to the Les Powell Trust, so why not expand?

On his drive to the Sunshine Centre, he decided to ask the staff there if he could help with the upcoming Port Berry Craft Fayre. It was time to get more involved locally. Thoughts of travelling had consumed him for so long, he'd forgotten what was closer to home.

Large colourful flowers painted on a whitewashed wall and a wide lilac door gave off nothing but cheer as Samuel entered the car park of the large building designed especially for people with disabilities. The front garden held an array of raised flowerbeds and large metal ornaments in the shape of ladybirds, hedgehogs, and hummingbirds.

Samuel decided to bring up their financial needs as well when he got a quiet moment with the person in charge, in case there was something needed that he could buy for the centre his sister adored so much.

Unpacking her artwork from his car, he headed inside, passing the sensory room, kitchen, and soft-play area. Arts and crafts were close to the back, with accordion doors leading to a large patio in the back garden, where there was a small nature reserve along with an allotment.

It was quiet inside the spacious room, as all occupants were outside, enjoying the beautiful weather.

Hannah saw him straight away and happily waved him over, showing where to place her paintings. A few members said hello and added some small talk before she introduced Felix.

Samuel tried hard to stop himself from scanning the twenty-three-year-old from top to toe. He knew Felix had started off as a volunteer, then became one of the paid staff when his older brother joined after losing three limbs as a soldier.

Felix happily shook Samuel's hand, showing no sign of awkwardness, and Samuel had a sneaky suspicion Hannah only had him come to the centre to get the meet-and-greet out the way on her own terms. 'Hannah's told me so much about you.'

'Not much about you,' said Samuel, holding back his intel and acting innocent, even though Hannah frowned at him.

'Not much to tell.' Felix laughed, and his eyes sparkled at Hannah, revealing his love. 'I'm pretty ordinary.'

Hannah playfully slapped his arm. 'You are not.'

Samuel watched them gush over each other to the point he could take no more. 'I'll just . . .' He let the sentence hang and made his way over to the woman in charge at the centre. 'Hey, Debra. Thought I'd join in with the fayre. Tell me what you need me to do, and I'm all in.'

Her bright eyes almost laughed. 'Oh, is that right? And what brought this on?'

Shrugging, he matched her laughter. 'Boredom.'

'That'll do it. Okay, come on then, let's find you a role.' The woman, who looked around fifty, guided him to a stack of boxes by the doorway. 'Well, you did offer, Samuel.'

'I bet you didn't make my sister do this when she asked to become a volunteer.'

'No. Hannah's better at settling new members.'

Samuel grinned. 'Is that your way of saying I'm not friendly?'

Debra grinned back. 'You're lovely, Samuel. Now, get lifting.'

Heavy lifting wasn't a problem. He was happy to build a sweat, having skipped exercise that morning.

'I was hoping you'd pop in soon, only I've got an app idea,' said Debra, flashing him her warm wide smile. 'And what with you being the app man.'

'I made one farming app when I worked on a few farms years ago.'

Debra nodded. 'Yeah, and look how that worked out for you. Anyway, we can chat later in the office, and you can give me some pointers.'

He saluted her, then got on with his task, only stopping when a blond man in an electric wheelchair came over to say hi. It was obviously Felix's brother, as they shared the same look.

Rupert wanted to know some family backstory, which made Samuel grin each time he turned away to sort the boxes. Seems he wasn't the only big bro out there looking out for his sibling.

It was hard to hold down a conversation with Rupert, because his strawberry-blond hair, flapping fringe, and wheelchair brought back the memory of the woman in the road.

*I wonder what she's doing now?*

How annoying was that? She had to disappear out of his head. There were boxes to stack and a fayre to get ready for. He *really* had to stop thinking about the pretty blonde. Enough was enough. He mentally shook her off and went back to his task.

# CHAPTER 6

*Lottie*

Sitting in the Hub with her friends, local newsagent Alice, and owner of the Jolly Pirate pub Robson, Lottie was checking through the helpful notes emailed from the Les Powell Trust. She tapped away merrily on her small red laptop, happy to feel useful.

There was a moment in her past when she first sat in a wheelchair and was told to push herself. She flat-out refused, crossing her arms in a huff while blinking back tears. Spencer didn't know what to do, and her aunt wasn't there to make everything better.

She glanced up at the framed affirmations on the wall, smiling at Sophie's work.

'You okay over there, Lott?' asked Robson. His piercing blue eyes playfully squinted as he wrinkled his nose. 'You've got a dreamy look about you. Anything we should know?'

Alice stopped unfolding boxes. 'Ooh, did you finally get a date?'

Lottie had to laugh. 'No. And I'm not being dreamy. I was just having a happy moment, that's all.'

Swirling her dark hair up into a ponytail, Alice tutted. 'Oh, I was hoping you'd met someone nice.'

'In all honesty, I have got a couple more lined up.' Lottie shrugged, not holding out much hope, going by her track record so far. 'Have to see how it goes.'

Robson headed into the back room, carrying some cartons of long-life milk. 'I don't know why everyone feels the need to date nowadays anyway.'

Lottie and Alice shared a look. They both knew Robson's wife had died a couple of years back so didn't expect him to want to be in the game.

'I can't remember the last time I was kissed,' said Alice, slumping further into her seat.

'You could try online dating, like me.' Lottie tapped something on her keyboard, then turned the screen to face her friend. 'See. This is the one I use.'

Alice scrunched her nose as her light-brown eyes homed in on the screen. 'Not sure anyone will want me. I'm not exactly in demand. I'm thirty and live with my mum, nan, and fourteen-year-old nephew above a newsagent's. And let's not forget I adopted my sister's son after she died. I'm Benny's mum now. Men will see me as baggage with no prospects.'

Robson came out the back room, kissed Alice on the head, and gave her shoulder a sympathetic rub. 'There's a kiss for you, and stop with the negatives.' He pointed at the dating website. 'There are all sorts on there, and if anyone's looking for perfection, they'll be looking forever because there's no such thing. Sign up if you want, Al. You're just as good as anyone else on there. And thirty isn't old. I'm thirty-seven, and I don't feel one bit old.'

Lottie beamed at Alice. 'Do you want me to open you an account?'

'Nope. I think I prefer the old-fashioned way.' Alice twiddled her hands in her lap, looking as though she was mulling over the idea.

Both Lottie and Robson laughed.

'What does that mean?' asked Lottie.

Alice grinned shyly, glancing out the window at the harbour. 'Oh, you know, a meet-cute, a friendly smile, serendipity.'

Lottie followed her eyeline, thinking how lovely it would be to meet someone by chance. But after Russ dumped her because she could no longer walk, it was as though she had something to prove, more so to herself.

'Maybe soulmates don't always show up in those ways,' said Robson, opening the Hub's door to thank a man for the bag of food he dropped off.

Alice took the bag, spreading tins of soup over the table so she could see what to add to the inventory. 'Maybe they don't always find you.'

Lottie scoffed as she clicked off the dating website. 'Well, that's cheerful. Remind me not to do shifts with you two again.'

'Hey,' said Robson, running a hand over his dark hair. 'What did I say?' He laughed at Alice. 'Anyway, Al, with all the psychic abilities in your family, I'm surprised you don't know your own future by now.'

'I think my nan does, but she's keeping tight-lipped on the subject. Tells me to just focus on saving up for my own B&B, which I haven't lost focus of, by the way.' Alice indicated at the window. 'She reckons I'll get one on the front, but I'm not sure I'll be able to afford that.'

'Don't see why not,' said Robson. 'You've been saving for your dream for an age, and the bank will help.'

Lottie agreed. 'You'll get there, Alice. I believe in you. Look at Ginny. She got her hands on Harbour Light Café, and that was her dream for years.'

Alice's head bobbed. 'Yep, this isn't the time for distractions that come in the form of hot naked men.'

Everyone laughed.

'Is that how you see your future man?' asked Lottie, thinking it not a bad visualization.

Alice shrugged as she grinned. 'Why not? Right now, he's my dream guy, so I can make him whoever and whatever. One thing I know for sure is, he's definitely kind. I can't have anyone like my ex in my life again. He was a narcissist, and that's not the life for me. To be honest, I'm a bit scared to date a man again after that experience. I know they're not all the same, but still.'

'You just need more time to heal from the trauma, that's all, Alice. You're doing great, and I know you'll meet someone as lovely as you one day.' Lottie smiled, hoping so much her dear friend did find someone nice. It was what she deserved. Not many came nicer than Alice Dipple.

Alice smiled softly. 'Thanks.'

Lottie glanced at her laptop. 'The men in my life are all real and nothing to write home about. Maybe I'd be better off with a dream guy instead. You know, I might take a break if these next dates don't pan out. I've got my garden to focus on now. Plus, I'm hoping to sell a couple of my paintings at the craft fayre. Spencer tells me to take time off from the shop when we're not busy, but I like doing that too.'

'And you've got the Hub's website to keep you out of dating trouble,' said Alice, chuckling.

'You've always liked being busy,' Robson added, putting the kettle on.

It was true. She hated having nothing to do and had certainly found more things to occupy her mind since losing the ability to walk.

'Hey, Rob, will you be up for an interview for the website? I want to include the volunteers in the videos, not just those we help.'

'Sure. What would I talk about though? You normally go down the mental well-being road, I've noticed.'

'Yes, and it's drawing in more support. People can relate to those kinds of stories. So, if you don't mind, I'd like to do a segment with you about grief.'

Both women pulled in their lips as they stared with soft expressions over at the man deep in thought. Lottie knew she was asking a lot of her friend, as it wasn't often he spoke of his late wife, Leah.

'Please don't feel obligated,' she added. 'I just think it might help someone out there.'

As Robson was hesitating, Alice chimed in. 'I can do one with you one day, Lott. Perhaps about adoption, seeing how I adopted Benny, and you and Spencer were adopted by your aunt too. Could be a good topic.'

'Ooh, yes, definitely. We'll raise that issue as well. Let me pencil you in.' She pulled up her digital calendar. 'When's good for you, Al?'

'Anytime during school hours would be best for me. Or we can leave my interview until after the summer school holiday. September would be better.'

Lottie agreed. 'Yes, let's put you in then. I've got someone for next month, and—'

'I'll do it,' said Robson. 'Book me in as well.'

'Are you sure?' She needed the confirmation because she felt so bad for asking and now figured he might feel awkward not joining in the website's interviews.

He nodded and smiled warmly. 'Yeah, it'll be good for someone. You can interview me. I'll be okay.'

She glanced at her calendar while chewing her bottom lip. 'I think we can work something out soon.'

Robson breathed out a small laugh. 'Sure. You get your schedule sorted, then let me know when you want me.' He went into the back room and started humming, which was a good sign, as Lottie knew he often hummed when pottering about, but only if his mind was clear.

Alice smiled as she winked Lottie's way, then went back to her tasks.

Lottie gazed outside, thinking about her upcoming dates. She would take a leaf out of Alice's book and stop worrying about having someone love her. There were other things to focus on and quite a lot on the calendar. For the first time since joining the online dating website, she was hoping the men she'd already agreed to meet were like the others. That way, she could go back to concentrating on the Hub, the

Port Berry Craft Fayre, her shop, and the food growing in her greenhouse.

It was decided. There wasn't room for anything else, especially men.

## CHAPTER 7

*Samuel*

Seeing the therapist that worked with the Happy to Help Hub, January Riley, sitting in the Food Bank Café made Samuel ponder over approaching her to talk all things agoraphobia. He hated anyone knowing, viewing his condition as a weakness that shouldn't be advertised, but now he was no longer seeing his own therapist, he figured it might be nice to talk to someone who had a smidge of a chance of understanding him. Her face had a glow about it that made her look friendly and caring, and he'd heard nothing but good things about her work.

He repeatedly passed by her table, waiting for the young man she was with to up and leave. They were chatting for ages, and he was starting to wonder whether this was such a good idea.

One of the regular volunteers, Kaz, was at least keeping him busy, as requested. It was his idea to help out for the morning, after all. He couldn't remember the last time he got involved and had been enjoying himself up until Jan entered and sat down.

The last time he'd seen her was when they'd met at a charity function over in Truro a couple of years back. He was a lot worse then but hid it well, suffering only in silence. The two hours he'd spent at the event was filled with dread, palpitations, and the need to rush home to his comfort zone. That was before he'd started to look into ways to help himself.

Finally Jan and the young man finished their chat. He left the premises and she was about to get up too, only staying seated for a moment while faffing with her large bag.

'Excuse me,' said Samuel, after swallowing a feeling of dryness. 'We've met before,' he added, offering a hand.

Jan's dark eyes glanced up. 'Yes, hello. You were one of the donators at the Olsham Memorial Fundraiser. Samuel, right?' She shook his hand, and he sat.

'Yes, that's right.'

'Mary Olsham is a good friend of mine. They raised a lot of money that day to help those grieving. So, well done for your contribution.'

Helping others grieving their loved ones was the least he could do with some of his money, especially knowing the work the charity did. He only wished he'd taken up the offer of grief counselling back when his parents died. Hannah had all sorts of therapy going on in the early years, but all he could concentrate on was paying the bills.

'I was wondering if I could speak to you about a personal matter, as a therapist, that is.' Samuel needed her to know anything he said was confidential. He studied the middle-aged woman clearly studying him.

'Of course,' she replied, reaching for her notebook. 'Would you like to book an appointment?'

He perused the café, making sure no one could listen in on their conversation. Kaz was behind the counter, showing a newbie how to work the till, and the elderly man at the back was heading to the toilet, leaving only two people sitting not far away.

Jan moved her half-empty mug of tea out of her way. 'Or is there something on your mind now?'

Samuel stopped bouncing his leg as soon as he noticed he was doing it. Taking a breath, he gave a sharp nod. 'I don't need therapy,' he blurted, then composed himself. 'I would just like some confirmation, of sorts.'

'Confirmation?'

'That I'm doing it right. Progress reports, that sort of thing.' He focused on one blonde curl out of her mass of bouncy locks, a dramatic contrast to her dark skin.

'What are you doing?' she asked softly.

Why was saying it out loud so hard? It was utterly annoying on every level. Anyone would think she wouldn't understand. Would she? He was sure she might, considering her job. He had to talk to someone professional. It was starting to drive him insane, if he wasn't already there, which, most days, he believed he was.

'Hey, Samuel. It's okay. Take a breath.'

Her voice was so gentle and soothing, the breath he took easily flowed through his normally tight lungs.

'I've been doing some exposure therapy. By myself. I had some therapy sessions to get me started and watched a few online tutorials, so I've got the gist of it, but my therapist moved away shortly into my course, and I haven't bothered to find a new one. It was hard enough reaching out the first time.' He felt stupid already. Taking another breath, he added, 'I have agoraphobia.' The words caught in his throat as his gaze drifted to the table.

'Exposure therapy is the way forward. Good on you for making a start. I can help with that, if you like. Give you some pointers, talk through your achievements, set some goals.'

He looked up. 'Erm, that would be helpful. I've been slowly pushing on my invisible walls for quite some time, but my progress is shockingly slow, and this therapy is time-consuming and, at times, aggravating.'

Jan smiled warmly. 'I bet. Tell me what you're doing.'

'I have a notebook where I document my journey. I write what I did, how long for, which fear level I reached, and how long it took for me to balance out.'

'All very good. Does it help?'

Samuel nodded. 'Yes, but sometimes I just want to tell someone other than my sister, who I'm not sure really understands the magnitude at times. In fact, she's the only other person who knows about this, so please, keep this information about me private.'

Jan almost looked insulted. 'Of course. I will say though, I'm a great believer in support, and it would benefit you more if you were open and honest about your mental health.'

'Mental health?'

'Agoraphobia isn't the same as being afraid of spiders, Samuel. It stems from anxiety in most cases. Sure, there are those who have a genuine fear of the outdoors. There are fears of all sorts, but with the majority of agoraphobics, it's a side order of their main course.'

Her wording made him breathe out a laugh. 'Sorry, I'm not laughing at you. It's just the way you described it.'

'How long have you had anxiety for?'

That was a no-brainer. It wasn't until his sister was allowed home that he noticed the changes in him. He shook his head at Jan. 'Ten years. Give or take.' Tapping his chest, he quickly added, 'But I wasn't always like this with travelling.'

'You see, the thing with agoraphobia is, it creeps up on you. It's a step-by-step process that, mostly, you don't see happening.'

That much he'd worked out already. 'I see that now. I didn't realize what I was doing to myself each time I ran home when anxiety struck.' He rubbed along his tense jaw. 'God, I've trained my own brain to be afraid to go far away from home. It's just so ridiculous.'

Jan reached over and lightly tapped his arm. 'No, it's not. It's just the mind doing its thing to stay safe. What you're doing now to reverse the process is good, but it will take time. Remember, it started out step by step, therefore it will require the same approach to retrain the mind.'

Revealing vulnerability in his eyes, he told her the truth. 'I get so tired of it all.'

Jan looked as though she understood. 'That's normal, Samuel. You're fighting a battle. You wouldn't be human if you didn't stumble a few times. Tell me, how far have you got?'

Twiddling with her cold mug, he puffed out his cheeks as he thought back to his quests. 'I've been conquering Cornwall, in small doses.' His index finger pointed out an invisible map. 'I'm heading upwards, going from left to right, stopping in each town until I feel comfortable, then moving on. Currently, I'm close to Looe, but I haven't quite made it in for a cuppa yet.'

Jan looked thoroughly impressed. 'Wow! And all this on your own. Do you even realize just how well you're doing?'

Samuel shrugged. He hardly ever praised himself.

Jan opened her notebook, revealing a calendar. 'Okay, here's what we're going to do. I'll book you an appointment, and you can bring your notes to show me, and we can work from there. So far, you're doing great, but I reckon, with help, we can break down that invisible wall once and for all.'

'Do you have any tips for the time being?'

Jan stopped flicking through pages and bit her lip for a second. 'Hmm, let's see. How about you go out a bit more to the places you're already comfortable with. Keep up the momentum, if you have time. Pop in cafés, have a coffee, go for walks, do some shopping. Anything to keep you outdoors for longer than you normally would be. Socialize.' She grinned at their surroundings. 'Like you're doing now. This type of thing helps. Keeps your mind from crawling back into its cave.'

Samuel nodded. 'I see what you mean. It's easy for me to stay home because I work from home. Plus, not going to lie, I actually like my home. I'm not much of a people person and enjoy my own company, so all this going out and about is forced, but I feel I have no choice if I want to beat this stupid thing.' He tapped his temple and sighed.

'Well, at least you've made a start, and I'm so pleased you reached out to me. We're in this together now. How about I book you in next week, and for now, you can escort me over to Port Berry. Hmm?'

'Sure.' He arranged a date in her diary, not even knowing what was on his own, and offered her a lift when she mentioned taking the bus. He'd done some bus routes as part of his therapy, but even without his condition, he much preferred the comfort of his car.

'I've got a shift at the Hub over there,' said Jan, heading out the door. 'You can grab a cuppa in the café or have a wander. Something to do, eh?'

'Yes. I've only been to Port Berry a few times, so it'll be good.'

Jan nudged his elbow. 'And I heard the Les Powell Trust is backing our little food bank over there, so thanks for that.'

'You're welcome. I'm thinking of opening a few more around Cornwall.'

'Great idea. They're certainly needed.' Jan beamed at him, a motherly smile filled with pride and admiration. 'You're a good man, Samuel Powell. Hey, have you met any of the volunteers at the Hub yet?'

'Only Sophie Moore. She emails me. A lot.' He pulled back his grin, but Jan was already smiling knowingly.

'I don't have much time today, but another day I'll introduce you to the team. You can even do a shift there too if you like.'

Samuel looked over his shoulder at his café, waving one hand to Kaz to let her know he was off. 'No, thanks. My spare time is consumed by this place, my little sister, the Sunshine Centre, work, and agoraphobia.'

Jan frowned. 'And you're healing, and it's one hell of a journey.'

That was one way to describe what was happening in his life. He closed his eyes for a second, enjoying the warmth of the sun on his face, then inhaled deeply, got in the car with Jan, and headed off to Port Berry. At least he could chill for a bit and not think of anything much.

It was a good feeling being in Jan's presence. She certainly was a positive person, and she was right, he had achieved so much on his own. He really needed to learn how to be proud of himself.

He perked up as he drove along, feeling a little weight drop from his tight shoulders. Perhaps talking about his problem would benefit him. He wasn't sure. It had always felt so embarrassing, and he wished it didn't, but it was how it had always been, and the longer he'd hidden what was happening in his head, the easier it had become to keep it a secret.

Samuel decided he'd consider being more open about himself. He'd see how things went with his new therapist first. At least now he had someone else to confide in.

# CHAPTER 8

*Lottie*

Much to Lottie's surprise, the date she'd arranged to meet outside Ginny's café actually sat down. It did make her wonder if he'd noticed her chair had wheels. Due to all the runners she'd encountered, she was suddenly a little lost for words. Luckily enough, tall, dark, and handsome spoke first.

'Lottie Jordan?'

She nodded.

'Thought so. Always best to check though. I'm Rio, as you know.'

'Hello, Rio.'

He pointed by her feet. 'What happened to you?'

'I was knocked off my bike last year.' She waited for the penny to drop. It wouldn't take him too long to figure out her injury was permanent, then he'd be off.

'Oh, so . . .' His sentence was left hanging.

'Yep. I can't walk anymore.'

It was a pleasant surprise watching his features soften, rather than twist into a grimace like the others, but still, she didn't hold out much hope nor did she actually care. She was only seeing through the dates she'd already fixed.

He leaned his elbows on the table between them, and there it was, the pity smile — just above the designer beard. 'I'm so sorry that happened to you, Lottie, but I have to be honest — I wish you'd mentioned it to me beforehand. Look, I don't want to come across like a horrible sod or anything, but I'm looking for a partner who can match me in my downtime. You said you were adventurous in your bio.'

*Yeah, maybe best to change that.*

'I used to be. I loved riding my bike.'

Rio smiled. 'I go skiing and climb mountains.'

'Oh, that kind of adventure.' Lottie straightened her back. 'I'm doing a marathon. Obviously in my wheelchair. I'm in training.'

*Oh, shut up!*

'That's brilliant. If I'm about at the time, I'll cheer you on. Feel free to contact me.'

'I will. Erm, sorry about the lack of full disclosure. I just—'

'It's okay. I get it, but, look, I might as well head off. No point us wasting each other's time.' Scraping his chair back, he offered a small wave, and walked off down Harbour End Road — and Lottie knew there and then she wouldn't contact him again, even if she did decide to enter the wheelchair event taking place over in Devon in a couple of months.

She'd seen it advertised on the noticeboard at the library and thought it sounded doable. Using the word marathon was pushing it, considering it was more a charity fun day and anyone in a wheelchair could enter.

Oh, how Lottie missed riding her bike.

Ginny came outside and filled the seat opposite. 'Another runner, Lott?'

'He sat and spoke to me, so excuse me if I seem a bit stunned. Anyway, I'm not bothered. I have my last date coming along in about fifteen minutes and then I'm officially off the dating books for a while.'

Ginny quietly laughed. 'I can't believe you set the dates so close together. What if that one stuck around?'

Lottie shrugged. 'I had a feeling he wouldn't. Not putting my money on the next one either. Hopefully, he'll arrive early and bugger off quickly, because honestly, Gin, I'm itching to get back to my garden.'

'Aww, don't give up, chick.'

'I'm not. I just have a lot on this summer. Maybe I'll try again nearer Christmas. Meanwhile, I'll have a spot of lunch. A cheese and ham toastie, please, and a pineapple juice.'

Ginny went back into the café to sort the order.

'Marathon, eh?' came a man's voice from behind her.

Lottie twisted her head as far as it would go, then snapped forward on seeing it was the man with the amber eyes sitting at a table.

*Oh my goodness. It's him!*

'Should be interesting,' he added, making her body tense.

'Yes, so next time you see someone out training on the road, perhaps you'll mind your own business.' Pleased with her retort, she grinned to herself, knowing full well he couldn't see her smugness.

'Perhaps I will,' he replied, and it sounded as though he was smiling too.

Thoughts rapidly fired around her head, but nothing she deemed good enough for a response. Finally she had something to say, but just as she was about to speak, Trey Seabridge, Councillor Seabridge's fifteen-year-old nephew, plonked himself down opposite her.

'Hello, gorgeous,' he said, flashing a cheeky smile that probably had a lot of girls his age swooning.

Lottie frowned in confusion at his presence. 'Erm, hello, Trey. What can I do for you?'

He leaned back in the chair, flopping one arm over the back as he twisted to his side. She figured he thought he looked cool, but his posture just reminded her of someone drunk. 'It's me. Fernando Augustus.'

It only took a moment for it to dawn on her. Totally her own fault for giving up the ghost and not bothering to vet the last date properly. With everyone else, she'd made sure she'd seen them via a short video chat first.

*Great!*

Trey catfishing her wasn't even the worst part. It was the man behind her watching the whole scene play out. Then there was Spencer, who would lose it once word got out she wasn't taking care when meeting dates, and word was definitely about to hit the Port Berry grapevine, especially if this kid had anything to do with it.

Lottie's arms jolted towards the table. 'Have you got someone filming this?' she snapped, unsure of his motives.

Trey's face turned serious as he sat up. 'No. Why would I film you?' His baby blues lit up. 'Do you want me to film you?'

'What I want is for you to bugger off,' she replied through clenched teeth.

'You haven't even given me a chance yet.'

'Why would I give you a chance? You bloody well lied to me.'

*And why am I acting like that's the only problem here?*

Trey grinned. 'Not the only one doing a bit of lying, eh, Lott.' He glanced at her wheelchair, then winked.

'Oh, shut up. And go away before I call your uncle.' She leaned closer, narrowing her eyes. 'I wonder what he would have to say about this, hmm?'

'Uncle Oliver always tells me to go for it. He'd admire my assertiveness.'

'Well, I'm not admiring anything. You've got a flipping cheek, and you know it!'

'A man's got to do what a man's got to do.'

'You're fifteen.' Lottie sat back, shaking her head. The decision to give up dating had well and truly been set in stone now, thanks to junior fluttering his long eyelashes her way.

'Don't be ageist, Lott.'

She lifted her brow as her mouth gaped. She went to speak, but he pulled out an e-cigarette, letting it hang from his lip until it almost fell.

'You can stop that,' she told him. 'You're not old enough. Besides, I don't want to breathe in your chemicals.'

'It relieves stress, and you just stressed me.'

Lottie huffed. 'I just stressed *you*!'

Trey stood, waggling a hand towards her lap. 'I thought you were nice, but it just goes to show you can't judge you women by your looks.'

A man's muffled laugh was all she heard next. Ignoring him, she focused on the rebel without a clue slouching in front of her.

'I'm telling your mum you're impersonating people online, Trey Seabridge.'

He shrugged, started vaping, and walked off.

'And you look like a dragon,' she yelled, waving away the smoke wafting in her direction.

*Little sod!*

'Can't blame the lad for trying,' said the man behind her. 'He's got a cheek.'

'At least that one would have bought you lunch.'

'I'm not hungry anymore.'

'Oh, I was about to offer to buy you lunch.'

'Well, you can buy me lunch.' Lottie quickly shot her head around. 'No, wait. I didn't mean you. I meant, a grown man can buy me lunch, not that you're not a grown man, obviously. What I . . .'

*Oh goodness, stop talking.*

She turned back to face the empty chair opposite her. The silence behind her was unnerving.

'You can take a rain check,' said his soft voice, causing a flutter to hit her stomach.

'Hmm,' was all she managed, and she wasn't entirely sure where that sound came from, because she sure as heck didn't authorize its release.

His presence was suddenly close to her shoulder. 'Good luck with the marathon,' he said quietly.

She went to reply but was momentarily seduced by the light woody scent she inhaled from his neck.

Ginny came out, carrying a tray filled with Lottie's lunch items, and Mr Eau de Sexy left the scene.

Lottie flapped away the heat creeping over her cheeks, blowing out hot air and little else. 'I'm never sitting in this spot again, Gin. I swear it's jinxed.'

Ginny gestured down the road, towards the Hub. 'What happened? Did he offer to pay for your lunch again?'

'Well, Trey . . . Wait, what?'

'That bloke you were just talking to when I came out. He's the one who paid last time. Did he not say?'

Between raspberry vape fumes and money-screaming cologne, Lottie's mind was far too befuddled to process the last half-hour of her life. 'Hmm,' was all she could manage, blinking hard, trying to wake herself from what must be a bizarre dream.

# CHAPTER 9

*Samuel*

Samuel was just about to say hello to Sophie as he entered the Happy to Help Hub, when a young woman burst through the door, sobbing heavily while clutching her stomach with one hand and a small boy in the other.

'Are you hurt?' he asked, quickly moving her towards a chair.

Sophie sprinted over, squatting to make eye contact with the woman. 'Take deep breaths. It's okay.'

The little lad slipped his hand out of his mum's hold and went over to play with the tins of vegetables in a nearby box waiting to be sorted and stacked out the back.

'Should I call the police?' asked Samuel, his attention on Sophie, who shook her head.

The woman caught her breath, sniffed, and raised her head. 'I'm sorry. I'm okay. I'm just so . . .' Her words faded, but Samuel was sure she said 'tired'.

Sophie patted her shoulder. 'I'll put the kettle on.'

Samuel sat by the woman's side, glancing at her child to make sure he was okay. The toddler was stacking tins, looking quite pleased with himself. At least that was one less worry. Now for the poor woman in front of him trying hard to compose herself. He offered a tissue from the box on the table, which she happily took.

'Thank you.'

'You're welcome. Now, tell me, how can I help?' After completing a short shift at the Food Bank Café that morning, then talking over his issues with Jan, he felt ready for anything the Hub had to throw his way.

There was so much sadness in her eyes as she blinked away the dampness on her lashes. 'I'm struggling to cope since my husband left a few months ago. I have three kids and two jobs, but it's just not enough. We hardly have any food at home, and I'm just so weak from not eating properly.'

Samuel immediately reached for the fresh pastries, lifting the glass cloche so she could choose for herself. 'Here, please. You can eat as many as you want.'

Her shaky hand reached out for a pain au chocolat, then ripped a piece off to hand to her son. 'He's already had his lunch, but if I start eating, he'll want a bite.' Her smile was weak before it disappeared altogether. 'I make sure my kids eat.'

Samuel nodded. 'I'm sure you do.'

Sophie placed a cold bottle of orange juice on the table. 'Here, get that down you while the kettle boils. It'll give you an energy boost, then we'll sort you a food parcel to take home.'

The woman quickly glugged the drink, then shook her head. 'I don't have a voucher.'

'You don't need one here,' said Sophie. She gestured at the child. 'Can he have a biscuit?'

The mum nodded, so Sophie got on with that task while Samuel finished making the tea.

Sophie smiled at the boy, then his mum. 'I'm Sophie, by the way, and he's Samuel.'

'I'm Victoria, and that's Harry. He's not long turned two. My other boys are in school.' She sighed deeply, removing the food from her mouth. 'Oh, had I known this was my future, I'd never have had three kids in seven years. I love them to bits, but I feel I've been tossed in the deep end since Neil left.'

In no position to talk relationships, Samuel thought it best to stick to what he knew. 'What work do you do?'

'I used to be in admin, but then I became a stay-at-home mum, thinking that was my life till the boys hit secondary school, then I planned to get back into work. Neil just left. No warning whatsoever, then calls me to say he's met someone else and would it be okay if he takes our Michael with him. He's my eldest. I said a few choice words I won't repeat here, and that was that. I got myself a morning cleaning gig, which I do as soon as I drop the boys off at breakfast club, then I do some house cleaning for a lady who lets me bring Harry, bless her. Still, it's not enough but all I have right now.'

If anyone knew how that felt, it was Samuel. Back when he quit university to look after Hannah, finding work to fit around her was hard, and the two farm jobs he'd acquired failed to cover their living costs. Sometimes he wondered what their life would be like had he not created that farming app.

'I have an idea, if you're interested,' he said to Victoria, knowing he also had Sophie's attention. 'I'm looking to expand the Les Powell Trust — that's my charity, named after my parents. Both had the same name. Different spellings. Although, it was only my mum who used the full name Lesley.' He smiled, and she smiled back, looking a little more settled. As she started to eat again, he continued. 'Therefore, I'll need more staff. How would you feel about working for me at the Trust? You'll mostly work from home, I'll have someone train you, and you can get started pretty much straight away. It'll be full-time, and you'll be doing admin work which you already have skills in, so that'll help. Your wages will be above average, so you will be expected to pull your weight and be a solid part of the team. And whenever you need your hours to be flexible, school holidays for example, we can find ways to work with that.'

'Oh my goodness, are you for real?' Victoria looked at Sophie for the confirmation she needed.

Sophie nodded. 'Hey, it's what we do here in Port Berry. Help, home, feed, find jobs, all sorts. Whatever we can.'

Samuel wasn't quite sure he was one of the Port Berry crew, but it sure did feel good being included. 'Let me go sort you a food parcel, then I can drop you home if you like, and I'll give you some more details about the job and also give you my assistant's number. You stay here and eat some more. Won't be a sec.' He gave Sophie the nod to step out back with him.

'Oh, Samuel, you're brilliant,' Sophie whispered, hugging him.

Not quite sure how to respond, Samuel left his arms hanging until she pulled away. There was no point her beaming his way like that. He'd hardly saved the world — he'd just helped one person. Life would have been a hell of a lot easier had more people helped him when it was needed. He shook off his bleak memories, choosing to focus on putting together a food parcel for the first time.

'You should volunteer here more often, Samuel.'

He glanced at Sophie, then back at the shelves. Not as well stocked as his café, but still, there were a few good meals he could sort, and he made a mental note to invite Victoria and her children over to the Food Bank Café for their dinner. 'I only popped in to see Jan. I dropped her off here before lunch. Thought she had a shift.'

Sophie nodded as she put together a brown box. 'She did, but something came up and she had to nip out which is why I'm here.' She pointed at the wall. 'I work a couple of doors down, Sea Shanty Shack, the fishmongers. My partner, Matt, is there at the moment, so when I got the call, I came right over.'

He knew where she worked. 'You're a very tight community here.'

'Not really. It's just a few of us that got together to make this happen. We all have businesses along Harbour End Road, you see. Plus, we're all old friends. My grandad planted the seed the day we saw two homeless people by the boats. A year later, and hey presto, here we are. And what you've just done for that woman goes above and beyond, so thank you, and that's from all of us here.'

'No thanks needed. I was just . . .'

*What was I doing?*

Sophie placed her hand gently on his shoulder and smiled. 'It's okay. I understand. So, shall I add your name to the roster? Ooh, we've got a stall at the Port Berry Craft Fayre. We're going to be advertising this place, and your café, of course. All part of the Les Powell Trust. Would you like to help out there?'

'I'll have to say no to both, I'm afraid. I'm going to be busy expanding the charity, and I've already volunteered to help the Sunshine Centre set up, as my little sister will be selling her artwork with them.'

'My friend recently joined that place. It's for people with physical disabilities, right?'

Samuel shook his head. 'Not just that. They help those recovering from long-term illnesses as well, and it's also a kind of respite for some with PTSD and depression, and there are those with neurodivergent minds who are members. There's a lot going on over there.'

Sophie gazed around the small room they were in. 'I wish we could offer more, but we're small fry here.'

'You're doing plenty. The door is always open, and help is at hand, so you just focus on that. This little hub is going places, you mark my words.'

'We are small, but we have a big heart.'

'Just what every community needs.'

Sophie smiled and leaned in for another hug, leaving Samuel at a loss for words. In the few face-to-face work meetings he'd had, no one had hugged him. Was it appropriate in the charity sector? He had no idea but refused to hug her back just in case he was breaking any laws. There was no way he was about to lose everything he'd worked so hard for over something so small as a friendly hug.

Samuel politely wriggled away and got Sophie's input on what to add to the food box for Victoria. Was he really so uptight he couldn't hug someone? And more to the point, why was it now playing on his mind? He was once cheerful and bubbly like Sophie Moore. What the hell happened to him along the way? He glanced out the door at Victoria, sipping her drink. She wasn't the only sob story in the Hub.

Perhaps it was time he started to build more than food banks. It was time to rebuild himself. Hannah was a grown-up, settled in her life, and dating someone decent enough. His business was secure, and even if it wasn't, he had enough money for the rest of his life without ever having to work again, and he had the security of owning his own home outright.

After he helped sort out Victoria, he was determined to find his inner sparkle once more. The serious rich grump he'd become no longer felt like the right fit.

He glanced at his surroundings as he brought over the box of food. Maybe Sophie Moore was rubbing off on him, or perhaps it was being in Port Berry. Either way, he kind of liked the small piece of happiness rippling through him.

Victoria chatted merrily away to him while Sophie nipped out to borrow a car booster seat from a friend who lived up the road. It really was nice to see the smile in Victoria's eyes.

The woman in the wheelchair was still sitting outside the café when he went to his car. He wanted to go back over to her and introduce himself properly, but she was talking to the owner, and Victoria was about to come out of the Hub for her lift home.

It was probably just Hannah getting inside his head with talk of relationships that kept the woman in the wheelchair on his mind. He didn't normally ask to buy a woman lunch. Why her? Why now? He mentally shook his head, then opened the car door for his new employee. It was for the best that he focus on work. No one would want to date him anyway once they found out his problem.

# CHAPTER 10

*Lottie*

Sitting in Lottie's kitchen playing Ludo with her was Spencer and George. Games night was always fun, but even more so when Spencer joined in — he'd been doing so a lot more since her accident. She was certain it had changed his life as well as her own.

Spencer ran his fingers through his copper locks as George shook the dice. 'So, what's this big surprise you've got for us, Lottie?'

Whether she felt excited or stupid about her decision she still hadn't decided — not that it mattered. The deed was done. All eyes were on her as she fidgeted her hands on her lap.

'Should we be worried?' asked George, rolling out a four.

It was time for Lottie to get to the point. 'No, at least, I hope not. I've signed up for a wheelchair fun run, of sorts. It's six miles, and I'll be raising money for the Les Powell Trust. It's in two months' time over near Tavistock in Devon. I've already opened my sponsor page, so feel free to start donating.'

Spencer's eyes were wide and with a hint of concern. 'Six miles?' That was all he had to say about the matter, but she was sure once her news sank in, more words would follow.

George looked supportive, albeit with a tight smile, so she couldn't be entirely sure what was whirling in his mind.

'I can do it,' said Lottie, feeling the need to defend her decision.

'Of course you can,' said George, staring only at the colourful board game on the table.

Lottie blew out her frustration at the lack of confidence coming her way. 'I was always fit before I ended up in this thing.' She tapped the armrest on her wheelchair. 'And now that I have a racing wheelchair I can build more upper body strength and get back out there doing what I love.'

George flashed her a sympathetic smile. 'I know you miss your bike, love, but this is a bit different.'

'I'm going to train, George. I won't just jump in at the deep end. Besides, it's just a bit of fun. You don't have to be an elite athlete or anything to take part.'

Spencer finally found his voice. 'How long have you been thinking about doing something like this?'

'A little while. Please support me, Spence. I really want to do this. It's not dangerous. The event runs yearly and is sponsored by a major brand. There will be volunteers all around the course, which is on someone's private land, and first-aiders will be on-site. Everything is to a professional standard, see.'

'Okay,' he said, after she watched him mull it over. 'If it's safe, and you'll be safe, then count me in. I'll even sign up to help out, if you like?'

She smiled as she nodded. 'That would be great, but I think they've got everything covered. Just come to cheer me on.'

'I'll come too,' said George, beaming her way.

'Thanks, George. Wouldn't be the same without you.' She watched him go back to the board game to move his counter, and it suddenly hit her just how grateful she was for him. Even though she didn't know her dad, it wasn't as though she grew up without one, as George had always been there, playing out the role. 'Hey, George. I just want to say thanks for always being here for me.'

Could that be a blush on his cheeks? He smiled warmly as he passed Spencer the dice.

Spencer nudged his arm. 'Yeah, that goes for me too. You're a good man, George Watson.' George went to speak, but Spencer quickly added, 'How come you never settled with a family of your own?'

Lottie was interested to know the answer as well. It wasn't something they had questioned George about, always minding their own business while enjoying his company and fatherly help.

'Aw, you know,' replied George. 'You two were enough.' He laughed, but Lottie felt he was hiding something.

'Have you ever been in love, George?' she asked, cringing inside at her intrusiveness. It wasn't the kind of thing they spoke about, but since she'd started interviewing people for the Hub's website, she found herself quizzing folk more often. She went to apologize but George got in first.

'Yeah, there was someone, but she loved someone else, and that was that.'

Lottie's heart sank on his behalf. She glanced at Spencer to see he held the same look as her. Oh, poor George. Perhaps it was time to get him into online dating.

'Sorry, mate,' said Spencer sincerely. 'But you're only young. There's still time.'

George chuckled. 'I'm sixty. I can't be doing with all that now. My heart has only ever been with one woman, and I'm happy for it to stay that way.'

'Didn't anything happen with her?' asked Lottie, wishing he at least spent some time with his sweetheart. She tried to do the maths. George having a love life must have been before she came to live with her aunt, because she couldn't remember a time when he was with someone.

Warm eyes flittered from Lottie to Spencer as George smiled a smile that seemed to be just for him. 'We had our moments, and that's all I'm telling you two. Now, I have my own surprise for you.' He indicated to the back door. 'I have a big greenhouse arriving first thing. Now we'll be able to grow more home produce for our neighbours.'

Lottie squealed quietly as she clasped her hands together. 'Oh, George, that's brilliant. Thank you so much.'

'Don't thank me. They're my neighbours too. I want to do my bit. I'll start coming out with you.'

'That's great,' said Spencer, giving Lottie a pointed look.

She huffed and folded her arms dramatically. 'Spencer thinks I'm taking on too much lately.'

He shrugged and tossed the dice. 'You work in the shop, go to that art centre place, help out in the Hub, feed the vulnerable, and now you're in training for a marathon.'

Lottie laughed. 'Hardly. But, yes, this is my life now, and I plan to keep busy and not shy away from the world.'

'Good attitude, love,' said George. 'Excuse me, I just need the loo.'

As soon as he was gone, Lottie leaned closer to her brother. 'Who do you think his woman was?'

Spencer breathed out a hushed laugh. 'How should I know, and anyway, mind your business. Whoever she was, she obviously broke his heart, so leave it alone.'

Lottie sat back, trying hard not to sulk at being told off. 'I bet I can get him a date.'

Spencer scoffed. 'Leave the man alone. Just because you love dating, doesn't mean everyone does.'

'I do *not* love dating! In fact, I've knocked it on the head for a while.'

'Good. It was starting to get embarrassing.'

'Oh, thank you very much!'

Spencer shook his head, adding a lazy smile. 'Sorry, sis. I didn't mean it that way. I was getting worried about you, that's all. Sitting outside Ginny's and getting stood up every five minutes. Even by Trey Seabridge.'

'Oh, goodness. You heard about that little runt? Wait till I see his mother. And just for the record, no one stood me up, Spence. They just didn't bother to notice me once they clapped eyes on the wheelchair, that's all. Nothing I can do about that. Anyway, you're always going back to some woman's house each weekend, so less of the embarrassment aimed my way, thanks.'

Spencer twisted his mouth to one side, then lifted his glass of cola in a cheers motion. 'At least I'll never be heartbroken like George, or pining away for love like you.' He tapped his chest with his free hand. 'I'm the happy one.'

'Are you really? Because bed-hopping is no life.'

He laughed into his glass, spluttering as bubbles went up his nostrils. 'Bed-hopping? Really? Anyway, it is a life. It's mine, and like I said, I'm happy.'

It was pointless trying to convince him otherwise. This wasn't her first time approaching the subject. Spencer had never wanted a family life other than the one he shared with her and George. She truly believed he'd be better off settled with someone, but she knew the trauma of their childhood weighed heavily on him. Having convicted murderers as parents, serving life, wasn't the best start for a kid. Oh, how she thanked her aunt for the stability and security she gave by taking them in. If only Spencer was driven by Rebecca's drive instead of their parents' failures.

She sighed to herself and took her turn on the game, staying quiet until George returned.

'Where we at?' he asked, sitting back down.

'Your turn,' she replied.

George smiled and rolled the dice.

'What do you think of online dating, George?' she asked, catching her brother's glare.

George chuckled. 'Get on with the game, little miss, then we'll talk fruit and veg, and you can show us your training plan.'

That was her told. She ignored Spencer's smirk of a smile and thought about what kind of plan she could have. One for the race, one for George's love life, and one more for her artwork.

'I've just remembered,' she said quickly. 'I need to get my paintings over to the Sunshine Centre. Everyone's already taken theirs.'

'I'll sort that tomorrow for you,' said Spencer. 'You're needed in the shop all week. We've got a lot of weddings on.'

It was time to set the alarm clock for an hour earlier — that way, she could get in some training before work. Yep, she was pleased with her schedule.

'Are you coming to the craft fayre, George?'

He nodded. 'I'll be there in case either of you need me. Might buy a few bits as well.'

'As long as you don't buy my work. I've already told Spencer I don't want any pity sales.'

'And I've got a shift at the Hub's stall,' said Spencer to George, 'so I won't need any help. The others are taking turns. You enjoy yourself, mate. Stop worrying about us.'

'What are you selling on the Hub's stall?' asked George.

Spencer shook his head. 'Nothing. We're raising awareness. Seeing if we can get people to donate money online, that sort of thing.'

George beamed at them both. 'Look at you two. Grew up to be a couple of good-uns. Your aunt would be proud.' He looked pretty proud himself, and that filled Lottie with warmth and happiness, and by the look Spencer was trying to hide, he was feeling the same.

Gratitude washed over Lottie. Her life had changed dramatically, but the people in it were just the same as they were before her accident, showing her an abundance of love and support and making sure she never felt alone.

*Who needs the likes of Russ anyway?*

She could see him in all his tainted glory now. Well, she was worth so much more than someone's trophy, and all those non-dates could get stuffed too, because she already had a ful-filled life, thank you very much. Anyone else coming into her home from now on would simply be a bonus, not a necessity. Spencer was wrong. She wasn't pining for love. It would just be nice to have it, that's all, but if she spent a life single like George, then so be it.

Right there and then, Lottie Jordan decided there wasn't a man good enough for her anyway, even if she did have a rain check with the gorgeous man with amber eyes.

# CHAPTER 11

*Samuel*

July had arrived, and the summer sunshine was on top form for the Port Berry Craft Fayre, being held at Old Market Square and Anchorage Park. Large cream tents over the park covered many stalls, selling an array of goods from books to crochet toys, and local honey to handmade small furniture pieces. All Saints Church had opened its doors, and also put out a bric-a-brac stall in the adjoining hall, and local shops welcomed tourists while the cobbled square held an abundance of clothing and haberdashery set up beneath colourful canopies. The air was scented with the sweetness of flowers and freshly baked cakes, enticing visitors to happily mooch around the annual event.

Samuel had already helped Hannah with her art layout over in one of the tents in the park so was free to wander. He slipped his sunglasses from his dark hair to cover his eyes, adjusted one of the brown leather sliders slipping off his foot, checked for creases in his peach polo shirt, then set off across the grass to check out the local glassblower's selection of pretty items for sale.

Hannah had already laid claim to a set of six yellow-and-green tumblers, so Samuel paid for those, then headed for the cake tent to see what was entered in the baking competition taking place later in the day.

A waft of chocolate hit him first, and he couldn't help but lick his lips. He used to love baking with his mum. It surprised her when he didn't go on to culinary school, as he enjoyed cooking so much. When he became Hannah's guardian, he didn't have time to heat a tin of baked beans, let alone anything else.

It was decided. Tomorrow he would make his little sister a cake. He was feeling generous, so perhaps he'd invite Felix to join them. It was definitely a move his mother would have made. Tea and cake with a side order of scrutiny. Yes, that would do just fine.

As it was still early in the day, and Hannah had already had the biggest breakfast she could manage, Samuel didn't purchase any sweet treats. Instead, he thought it worth checking out the Hub's awareness stall, seeing how their food bank was under the Les Powell Trust — not that he wanted to throw out any CEO vibes. He just figured it would be rude not to show his face when in the vicinity.

Sophie was the first he saw as he closed in on the Hub's stall. He stopped and watched for a while, scanning over the noticeboards around a trestle table. It wasn't just their food bank advertised. They had included the Food Bank Café, which he thought pretty decent of them.

Samuel approached the copper-haired man behind the table while Sophie chatted to someone, handing them a leaflet. She was quite animated during her discussion, gathering a small group of onlookers to step closer to collect some information.

'All right, mate,' said Spencer, pointing at the tall board to his side that showcased homeless stats and help numbers. 'You look like a man with a donation ready.'

Samuel smiled, absentmindedly touching his wallet in the pocket of his cream shorts. 'Yes, I do like to donate, but

I was thinking of buying some artwork from the Sunshine Centre's tent today.'

Spencer stretched his neck to peer over that way. 'There's a beautiful painting of Port Berry's harbour over there. I say check that one out. It's the view from the very top of Berry Hill. Stunning sunset. Can't go wrong.'

Samuel laughed. 'You the artist?'

'Nah, it's my little sister. She's a member there. I've not long helped her set up. We were running late. But don't tell her I sent you. I'm under strict instructions not to interfere in any of her sales.'

'Same. My little sister started as a member but is one of the volunteers now as well, and I'm not allowed to buy any of her work.'

The two men shared a smile before Sophie came over, pointing out to Spencer who Samuel was.

Spencer's head bobbed as he laughed. 'And there was me about to hit you with my spiel.' He reached out a hand. 'Pleased to meet you, mate. And thanks for all your help with our Hub. You'll have to have dinner with us all one night in our mate Robson's pub. It's just at the corner of Harbour End Road. The Jolly Pirate. You'll always be welcome. We often have our meetings in there or the beer garden, when the weather's nice.'

Samuel wasn't used to being asked to go anywhere. Since losing his parents, quitting uni, and being evicted from his family home, his circle grew smaller by the month. All he had now were work acquaintances, and they were mostly online faces he'd rarely met in person. 'Thanks,' he replied, and he meant it.

Spencer turned to Sophie. 'About time the gang met this fella, eh, Soph?'

She nodded her agreement. 'I've already asked him to volunteer in the Hub anytime he wants.'

Spencer met his eyes. 'Oh yeah, I heard about you offering a woman a job. I hope it works out for her, and you. We had a bloke once who was just taking advantage of us.'

'He stole from our charity funds,' said Sophie.

Samuel knew all about it, as the story had made the local news. Like everyone else, he was glad the culprit was caught and put behind bars.

'I think Victoria will be just fine. She's in training with my assistant already. I'm hoping to expand the food banks all over Cornwall, so what you're doing here today is incredibly helpful. Thank you.'

Sophie quietly clapped. 'It's exciting, isn't it, Spence? Well, about Samuel's help, not the fact people need us.'

He understood. They all did.

Samuel wished them luck for the day, telling them he was off to check out some more stalls. He left, heading back to his sister to give her the glasses she wanted and use the sunscreen she had in her bag. The back of his neck had started to burn when he was talking to Spencer. He was glad Hannah had the shade inside the tent. Figuring she might need hydrating as well, he stopped off at a soft drinks stand and bought her a cold bottle of water.

Hannah was already sipping freshly squeezed orange juice that Felix had managed to get from who knows where, leaving Samuel feeling like a spare part all of a sudden.

'Ooh, are they the tumblers I spotted earlier?' she asked, eyes alight with glee.

Feeling ever so smug because Felix hadn't bought them, Samuel placed the small box behind her and kissed her cheek. 'Yes, now you can stop worrying. So, tell me, sold anything yet?' He glanced around him at the paintings everywhere, then stole a quick look at Felix, whose attention was on his little sister's mouth.

Hannah nodded. 'One. But, hey, it's a start.'

'And it's not even lunchtime yet,' said Felix, giving her a peck on the lips.

Samuel turned away so they didn't see him roll his eyes. 'Well done, sis.' He made sure his tone was light and filled with meaning. After all, just because Felix irritated him for taking care of Hannah, it didn't mean he wasn't proud of her. He glanced over his shoulder as he reached for the sunscreen — they were going dreamy eyed over each other again.

At this rate, they'd miss any potential customers. 'Keep an eye out, won't you?' he said, waggling an index finger over the pictures at the front. 'I'm going to check out your competition.' He rubbed some of the tropical-scented cream around the back of his neck.

Hannah snorted. 'We're not in competition, Sam.' She waved him away, then went back to stroking Felix's jawline. Something else Samuel didn't need to see.

As he walked around the large tent, perusing the artwork, he wondered if his parents would expect him to do something about Felix's lips touching their daughter's.

Samuel wondered if perhaps it was time he found his own partner, but how would it work? What if she wanted to go on holiday? And how on earth would he even approach the subject of his demon? It wasn't exactly the best opener, and it wouldn't be fair to keep it a secret. He hated the thought of wearing a mask. He prided himself on honesty, even if he could be quite blunt at times. It was pointless having the thought. No one would want to take on his issues. He didn't want them either.

It wasn't until he spotted the painting of the harbour in Port Berry that his chatterbox brain shut up. He lowered his sunglasses to take a closer look. Spencer was right. It was lovely, and if Hannah's paintings were off limits, then he would buy another.

Picking it up to angle the canvas in both hands, he couldn't fathom why he suddenly wanted the picture so much. All rooms in his house flashed through his mind, and he still wasn't sure where he could hang the image.

'Excuse me,' came a sweet but firm voice from the other side of the painting, sounding awfully familiar.

Samuel lowered the picture, revealing his shaded eyes. 'Yes?' It was the woman he'd offered to buy lunch for. 'Oh, it's you.'

'What are you doing?' she asked, looking only at the painting.

He paused, then lifted his sunglasses to sit on his head, scanning the beauty before him. She really was gorgeous, even with pursed lips. 'Is this yours?'

'Yes.'

That was it. One short sharp word.

Why was he suddenly feeling intimidated? He decided to let her see his business side. Taking a step closer, he put on his work face, leaned slightly over her artwork, and asked, 'How much?'

She swallowed hard. He noticed. But then her glance fell to his lips for a split second, causing him to straighten and swallow the dryness clogging his throat.

'It's not for sale,' she told him flatly, adding a tight smile, which made the edge of his mouth twitch.

'Has someone already bought the painting?'

The fact she was mulling over her answer was entertaining, but he kept his cool and waited, not once removing his eyes from her face.

'No,' she replied quietly.

'So, why can't I buy it?'

She met his eyes, and fizz met his stomach. 'Why do you want to?'

Samuel softened his features, wanting her to relax around him. 'I like it.'

Her bottom lip juddered and she quickly bit down on it to keep it in place. It was all a bit too much for him, staring at her mouth. He broke contact with her face just as she straightened in her seat.

'One hundred pounds.' She had said it slowly and with such conviction, Samuel almost burst out laughing. They both knew the pictures on display were selling for around a tenner each, if that.

He met determination mixed with smugness in those beautiful sea-blue eyes of hers. Was she testing him or merely trying to flick him away as though he were an irritating bug?

'Sold,' he announced, reaching for his wallet, ignoring her gaping mouth.

*Don't laugh. Don't laugh. Don't laugh.*

He repeated his mantra before gazing back up to see what her expression was this time.

She looked quite taken aback, but she held herself well, he thought. She gestured to a table at the back of the tent. 'You have to pay over there.'

Samuel went to walk away but stopped at another painting of the harbour in Port Berry. It held the moonlight shining down upon three small boats. 'Is this one yours as well?'

Silence seemed to fill the area when she didn't reply, and Samuel reached a point where he started to think she didn't like him at all. He really didn't know what to say.

'Yes,' she said, finally.

He gave her a warm smile. 'You're very talented.'

A beat passed.

'Thank you,' she mumbled.

Samuel tensed his shoulders. 'How much?'

Her eyes narrowed as her jaw clenched. She'd never make it in a game of poker.

'Same price, I assume?' he added, seeing how she hadn't replied.

Her head bobbed so slightly it wouldn't have been noticeable to anyone not paying close attention.

'I'll take them both. Won't be a sec.' He heard her electric wheelchair move as he went to pay for her paintings.

*Oh, Sam, what are you doing . . .*

It was so hard to keep a straight face when he returned to her, picked up the two pictures, nodded a *good day*, then left.

Hannah's face was filled with curiosity when he placed the items behind her, adding to their collection of bought goods. She frowned but didn't say a word.

'You hungry yet?' he asked her.

'No. But Felix said he'll buy me lunch later.'

Not even good old Felix could dampen his mood. 'I'm making a cake tomorrow, sis. Mum's recipe. Bring Felix over to join us. Say three o'clock.'

Hannah's big smile quickly faded. 'Oh, we've already agreed to meet up with Lottie. She's my new friend. I've mentioned her before, but you never listen, so—'

Samuel had a real skip in his step. 'Bring her too. The more the merrier.'

'Really?' Hannah didn't sound too convinced, and he couldn't blame her. When was the last time he invited anyone to their home? Never.

'Yeah, sure. Chocolate fudge cake for everyone.' He ignored his sister studying him and went to see what else he could buy that would have him walk past the blonde with the pretty smile.

The Port Berry Craft Fayre was turning out to be a wonderful day.

# CHAPTER 12

*Lottie*

The tropical smell that came from Lottie's customer was still lingering in the air, swirling around her head, making her a tad dizzy.

*Did that just happen?*

She stilled as he passed by the art tent where she sat behind a small now empty table covered only in a white sheet. Where was he off to now? And would he come back? She hoped so. Did she? Not wanting to think about him anymore, she found the woman who ran the Sunshine Centre.

'As I've sold both my paintings, Debra. I thought I'd go over to the Hub's stall and help out there.'

Debra smiled and nodded. 'Good idea. Oh, and, Lottie, well done.'

Heat trickled up Lottie's neck as she headed out the tent. She wasn't feeling best pleased with herself. After all, had she just conned some man into paying over the odds for her pictures? Partly, it seemed that way, but judging by the way she'd acted, it did come across more like a weird stand-off.

She tried to hurry her wheelchair across the bumpy grass in case the stranger, who was becoming less of a stranger as the days went on, made another appearance. Who was he and why did he keep popping up in her life lately? It was all too much, especially those captivating eyes of his and that athletic frame.

She told herself to stop thinking about him, but it was no good. He stayed in her mind all the way to the Hub's stall.

Relieved to see Spencer still there, and Robson too, she happily joined them, thinking it would be a good opportunity to tell potential donors all about her upcoming race for charity.

'What you doing over here, sis?' asked Spencer.

'I already sold my artwork, so I thought I'd help here.'

'Oh, well done. I'll go grab us some lunch. What would you like? There are loads of food stalls.'

Lottie gestured towards Old Market Square. 'I spotted quiche and salad somewhere over there. That would be good.'

Spencer took a food order for Robson as well, then set off.

Robson turned her way and smiled. 'Well done on your sales, Lott, and I heard about the charity race you're doing. I'll sponsor you later.'

'Thanks, Robson. Every little helps, right?'

His eyes sparkled. 'Exactly.' He waved her closer. 'Come over here under the shade. You'll end up with sunburn that side. It's strong today.'

She moved his way and picked up some leaflets, ready to hand out. 'Have you had much interest so far?'

'Yeah, it was busy just before you arrived. A lot of people have promised to bring food into the Hub in the week, so we'll see, and we've had a few make donations online while they stood here, so that was good.'

'Ooh, I hope I have as much luck. When's Ginny due over?'

He checked his watch. 'Just after two, she said. No doubt, she'll wake the crowd up when it's her turn. You know what she's like.'

Lottie giggled, thinking of her friend's loud voice that came out when needed.

'So, Lott, do you know who bought your paintings?'

'No.' Was that a lie? Not completely. Peach top and sun-shades needed to be gone from her mind. 'How's business at the pub?'

There was a brief crinkle that hit Robson's brow, and she knew his confusion was because she didn't normally ask questions like that.

'Good,' he replied. 'You okay?'

Having taken part in quite a few beauty pageants over the years, Lottie knew how to fake the perfect smile. She flashed one at her friend. 'Yep. I'm having a lovely day.'

Robson didn't look too convinced but didn't get time to say anything else because a couple of young women came over to ask what he was selling.

Lottie was pretty sure they were just trying to chat him up. She secretly timed how long it would take before they realized they had no chance with the widower. Robson still wasn't ready to date and had no interest in flirting either.

She had just reached thirty-seven seconds when a tropical scent entered the light breeze doing little to shift her fringe. She slowly left Robson's party to land her gaze upon the man who had bought her artwork.

'Hello,' he said, sounding so smooth, so composed.

'Hello,' she managed, not sounding half as cool.

He lifted his sunglasses from his nose to his head and scanned the noticeboard to her side. 'Are you a volunteer here?'

'Yes. I help run the Happy to Help Hub, here in Port Berry. We help anyone in need, from the homeless to the hungry. We find jobs, homes, and now offer food parcels at our food bank, under the guidance of the Les Powell Trust.' She took a breath. 'We accept online donations, non-perishable food at the Hub, or you can sponsor me in a wheelchair race I'm participating in soon. All proceeds go straight into the

Trust, which in turn helps the Hub.' Feeling mighty proud of her professionalism, she sat back in her chair and smiled.

He took a leaflet from her. 'This park would be a good place to train for your race. Safer than the road, don't you think?'

Lottie tensed. Oh, so he was going to bring that up again. 'Still looking out for me?' she asked as calmly as she could muster.

'I can't have lunch with you if someone runs you over,' he said, just as coolly, catching her eye and holding her gaze.

Lottie found she had no words. Her tummy was in knots, and her throat extremely dry all of a sudden. She pulled her bottom lip inwards and took a silent calming breath.

Robson was still chatting merrily away to potential donors, and Spencer wasn't back yet. So she was front of house for the Hub. She had to say something.

'Would you like to donate, sir?'

He lowered his sunglasses to peer down at her with a look she couldn't fathom. 'Another time.' And with that, he left.

Luna approached with Mrs Hopkin. 'Going well, love?'

Lottie was so pleased to have a distraction, she practically squealed out her reply. 'Yes, we've had loads of attention.'

Mrs Hopkin started to read a leaflet while Luna scrutinized Lottie.

Lottie hated when she did that. There was no way of telling if the old woman was seeing the future or delving into parts of the soul.

Luna tucked away a piece of hair that had fallen from her bun, and all Lottie could focus on were the midnight-blue eyes boring into her private life.

'Bought anything, Luna?' Lottie tried for casual but was having a weird day so didn't pull it off well.

'I thought I'd sponsor you, dear.'

'Oh, no need. Your granddaughter already did that for all of you lot at the newsagent's. Family donation.' She smiled, thinking of her friend. 'Speaking of which, where is Alice? She said she'd be along today.'

Luna made a circle in the air with her index finger. 'Around with her mum. Lizzie's taking her lunch break here while the Saturday staff are working the shop.'

Lottie hadn't seen Lizzie either. She didn't mention it, but she was surprised the three of them hadn't booked a stall for the tarot readings they could all do. Luna often did a quick reading for customers back at the Treasure Chest newsagent's when they popped in to buy a lottery ticket, as did Lizzie. The running joke was why couldn't they just predict the winning numbers?

'And how are you, Lottie?'

'I'm good. Training hard.'

Luna smiled tightly. 'And the dating?'

'On the back burner.'

'Love finds you, you know.'

Lottie snorted out a laugh. 'I think you'll find a lot of couples meet online. Sometimes, Luna, you have to go find love for yourself.'

'And sometimes, you just have to open your eyes and see what's right in front of you.' Luna nudged Mrs Hopkin, and they set off towards the cake tent.

'What is she . . .' Her mumbled words drifted off as Robson flashed her a brief smile.

*Surely she didn't mean him.*

Not once had she ever looked at Robson in that way. He was her friend. She had been friends with his wife. No, that can't be right. Just thinking about it felt odd. Robson was more like a brother.

She dipped her head to her hands. 'Oh, what a day!' she whispered, then wished she hadn't looked up so soon, because over in the near distance was the man who'd bought her paintings, once more passing by. And he caught her looking.

*Blimming heck!*

She smiled to herself as she turned away. The thought of having lunch with the man didn't seem so bad after all.

# CHAPTER 13

*Samuel*

Don't think, just do, was Samuel's mantra all the way to Looe. The road had been unusually quiet and he'd made good time. The thought of that being a good omen didn't pass him by completely, even if he wasn't sure he believed in such things.

Approaching the road sign that tormented him, he turned his attention to the chocolate fudge cake he'd baked early that morning. Pulling out his mum's old recipe book and flicking through scribbled notes left behind from her and her grandmother was emotional. So much so, he was going to give today's exposure therapy a miss.

Samuel's heart had ached as each ingredient hit the big cream bowl. The times he'd baked with his mother all taken for granted. He missed her terribly and wished so hard he could speak to her just one last time.

The choccy cake was cooling back home. Hannah wasn't due back till three, so it was a good opportunity for him to grab some lunch in Looe. Today was the day he conquered that place and made his mark. And now he had Jan to report back to about his progress, things seemed a little easier.

With thoughts of his mum, the cake, Hannah, and the woman in the wheelchair, who also had a place in his head, he drove all the way into Looe and didn't stop until he parked up.

*Whoa!*

No matter how many times he won a battle, it always felt surreal. Being somewhere for no reason other than to be there wasn't ever as exciting as he'd imagined. He'd reached a point months back where he gave up thinking it a win.

Brain training was boring, scary, and plain old weird. What a combination.

Samuel walked until he reached a sea view and took a moment to simply stare at his new surroundings, which wasn't that different to the one he had at home. He had one of those moments where he wondered why he was bothering.

He found a café with outdoor seating, ordered some lunch, and sat outside. He'd come this far, might as well do what he always did. Sit. Eat. Feel bored. Fight for a touch of happiness to hit, and then head home to study where to head off to next.

Seagulls circled the overcast sky, making themselves known, as strangers sat around him, chattering away to their company. Perhaps that's where he was going wrong. Hannah would accompany him, he was sure, but it was difficult to ask for help. Plus, what if he wanted to turn around and go home before they'd arrived at their destination? Or what if he wanted to suddenly leave. That would spoil her fun, and that thought alone weighed heavily on him.

Samuel hated being a burden, so life alone worked.

Looe was tougher than the others, but he figured it was because he wasn't having a good day anyway. All over a stupid chocolate cake. The slice sitting on the plate at the table next to him brought back his memories. They were supposed to lift him. Make him smile, not cry into the food mixer.

*Jeez, what a morning!*

Any onlookers would see a thirty-year-old man enjoying lunch and little else, as Samuel knew how to hide his demon well. Glancing around, he wondered how many around him had secrets destroying their souls.

Pulling out his notebook, he wrote down how he was feeling, what level of fear was attacking, and how long it stayed for. Looking it over, it showed he wasn't doing too bad. Even so, it failed to lift his worn spirit. Maybe he needed a break from his disorder, but that would mean ignoring it altogether, which had the potential to take him straight back to square one.

A quick flick through his phone and he was watching a short video of a young man talking about how he now travels after years of agoraphobia. It did help. Strangers online showing him the end game always helped, but today was a low day. Today, he was losing. He wrote that down. All thoughts and feelings had to come out one way or another.

He'd had enough of Looe already. Unable to appreciate its beauty, he made light work of his ploughman's and walked back to his car, feeling deflated on every level.

The drive home was a little faster, as he was short on time. Hannah would be back with Felix and her friend soon, and he wanted to have a nice tea and cake spread laid out for her. He'd even bought a red gingham tablecloth at the Port Berry Craft Fayre the day before.

It looked good in his mind. All he had to do was make it pretty for Hannah. She loved that sort of thing, and he loved making her smile.

Hannah was leaving him soon, he could tell. She was in love and full of confidence. She'd come a long way since the accident, and it had been one hell of a trip. All he hoped was that Felix really was a good guy, because his little sister deserved only the best.

The perfectionist in him was surfacing as the time ticked louder and louder, telling him to get a wriggle on. The numbness inside rapidly changed as adrenaline took charge, causing sweaty palms, a racing heart, and a thumping headache.

The gates to his driveway couldn't open fast enough. There was still time to set everything up. He jumped out of the car, rushed into the house, tossed his notebook and keys on the side table in the hallway, and headed straight to the kitchen.

He pulled the table closer to the ceiling-to-floor windows, showing off the sea view. Red gingham stole the show, and teacups and saucers, a plate of fancy biscuits, and his mum's choccy cake made the rest.

He stood back, admiring his handiwork, knowing his mother would have done the same.

Felix was getting a friendly welcome to the Powell's, whether he liked it or not.

A text came through from Hannah, saying she was running late but would be home soon. He placed his phone on the white worktop and sighed. It wasn't fair that his parents weren't there to meet their daughter's boyfriend.

*Bloody hell. Stop.*

He blinked away the threatening tears and took a deep breath, grabbing his bottle of water. It was time to step up, get a grip, and make his parents proud. There was nothing else he could think to do.

Balloons sprung to mind, but that would make it look like a birthday party or something. No, that was taking things too far.

'I could . . .' A noise came from the hallway, startling him. His housekeeper wasn't rostered on, and Hannah had just told him she wasn't home. He suddenly remembered he'd left the gates open . . . and his front door.

# CHAPTER 14

*Lottie*

Lottie had told Hannah she would meet her at her house, so George dropped Lottie off inside the opened gates of the address. She glanced up at the big house, pleased to see a wide slope at the foot of the main door, which was also open.

She raised one hand, waving George off.

The dark-blue wheelchair accessible vehicle he drove was bought just before she came out of hospital and was such a surprise for her, not to mention Spencer, who was also kept in the dark about the purchase.

As soon as he was out of sight, Lottie manoeuvred up the slope, taking a moment to admire Hannah's house. It was absolutely stunning for an old coastal home. It's whitewashed walls and huge windows added a modern touch to a home that had clearly been renovated. The big building screamed wealth that Lottie didn't know Hannah had.

Hannah was just Hannah from the Sunshine Centre. The first friend she'd made when she joined. Why would they talk bank balances?

The hallway to the house was large and vacant, with not a lot of furniture going on. A wide stairway was to one side and a few closed doors dotted about. There was a glass lift at the back, which made her smile. She knew Hannah wore prosthetic legs and sometimes used a wheelchair, so she guessed the lift was an asset at times. She could have done with one back when she first had to use her manual wheelchair to climb Berry Hill.

'Hello,' she called.

Silence.

She moved over to a shiny white sideboard to pop down the bunch of flowers she'd bought for Hannah as a gift, but she accidentally knocked the large vase of blooms already there alongside a notebook and keys. Her body didn't have time to freeze as the water completely drenched her and the cream vase landed on her lap because she was too busy struggling and juggling with the notebook mid-fall.

'Oh, blimming heck,' she mumbled.

There was no way she was going to be able to scoop up the car keys from the floor. They were a lost cause.

She sat there, soaked through, knowing there was little she could do about the state she was now in. She was about to close the notebook and put it back on the side, when the man who'd bought her paintings at the craft fayre appeared from a side door.

*Goodness, it's him!*

Confusion in his eyes quickly turned to embarrassment as he looked at what she was holding.

'Oh,' said Lottie, holding the notebook a little higher. 'I was—'

'That's mine,' he snapped, making her jump.

Lottie recoiled into her seat. 'I'm sorry. I—'

'Did you read it?' he asked, sounding rattled.

'No, I—'

'What are you doing here?' She went to speak, but he quickly added, 'Never mind . . . I . . .'

Lottie had no idea what was going on. All she knew was she had better go, as he looked so upset. She didn't even ask what he was doing in Hannah's house. 'I'm sorry,' she said softly, handing him the book.

He took it and hugged it close to his chest.

Lottie had no idea what to say. She removed the vase from her lap, awkwardly tried to rearrange the colourful flowers, placed it back on the sideboard, then spun her wheelchair around, with the attention of heading for the doorway.

George was probably halfway home, so she decided to head for the gate first, then call him to come back. That way she'd be away from the man in the hallway, even though part of her wanted to find out what was wrong.

'Please, don't leave,' he blurted. 'I'm so sorry. I didn't mean to be weird. I just . . . I . . .' His words drifted again, but Lottie was only half listening. She was painfully aware that her pink dress was soaked through, and she still had a couple of buds on her lap.

'I don't know what's wrong, but it's okay, I'm leaving. You don't have to worry about me being here much longer.' She pointed forward.

He stepped back, giving her space. 'Please, let me explain.'

Lottie was having a hard time figuring him out. Clearly something bothered him about that notebook. 'I wasn't being nosey with your book.' He had to know that much.

His eyes dipped. 'I . . . It's just, well . . .'

Whatever he was trying to say, he wasn't doing a good job of it, and she couldn't concentrate on him any longer, as she was starting to feel a tad shivery.

'Please let me explain.' His voice sounded wrecked. 'I'm guessing you're Lottie, right? Hannah's friend?'

Lottie nodded.

'I'm Hannah's brother. Samuel. Please, I'm so sorry. I just, well, you were, and I . . .'

Lottie offered a small smile, as he sounded sincere, and she wondered if it was just her unexpected appearance in his house that had rattled him so much. 'It's okay. I'm going home. I just have to call my friend to pick me up. I won't be here much longer, and I promise you, if I could have, I would have left by now. I can't always get away as quickly as I want. Sometimes it's like being trapped. Sorry, I don't expect you to know how that feels.' She mentally shook her head at her rambling.

A beat passed.

'I'll take you home,' he said softly.

Lottie was already on the phone to George. 'Hello, George. Can you come get me, please? I'm ready to go home.'

George told her he would be there in a jiffy, so she hung up the call and stared at the flowers, knowing they needed a drink, seeing how she was wearing their last one.

Samuel moved closer to push the vase further back from the edge. 'You're not trapped here,' he told her quietly.

Lottie felt her heart break slightly at how sad he sounded, but she also felt cold, wet, and in need of dry clothes. 'I know I'm not trapped here. I just wanted to get out of your way, as clearly you're not happy me being here.'

'I am really sorry I made you feel uncomfortable, Lottie. Please know I didn't mean it.'

She turned her chair and leaned forward, staring into his worried eyes. 'I don't know what happened here, but right now I have bigger things to worry about.' She picked up a damp bud and frowned.

He lowered his head. 'I was upset because you were reading my private—'

'I did not read your book,' she said sharply, startling herself.

Samuel's mouth opened for a moment but then closed.

The silence between them was suffocating, and she wondered why he was still standing there. There had been a misunderstanding, and as far as she was concerned, it had been cleared up. He'd got upset because he thought she had read something private. She'd explained she hadn't. Job done. They both had calmed, and all that was left was for George to pull up and take her home, so there was no need for Samuel to keep apologizing.

'Would you like some cake?' he asked.

Lottie almost laughed, the question was so bizarre.

'It's chocolate fudge,' he added softly.

'Another time.'

'I feel terrible.'

She glanced at her lap, picking off the remaining bud and slowly placed it on the sideboard.

'Bloody hell!' He gasped, noticing her wet dress. 'The vase. Your lap. You're soaked.'

Lottie pulled her lips in as she nodded.

Samuel frowned, looking angry at himself, if his head shake was anything to go by. 'Let me get you a towel. Erm, there's a bathroom just here.' He gestured at a white door.

'Thank you.'

Samuel sprinted across the hallway, bowing and waving her forward like he was some sort of Disney royal servant. His dark hair flopped into his eyes, looking somewhat amusing. 'Just here,' he pointed out.

Lottie brought the wheelchair to a halt in the bathroom, so pleased to see it was adapted for her needs. She quickly sorted herself and sighed with relief. But what the hell was she going to do with her wet clothes? She frowned at her lovely pink summer dress now sticking to her.

There was a pile of stripy towels close by, so she figured she'd absorb some of the water using one, then sit outside until George returned. Should be okay. It wouldn't be long before she was home and could get changed.

'Oh, what a flipping disaster!' she scoffed, shaking her head. 'And *him* being here, of all people.'

She glanced at the white ceiling, taking a moment to clear her head. All she did was go to her friend's house for tea and cake, and now look. She almost laughed at the madness.

*Oh, Rebecca. Why me?*

A light tapping came at the door.

# CHAPTER 15

*Samuel*

Never before had Samuel felt so utterly mortified. This poor woman had come into his home for tea and cake with his little sister, and what did he do? Made her feel awkward, accused her of reading his notebook, and didn't even notice the water all over her lap.

Lottie was in his downstairs bathroom, soaking wet and needing assistance, and he was just standing there like a right lemon. He had to do something.

When Hannah first came out of the recovery centre, Samuel had to do most things for her. She was so depressed and flat-out refused to try artificial limbs. Those were the bleak days, but somehow, along the way, they'd found methods that worked for them both. He had grown with her, learning how to navigate tough situations, so he could surely get a grip and help Lottie.

He tapped on the door, hoping she would answer him. 'Do you need any help, Lottie?' He shook his head at how feeble he sounded.

'My dress is wet. I'm just drying off a bit.'

'I can fetch you something of Hannah's to change into if you like,' he called through the door, knowing they were around the same size.

'Yes, please. That would be helpful.'

'Won't be a sec.'

Lottie's small voice called back, 'Thank you.'

Samuel sprinted upstairs and rummaged around in the wardrobe in Hannah's bedroom. 'Ah-ha!' He removed the soft pink tracksuit, thinking it would do the trick, as he knew it was one of Hannah's favourite loungewear items.

Sitting on his sister's bed for a moment, he took some much-needed deep breaths. He didn't have time to wallow, as Lottie needed him to step up, not crack up.

Why did he have to be weird about things? He knew why. Panic hit him hard when he saw her with his therapy notes. The shame took over, morphing into embarrassment at the speed of light. It didn't take long for his senses to return. And now look. What a mess!

*Stupid agoraphobia. I bloody hate you.*

He went back downstairs and tentatively tapped on the bathroom door. 'I'm back.' He had no idea why he'd stated the obvious, but seeing how his brain had turned to mush somewhere in the hallway, he simply accepted his stupidity.

'You can come in,' said her delicate voice on the other side.

He entered to see her dress on the floor along with the flowery cushion from her wheelchair. She was sitting on the soft chair by the sink, her body wrapped in a large red-and-white stripy towel.

Hannah had chairs everywhere, as sometimes tiredness would strike and she just needed to flop to a seat.

Lottie gestured at the beach towel around her. 'This reminds me of the tent for the Punch and Judy show.'

Could they really make light of their situation?

'Yeah, go on, laugh,' she added. 'But remember, it's your towel.'

96

Samuel twisted his mouth to one side as he handed over Hannah's clothes. 'I wasn't going to laugh.'

'Hmm. At least I'm dry again, so that's something. Thank you.'

'Please don't thank me. I should have helped you sooner.'

'It's okay. You didn't notice.'

Samuel bent to a cabinet, pulling out a small laundry basket to gather up her wet things. 'I should have.'

'I don't want to argue, Sam.'

His name rolling off her tongue so gently made his stomach flip. 'You get dressed. It's just Hannah's loungewear, but she swears it's the best outfit ever.' He breathed out a quiet laugh, then gestured at her wheelchair. 'Is this dry? I could put it outside in the sun?'

'Oh no, please don't take it away. I get a bit funny if my wheelchair isn't close by. I know it sounds silly, but if I can't see it, I feel . . . trapped.'

His heart sank as his thoughts went back to her words before. There was no way he wanted her to not feel freedom. He knew all too well what trapped felt like. His was just in a different way. 'Sorry, I'm not thinking straight.'

'It's okay. Not everyone thinks about such matters.'

Samuel nodded. 'I do. Normally.'

'Yeah, well, you got a little flustered seeing me in your home.'

He shook his head. 'It was just the book. It's a, erm . . . I'll pop your bits in the dryer. Shouldn't take long. What do you think?'

'Thanks, that would be great, if you don't mind me sticking around.'

Samuel turned in the doorway. 'You're welcome to stay here for as long as you want.' Her gentle smile warmed him all the way to the tumble dryer, where he got on with his task.

There was a message on his phone from Hannah, apologizing for her lateness, saying she shouldn't be too much longer at the centre and to look after Lottie should she arrive first.

He grabbed a cushion from the living room, hoping it might replace the one drying, then headed back to the bathroom and once more knocked and waited.

'Come in, Sam.'

He was starting to like it when she said his name, and he didn't favour people shortening Samuel. Only Hannah got away with it, and now Lottie, it would appear.

'What do you think?' she asked, gesturing to the pink tracksuit she wore.

'You look beautiful.' He meant it, as she'd even managed to look good wearing the stripy towel. And he'd thought his behaviour towards Lottie since her arrival couldn't have got any more inappropriate. He got on with double-checking the wheelchair was dry.

'It's okay, I already dried it off, but it wasn't too bad. My lap and cushion took most of the water.'

Samuel glanced up. 'I'm so sorry.'

'I can see. Let's move forward now. Just because we had a bad start, doesn't mean it has to continue.'

He smiled at her generosity. She really was very kind.

'So, do you really have chocolate cake?' Lottie asked, making his smile widen.

'I do. Made it this morning.'

'You bake?'

'Don't sound so surprised. I'm Jack of all trades.'

Lottie snorted. 'Master of none.'

Samuel grinned, placing the cushion on her wheelchair. 'I can master a lot, thanks.' He avoided her eyes as he took the towel she handed him.

'That needs a wash now.'

'It can wait.' He flopped it over his arm. 'How are you feeling now?'

'Better, thanks.' She motioned to the cream cushion. 'And thanks for that. Very thoughtful of you.'

Samuel wrinkled his nose. 'Yes, well, least I can do.'

'Hey, stop being so hard on yourself. You got me dry clothes, I had a bathroom and towel to use. Everything's fine.'

He looked at the towel. 'Had I known, I would have put new towels in here.'

Lottie chuckled. 'I like that towel. It brought on a funny memory when you went a minute ago.'

'Oh, what was that?'

'My aunt took Spencer and me to the beach one day when we were little, and there was a Punch and Judy show going on. Well, she got so mad. Marched up to the tent and started ranting about how the show makes light of domestic abuse, and how it was outdated and should never have been allowed to make boys and girls think violence towards women is funny.'

'Oh, I've never thought of that before.'

'Neither had a lot of the audience till Rebecca educated them, pointing out that Punch murders his baby and wife. One man swore at her and told her she was ruining the show and that it wouldn't be funny without the violence. Well, it all kicked off. One woman threw something at him and asked if he thought that was funny. The police ended up on the scene, and the show was cancelled.'

'Sounds like the type of thing my mum would have done.'

Lottie covered her mouth with one hand. 'I have Judy sitting on the bookshelf in my living room. My aunt swiped her away during the chaos. Said it was one woman she could save.'

Samuel laughed, then mimicked the words from the show. 'That's the way to do it.'

Lottie laughed with him, then transferred herself back into the wheelchair.

'Would you like that cake now?'

She nodded, and Samuel was pleased the air felt clearer between them.

'Follow me.' He led her to the kitchen and smiled as her eyes lit up at the view of the sea in the near distance.

'Wow, what a room. I think I just fell in love with your kitchen. I could sit here for hours and paint.'

'You're welcome to paint here anytime,' he blurted, then chastised himself for being a tad forward.

'I might just take you up on that.' Her smile was so warm, it settled him.

'You can paint now if you like. Hannah has loads of art equipment here.'

Lottie smiled. 'Another time.' She stared back at the view. 'I probably wouldn't get any work done if I had this to look at every day. It's a great spot to sit and have your morning cuppa.'

Samuel didn't do much in the way of sitting around, as he tried hard to keep busy to keep his mind occupied.

'There's a lot of space in here as well.' She gazed over her shoulder. 'You have such a lovely home.'

'I wanted as much room as possible so when Hannah's in her wheelchair she could move around with ease.' He quickly brushed off the memory of their old life when the money ran out and they were living in a small place, wishing they had more space.

Lottie moved over to the table. 'She's a nice lady, your sister. She was the first friend I made when I joined the centre. And then Felix.'

'Do you know much about him?'

She breathed out a small laugh. 'I know he's Hannah's boyfriend, and that's why you asked.' She flapped a hand. 'My big brother is protective too.'

Samuel went over to the kettle. 'I just worry about her, that's all.'

'Can't be helped when you're close.'

'I guess.' He waggled a cup. 'Do you take sugar?'

'No, thanks. Just milk.'

Samuel got busy with his task, wondering what to talk about next. He was having such a strange day, and being in Lottie's company was completely unexpected. 'Would you like some lunch before having cake?' He turned and grinned. 'I believe I owe you a lunch.'

Lottie's eyes widened. 'Oh, yes, about that. I heard you already paid for my lunch at Harbour Light Café. My friend told me.'

'Ah, that. Well, I saw your date walk away when he noticed your wheelchair, and I wanted to help cheer you up.'

'Thank you, but I was fine. It was my own fault for not telling him.'

'I thought you were brave meeting someone you'd met online.' He shrugged one shoulder. 'Sorry, I kind of overheard everything.'

'I don't see it as brave. Those sites are set up for people looking for love.'

'You get all sorts on those places. Liars and cheaters.'

Lottie's lips twisted to one side as her gaze fell to the table. 'I guess I was one of the liars.' She looked over at him. 'I hid the wheelchair from all my dates.'

'What made you decide to do that?'

'I just wanted to be seen for who I am. I wasn't trying to deceive anyone.'

'I understand.'

She didn't look as though she believed him. 'Really?'

Samuel nodded. 'Of course.' He knew how she felt. If he dated anyone, he'd want to hide his condition from them, even though he knew it wouldn't be fair. He pondered over telling her. She must have questions about his notebook after the way he'd reacted.

Lottie glanced at the door leading to the hallway. 'I have no idea where George is. He should have been here by now.'

'Hannah said she's running late, but she should be here soon as well.'

'There were some roadworks on the way here, but nothing much.'

Samuel went over to check the security camera showing the front gate. 'No one there.'

Lottie peered at the screen. 'The gates are closed.'

'Yes, if I forget to close them, they close by themselves after a while.'

'Ooh, flash.'

He laughed and got on with making her tea. The atmosphere had changed between them, bringing a lighter, calmer mood. 'You know, if you want to stay now, you could always call him again and tell him to head home.'

'I think I might go back with him when he arrives.'

'Oh, okay.' Samuel tried not to show how disappointed he was. He understood things weren't exactly normal between them. Perhaps it would be best to start over another day. He sat to her side, leaning one arm on the red gingham tablecloth. 'Lunch another time. I still owe you.' It took a moment for him to stop staring into her eyes.

'You don't owe me anything. It's the other way around after what I charged you for my paintings.'

Samuel grinned. 'Hmm. I think I can still buy us lunch though.'

'Okay,' she said softly.

He suddenly felt like a fake. How could he start something with her when he was hiding his own truth? It wouldn't be fair on her. His overreaction to her holding his notebook proved that. An explanation was long overdue. 'I need to tell you—'

Lottie's phone rang in her bag hanging on her chair. 'Ooh, I bet that's George.'

Samuel controlled his sigh and went off to finish making the tea.

'Oh, it's Spencer. Hello.'

Even with the kettle on its final boil, Samuel could hear Lottie's side of the conversation. The front gates opening caught his eye on the monitor, and he watched as one of the Sunshine Centre's wheelchair accessible vehicles pulled in. Knowing it was Felix driving, he left Lottie to her call and went to the front door.

Hannah looked flushed as she left the vehicle, swiftly followed by Felix. 'Sam, there's been an accident up the road. Someone crashed into a roundabout. People were saying a man died. There were blue lights everywhere. It took ages to get by.'

Samuel looked to his side as Lottie came powering through.

'It's George,' she cried. 'He's been in a road accident. Spencer got a call from someone. He's on his way to the scene. I have to go too.' She turned to Felix. 'Will you take me please? It's not far.'

Felix's worried face didn't go unnoticed to Samuel. He cottoned on straight away. Lottie hadn't heard a man had died in a local accident. It had to be the same one, and in case it was, it wasn't something Lottie should see.

'You can't, Lottie,' he told her softly. 'They've just driven past an accident, and it's taken them ages to get through, so by the time you try, George will no doubt be at the hospital if that was his accident.'

Lottie wasn't looking at him. Her eyes were only on Felix. 'Take me to the hospital, please. I'll meet my brother there.'

Felix nodded, but Samuel jumped in.

'I'll take you.'

Her head snapped his way, and the gentleness he'd witnessed in the kitchen moments ago was gone. 'If it wasn't for you and your stupid book, George wouldn't have been on his way back here and he wouldn't have got into an accident, so you can get lost. I never want to see you again.'

Samuel had no words after that hit to his solar plexus. All he could do was watch helplessly as Felix drove off with Lottie and Hannah.

# CHAPTER 16

*Lottie*

Lottie could hear Ginny talking to Spencer outside her bedroom door. They were keeping their voices low, but she could hear every word, not that she cared what they had to say. She didn't care about anything.

'I managed to get some soup down her, but that's it,' said Ginny. 'She's still refusing to get out of bed unless she needs the loo. She won't even take a wet flannel for her face.'

'Thanks, Gin, for everything,' said Spencer, his deep sigh slipping in through the crack in the bedroom door.

'Hey, it's what friends are for, and right now, she needs all the friends she can get.'

Lottie punched the quilt, tugging it away from her neck. She didn't need friends. She needed George to still be alive and living right next door. What was she going to do without him?

Spencer's head poked around the door. 'You getting up today, sis?'

'Go away, Spence.'

He entered and sat at the end of her double bed. 'No can do, I'm afraid. You're stuck with me.'

'I just want to be left alone.'

'You haven't left your room in two weeks. It's time, Lott. You can't carry on like this.'

Lottie glared at him. He meant well, but George was dead so she was perfectly entitled to carry on any way she wanted. 'Rebecca is gone, and so is George. Don't you feel anything, Spence?' She tapped her collarbone. 'I feel like an orphan. We don't have anyone anymore.'

He grabbed her hand and slid it towards him. 'We've got each other, and neither Rebecca or George would want to see you like this.'

'They can't see me. They're dead,' she snapped, snatching her hand back.

'What if they can? What if they're both looking down on you right now? What would they say to you?'

It was obvious what they would say. George would have her up and out the door, doing something productive, and Rebecca would whisper soothing motivational words, then sing something cheerful. Oh, how her heart ached from the weight of a thousand unshed tears.

'I don't want to do anything, Spencer.' Her voice was broken as she'd swallowed hard while trying to form words.

Spencer gestured at the door. 'Ginny's still here. I think she's moved in.' He breathed out a laugh, and Lottie smiled softly. 'She's kept house for you, so there's nothing for you to do except get up and have a wash.'

'You trying to say I smell?'

He pinched his crinkled nose and grinned. 'No.'

Lottie went to laugh, but it felt wrong. Nothing would ever feel right again, she was sure. 'I'm so tired, Spence.'

'I know, but it's George's funeral in a couple of days, and I need you to arrange his flowers. You're the best one for the job. Come on, sis. Get back in the game and make him proud one last time.'

Lottie sniffed, rolling back tears. 'Do you think he was proud of us?'

'Definitely, especially you. He loved you to the moon and back.'

'He loved you too.'

Spencer nodded. 'He was a good man. We were lucky to have him.'

Lottie pulled herself upright. 'I know we didn't have the best start in life, but between Rebecca and George, we certainly were blessed.'

'Yeah, we were. But just like we had to sort things for Rebecca after her death, we have to do the same for George. We were all he had. We can't let him down.'

Scrunching the top of the quilt, Lottie shook her head and cried. 'It's my fault he died. I asked him to come and collect me from Hannah's. If he hadn't—'

Spencer pulled her into his arms. 'Hey, hey. It's not your fault. Christ, is that what you've been thinking these past weeks? He had a heart attack.'

'I know.' She continued to sob on his chest. 'Because he crashed.'

Spencer pulled her away slightly and wiped back her damp hair. 'No, Lottie. He had a heart attack, that's why he crashed. The doctor at the hospital said it wouldn't have mattered where George was. He would have died anyway. Honestly, I'm just glad you weren't in the car with him at the time.'

Lottie's mind drifted back to the day, bypassing anything to do with Samuel Powell. 'You know, I saw him rubbing his shoulder that morning. When I asked about it, he blamed the usual aches and pains. Maybe he was suffering then, and I didn't do anything.'

'You weren't to know. Look, you can't put this on yourself. George would hate that. It was just one of those things. We have to be grateful no one else died, and that it was quick for him. That he didn't suffer. And he certainly wouldn't want you to suffer.'

Lottie had been far too zoned out to take on board any information about George back when it happened. All she could do was cry and hide away from the world. Knowing George would have died anyway released the weight from her back. Her breath came a little easier and visualizing George smiling at her eased the ache in her heart.

'I thought it was because of me, Spence.'

'I wish I'd known that sooner. I thought you were listening when it was explained. Never mind. You know now.'

A light tapping hit the bedroom door. 'Hello,' said Sophie, peeping inside the dark room. 'Is it all right if I come in?'

Lottie smiled and waved her over. 'Yes, I was just about to get up and sort myself out. You can help me if you want.'

Spencer got up and left them to it while Sophie made a beeline for the curtains, pulling them back to allow the sunlight to pour in and wake the room. She opened the window, and Lottie could smell the salty sea air.

'Now, isn't that better?' Sophie smiled, heading for the wardrobe. 'I'm thinking one of your pretty summer dresses would be suitable for this weather.'

Lottie grinned at her friend fussing and taking charge. 'I was going to get up anyway, Soph. You won't have to frog-march me to the bathroom.'

'Oh, and I had it all planned as well.' Sophie laughed, holding out a flowery green dress.

'As long as you weren't planning on giving me a bed bath.'

'If I had to wipe your bum, I would.'

They shared a laugh, then Lottie frowned as the memory of drying herself in Samuel's bathroom hit hard.

'What's wrong, Lott?' Sophie sat on the bed and held her hand. 'Are you worried about the funeral?'

'No, it's not that. It's just . . . well, the day George died, I was at Hannah's. You know, my new friend from the Sunshine Centre.'

Sophie nodded, stroking over her hand.

'I met her brother,' added Lottie. 'And it was all a bit weird. I knocked a vase off the side and got covered in water, then I ended up in his bathroom, wrapped in a towel until he brought me one of Hannah's tracksuits to wear.'

'Oh no. I bet that was awkward.'

Lottie nodded, remembering the feeling. 'It was at first, but then he was so kind to me, helping and doing everything he could. He even put my dress and cushion in the tumble dryer. I hid my knickers in my bag, as I wasn't about to let him see those. Goodness, Soph, it was one of the weirdest moments of my life.'

'I'm glad he helped.'

'Me too. I had planned to sit outside to dry off while I waited for George, but the change of clothing was a better idea, plus comfier.'

'I can imagine.'

Ginny appeared in the doorway. 'I'm thinking we could sit in the garden today. Check out your salad and bits. You and George grew so much out there.'

She inhaled deeply, glancing at the window. 'I'm going to miss having him next door.'

Sophie lightly squeezed Lottie's hand. 'He was a good man, wasn't he?'

Lottie smiled as her heart warmed. 'He was.' She grinned at Ginny. 'You can get involved with the gardening now.'

'No one needs me around their plants. I'm more brown thumb than green finger. My skills in that department won't exactly impress anyone.'

'You don't garden to impress someone, Gin. People do it for enjoyment,' said Sophie.

Ginny laughed. 'I remember trying to impress some lad back when I was a teen. I was all roller skates and stunt jumps. Ended up with a twisted ankle and a bruised nose.'

'Bruised ego more like,' said Sophie.

Ginny shrugged. 'Hey, teenagers are complicated.'

Lottie frowned. 'I'm not sure we grow out of it, Gin. Look at Sophie.'

'What do you mean, look at me?'

Lottie grinned at Ginny. 'Remember what she was like when Matt turned up?'

Ginny nodded. 'Yep. Started dressing a bit smarter just to work in the fishmonger's.'

'I did not.'

'You did, Soph. Didn't she, Lott?'

Lottie gave Sophie's hand a friendly squeeze. 'It was instant attraction, wasn't it?'

'No. I was wary of him at first.'

Ginny scoffed. 'Oh, is that why you gave him a room at yours before you even knew his middle name.'

'Hey, I was being thoughtful.'

Ginny laughed.

'I felt sorry for him,' added Sophie. 'Anyway, lots of people take in lodgers, and Grandad trusted him. Trustworthy men are welcome in my world.'

Ginny looked at Lottie. 'Mine too.'

Sophie turned to Lottie as well. 'So, tell us, what about you and men? Who is Hannah's brother?'

Just thinking about him made Lottie's stomach flip. They'd know his name as soon as it left her mouth, that was a given. But what would they have to say about him buying her paintings and paying for her lunch?

'Spit it out,' said Sophie, giving her hand a nudge.

'Samuel Powell.' Lottie watched their eyes widen along with their mouths.

'Ooh, he helps our food bank,' said Ginny, approaching the bed to sit down. 'The founder of the Les Powell Trust. That's him, right? I've not met him yet.'

Lottie nodded. 'You have, Gin. He was the man at your café who paid for my lunch.'

'He did what?' asked Sophie.

Ginny looked way more surprised. 'That was him?'

'He's been working in the Hub this week,' said Sophie. 'He's getting more and more involved, although he seems a bit different lately.'

109

Without her consent, Lottie's interest woke. 'What do you mean?'

Sophie shrugged. 'He was very assertive when I first met him. All shiny shoes and expensive tie. You know the type. But this week, he's been pretty quiet, not that he was a fan of small talk, but still. I don't know, he just seems sad. I've tried to lift his spirits, but so far, nothing's worked.'

After George's death and confining herself to bed for two weeks, Lottie didn't need to feel any worse, but she did. 'That might be my fault.'

'How?' asked Ginny.

'I blamed him for George's death. That was before I started blaming myself. I was in such a state, and it just came blurting out. But now I know George would have had a heart attack no matter what. I feel absolutely terrible. Sam's probably walking around out there thinking it's his fault. That's what you're seeing, Soph. Someone with guilt on their shoulders.'

Her friends looked confused, which was understandable. They didn't know the full story, so it was time to fill them in about her run-ins with the millionaire businessman from Penzance.

'There was a misunderstanding at Hannah's house between Sam and me, so I called George to pick me up. He died on the way, so I told Sam it was his fault.' Lottie covered her face with one hand. 'What a terrible thing to say to someone. I don't think I could face him again, and he still has my dress and cushion.'

'I'm sure you can sort this with him,' said Sophie softly. 'How well do you know him?'

'We've seen each other a few times, but we only started to get to know each other that day.' She went on to tell them about her encounters with Samuel Powell, knowing they would be left intrigued. She, however, was left wondering how he was and if it was possible for her to face him and apologize. She felt such a fool, perhaps bed was the best place to hide forever.

# CHAPTER 17

*Samuel*

Thanks to Sophie's grandfather, Jed, bringing in fish and chips for lunch, the Hub now ponged like a chippy. However, Samuel failed to care, as the food went down the hatch quite nicely.

Samuel glanced over at the seventy-year-old man staring out the window, wondering if he'd ever feel as carefree as the old fella looked. He could just imagine having the same salt-and-pepper hair, but perhaps not the wiry grey beard. The sailor vibe wasn't hitting the spot, as business was more his thing, but maybe Jed could help with something.

Out in the harbour of Port Berry, among the bobbing boats, was a large white yacht Samuel had bought two years ago. He didn't want to sail the world or anywhere in particular. It was just a nice vessel he saw at an online boat show, and an impulse purchase had it moored in Penzance a week later. Only, he hadn't bargained on it taunting him from his bedroom window, so he had it moved to the fishing village next door, out of sight.

'I have a boat out there,' he told Jed, still unsure why.

Jed turned from staring out to sea. 'Been anywhere nice on her, son?'

There was no way Samuel was about to talk all things agoraphobia with the old man, so he gave a warped shrug as his nose twisted up.

A twinkle hit Jed's slate-blue eyes as he grinned. 'Got a name for your lady?'

Lottie sprung to mind at the mention of the word "lady", but he quickly brushed her face from his mind. Since the moment she'd put someone's death on his shoulders, he had shooed her away each time she popped up, which was daily.

'*Hannah's Dream,*' he replied.

Jed sat by his side. 'I have a trawler for work called *Ursula*, and my *Mrs Berry* is where I live.'

'You live on a boat? I thought you lived with your granddaughter.'

'Sophie would love that, but nope. I love the open space, me. I stay with her during the winter, that's all. When was the last time you were on that fancy vessel of yours?' Jed nodded as he smiled. 'Yeah, I've seen her. Big oaf of a thing.'

Samuel laughed, and it seemed weird because he hadn't heard his own laugh in a while. 'I guess it's a little big.'

'Seen bigger, but yeah, she sticks out around here. Looks lonely too.'

'You think a boat can look lonely?'

'They have feelings, son. Take it from a fisherman. I'm telling you they pick up on things. So, tell me, why doesn't anyone ever, at the very least, sit on deck?'

Hannah had said that once, but he told her she wasn't allowed on board in case she fell off. She assured him she could swim, but he still wasn't having it. Why he hadn't sold the thing, he couldn't say. Well, he could, but it was easier to lie to himself at times than face the truth of wanting to sail.

'I have a cleaner go on board.' As soon as the words left his lips, he felt stupid.

Jed laughed. 'Why don't we go on board as soon as Matt gets here for his shift?'

A flutter hit Samuel's stomach, waking the fish and chips just consumed. 'You want to look at the yacht?'

'No, son. I want you to board her. Make her your own. Look, I know the sea can be a scary place. Lived here all my life. Seen it all. But, with small steps, anything can be accomplished. I can see you're worried about something, and that's none of my business, but one thing I do know is, being on the water takes away many a trouble.'

Samuel wished the answer to his problem was as simple as that.

As though reading his mind, Jed added, 'One way to find out.'

There was a shrewdness to the fisherman that oozed from his very existence and something else almost touching on angelic. Samuel had to laugh to himself. Was it at all possible he was going to sit on his boat today? By the look on Jed's face, a trip to *Hannah's Dream* was on the cards.

The door to the Hub opened, and Samuel hoped it was someone he could help so that he had a good excuse not to go to the harbour.

'Hello, Jed,' said a man, rushing in. 'Can't stop. Got a lot on.' He pinned a small card to the noticeboard. 'Just want to pop that up.'

'What's that, Shaun?'

'Just an ad for anyone looking for some labouring work. If anyone comes in who could do some shifts, point them to me.'

'Will do, son.'

Samuel peered over Jed's shoulder to glance at the note as Shaun waved a goodbye as he left the Hub.

'That'll do someone a favour, I'm sure,' said Jed. 'Shaun's got his own building company so agreed to place ads here whenever he needs help. A young woman got a cleaning job off the board just the other day as well. Comes in handy that.'

113

Matt entered, swiping back his dark hair, caught off-guard by a light breeze. 'Sophie's back in the shop,' he announced on arrival. 'Blimey, it smells of salt and vinegar in here.' He jammed the door open. 'Let's get a bit of air in here. I've got a couple of homeless people coming in soon to talk to me about the hostel. Not sure what advice I can give them, as I haven't stayed in it, not many have yet, seeing how it's not long opened, but Jan reckons they'll feel more comfortable talking to me than someone over there. She'll be along in a minute with them, so you two can head off if you—'

'Great,' sang out Jed, making a dash for Samuel's arm.

Before Samuel had a chance to respond, Jed tugged him out onto the pavement, looked left and right, then pulled him across the road.

Jed started singing a sea shanty, which did help occupy Samuel's mind, as it was set to swirl as much as his stomach. Reminding himself he didn't have the boat keys somehow failed to settle the acrobats practising moves all over him.

'There she is,' said Jed, pointing to the jetty. He indicated towards his own vessel, *Mrs Berry*, then pretty much dragged Samuel all the way to *Hannah's Dream*, the last boat bobbing in the deepest water.

Samuel dug his heels in. 'I don't have the keys.'

'We're not going anywhere, son. Just sitting up top. Come on.'

Samuel stared out at the calm sea. Gulls circled above as sailboats cruised the waves in the near distance. The sun was bright and the clouds few, and the smell of the seaside filled the air, clearing Samuel's head for a moment.

Feeling a tad dazed, Samuel boarded his yacht and sat on a hard, built-in bench seat, facing Harbour End Road. It was quite surreal and totally unexpected. It certainly wasn't on his to-do list when he woke that morning not wanting to face the world. The Hub wasn't on his list either, but he had to do something other than hit the gym, as he couldn't concentrate on work.

Jed flopped back on another seat, held his face to the sky and closed his eyes. 'Ah, this is the life, eh, son?'

Samuel wasn't sure what made life anymore. He glanced around at his floating asset. What would his parents think about him owning a boat? His mum would probably say it was a waste of money if he wasn't going to use it. She said that about a camera he once bought. She was right. He used it twice. The yacht, never.

Harbour End Road looked like something out of a painting from his viewpoint. It certainly was picturesque and deserved to be on someone's wall.

Lottie's paintings were on the wall in his office. She would love the view from *Hannah's Dream*, he was sure. If they were, at the very least, friends, he could invite her on board and have an easel, brushes, and paints ready. He really needed to stop thinking about her. He had enough on his plate.

*I wonder what she's doing now?*

Samuel glanced at Sea Shanty Shack, the fishmongers Jed owned with his granddaughter, then he shifted his gaze a few doors down to Harbour Light Café and smiled, remembering watching Lottie's failed dates. He had so much admiration for her putting herself through that. She had guts, that was for sure. How would he have handled that kind of situation? Probably not as well. He could see her chin held high and the stubbornness in her gorgeous eyes.

*Oh, go away.*

He didn't want to think about her. It was pointless. She hated his guts, and that was that. Not much he could do about it.

Jed had said the water took away worries, but Samuel was still tightly wound. For one whole week, he'd not left his bed, feeling gutted he'd caused someone's death. If it hadn't been for Hannah bringing Jan around to see him, he'd never have known about George's heart attack being inevitable. It wasn't his fault. It wasn't anyone's, but had Lottie reached out to let him know? Nope.

If he could sail away, he would. Maybe the old man had the right idea about boating life. What was there to worry about in the middle of the ocean? Storms entered his mind, swiftly followed by man-eating sharks, tsunamis, and pirates.

Closing his eyes for a moment, mimicking Jed, who'd possibly fallen asleep, Samuel once more tried to rid his thoughts of Lottie. It wasn't an easy task. She'd been part of his day since he first laid eyes on her, and truth be told, it was getting annoying. Why should she occupy his mind? She obviously gave little thought for him, judging by her radio silence. She wouldn't even take Hannah's calls, and there was no thank you for the flowers he'd sent the day after George passed away.

Perhaps he shouldn't have bought them from her own shop. The rights, the wrongs, he couldn't tell the difference lately. When Hannah told him George was like a father to Lottie, all he wanted was the ground to open up and swallow him whole and never spit him out. It was all too much. Even Jan, with her kindness and logic, couldn't pull him through at first.

Helping at the Hub was something positive, especially as Victoria had settled into his business nicely. He was sure he could recruit more for the charity. She had become an inspiration to him, handling her kids, finances, and job like a pro. If he could get together a whole team just like her, the Trust would expand with little worries.

Samuel opened his eyes and stared over at Berry Blooms flower shop, unsure if Lottie was at work. Last he heard, she was still at home, in mourning. He knew the feeling. He couldn't remember how long it took for him to pull himself together after the loss of his parents. Sometimes it seemed so far in the past, and other days, it felt like yesterday.

Another thought hit, so he pulled out his phone to add some notes. Sitting on the boat could count as therapy, and seeing how he'd not driven anywhere in the last two weeks, having given up, he figured Jed's outing was better than nothing. He jotted down his feelings. At least he could talk to Jan about it later.

There wasn't any anxiety to write about, as all was calm. Step one of boat therapy was complete. Perhaps next time, he could ask Jed to teach him how to manoeuvre the thing. He could go out to sea, but not too far. As long as he could still see the land, he should be okay. Baby steps. Worth considering.

'See what I mean,' said Jed, making him jump out of his trance with the deck.

Samuel glanced his way to see the old man still hadn't opened his eyes. He had to smile. There was something so therapeutic about being in his presence, let alone bobbing on gentle waves.

'So much beauty,' added Jed.

Just at that moment, Samuel spotted Lottie outside her shop. Her head turned in his direction, but he was sure she was just taking in the view.

Not much mattered once more. She seemed further away than ever, and perhaps that was for the best. She had enough on her plate without him adding agoraphobia into her mix. He didn't want it in his own life. Besides, she hadn't reached out to him, and the least she could have done was apologize for laying blame at his feet.

He still felt so bad for their hallway interaction. If only he could go back and change that moment. He sighed silently and continued to watch Lottie.

*Could we have been something?*

Nope. It wasn't meant to be, and he wished he didn't feel so rundown about it. Why did he want her to like him so much? He tried to shake it off. He wasn't the type of person who could have a happy healthy relationship, and she wasn't talking to him anyway, so there wasn't much point trying to think of a way forward. He needed to get a grip and stop pining for someone he hardly knew, or more importantly, stop pining for a life that just for a second he thought was possible to have.

She crossed the road, still gazing at the view, and just for a moment he wondered if she'd spotted him. He even sat up straighter, debating whether to raise a hand. But then she looked away and a chill hit his heart.

Samuel sank into himself, putting his legs up and resting his arms behind his head. Sod the world. He was taking a leaf out of Jed's book. An afternoon nap was long overdue in his life, so he closed his eyes, blocking out the sun. Blocking out Lottie Jordan.

# CHAPTER 18

*Lottie*

Making wedding flower arrangements in the back room of Berry Blooms had Lottie thinking about George's funeral the week before. It had gone well, and she was sure he would have loved the flowers she chose for him, especially as she picked some from both their gardens to add into the mix.

It was sad when she was pottering around in the new greenhouse he'd bought, not having him with her. The community still needed any salad on offer though, so she was getting on with the gardening by herself in both her own and George's garden.

As Ginny lived the other side of George's house, she popped over after work to lend a hand as best she could, but she often squirmed if any dirt entered her fingernails, which always made Lottie laugh.

Having Ginny so close was helpful, even though Spencer was only in the flat above the shop. None of her friends lived far away. Sophie's cottage was a few streets back, Robson's pub was along by her shop, and Alice lived with her family over the newsagent's along Harbour End Road. Everyone had rallied round, seeing where they were needed in her life, but still, George left a big hole, and she'd never felt so lonely.

With weddings on her mind, the last thing she needed was to think about Samuel, but seeing as she was twiddling with one of the flowers similar to the ones he'd sent her from her own shop, he was there again, invading her thoughts.

She'd questioned many times why she had ended up feeling so comfortable with him in his bathroom, and how quickly they had gone from him biting her head off to them making friends to her telling him to get lost.

Everything about the man occupied her. It was daft and needed sorting. The least she could do was apologize for what she'd said.

She shook her head at herself. The least she could do was concentrate on her job, because a bride needed her wedding flowers to be delivered at seven the next morning. Dithering and daydreaming would have to wait till a more convenient time, like two in the morning, which seemed to be her inner alarm clock lately.

The small antique bronze bell above the flower shop's door jingled, announcing someone's entrance. Spencer was out front, so she left him to deal with the customer while she carried on with the bouquet she was making.

Muffled chatter and some laughter floated through to the back of the shop before Spencer poked his head around the doorway.

'Caroline Gately's here.' He stepped aside, gesturing for woman to enter first.

Lottie looked up and smiled. 'Hello, Caroline. Not seen you in a while. Are you here for flowers or an official visit?' She laughed inwardly at her question, because there wasn't any reason for a local solicitor to have an official visit with them.

Caroline looked every bit official, with her dark suit and clutched thin briefcase. 'Actually, this is official, in an unofficial way.'

Both Lottie and Spencer frowned.

'Let me explain,' added Caroline. 'George wanted me to do it this way. Normally, I'd call you in to my office, but . . .' She shrugged at her surroundings. 'At least your office is colourful.' She smiled, then cleared her throat. 'Long and short of it is, George left you two everything. Yep, he made a will, and he had it written that I wasn't to tell you until after his funeral. He left you his house, which I believe you know is fully paid for, thanks to his small lottery win.'

Lottie turned to see Spencer was as gobsmacked as her. Not once had she thought about George's worldly goods since his death. All she thought was he might walk into his garden one day and the nightmare would be over.

Caroline continued. 'I don't know how much you know about inheritance, but I'll talk you through it all. Just know, you won't be able to sell the property straight away, but you can have a clear out, even line up a buyer.'

She waffled on, using words like probate and capital gains, but Lottie had zoned out of the conversation. There was no way someone else could live in George's home. It was unthinkable. And as for clearing out his belongings, how could she? Those were his things.

Without warning, Lottie burst into tears. Just as she had started to come to terms with not having George around, she was back to square one. They'd only played Snakes and Ladders a few days before he died. She felt as though she were playing it now, and she'd just slid down the longest snake in the game.

Spencer handed her a box of tissues and told Caroline he would make an appointment to see her soon to discuss the matter further. As soon as she left, he put the kettle on, acting as though nothing had just happened.

Lottie sniffed and wiped her nose. It had happened. It was real. George was gone and now so were his things, because they didn't belong to him, they belonged to them, and it just didn't sit right. 'Spencer, I can't cope with this right now.'

'It's okay. You don't have to do anything. I'll sort it.'

'But you heard her. She was talking about selling George's home.'

'No one's selling his house, Lott. She was just telling us it's ours now, and if we want to sell it, we can't straight away because—'

'I'm never selling it. It belongs to George. It's his home.'

Spencer sat by her side and held her hand, lowering the scissors she clutched. 'Hey, we don't have to think about any of this right now. But, sooner or later, we do have to sort through George's things.'

She knew he was right, but logic could bugger off. Even if George did once say that if he died he wanted his clothes to go to a charity shop so they could be put to good use, it didn't matter. How on earth was she supposed to riffle through his private things and decide what should go where? It was so much easier when it was Rebecca, because most of her stuff stayed in their family home, seeing how Lottie was still living there.

'I need some fresh air, Spence.'

'Take your time.'

Lottie went outside, inhaling the warm salty air that hit her immediately. The sun healed some aches and the beauty of the harbour helped soothe her soul.

She really needed a break so made her way towards the jetty, ignoring the people pottering around, in no mood for chit-chat or friendly smiles. She put on her sunglasses and kept her head low, and as soon as she stopped in one of her favourite spots, she took some deep breaths and stilled her fluttering heart.

Tourist season kept Port Berry busy, but down by the boats was a bit quieter, and Lottie was grateful for the peace. Part of her wanted to go home, but it was also wedding season, so she knew she'd have to get back to the shop soon, as there was so much to do.

She took some time to do nothing but gaze out to sea, knowing she would be fine in a minute or two.

Luna passed by, and Lottie wondered why the local psychic couldn't have warned her about George's heart. She had to stop with the blame, as it was starting to get on her nerves. Jan had told her acceptance was needed to help with grief, and she knew her friend was right.

'There's not a thing you can do about death, love. It comes to us all,' said Luna, staring out at the boats.

Lottie wished she would go away. She didn't want to talk to anyone.

'But life is for the living, young girl. Remember that.'

Lottie had a hundred and one replies to that statement, but Luna walked away before she could respond.

'What blimming life?' Lottie mumbled to a lifebuoy ring attached to a nearby post.

One minute she was living with her boyfriend, Russ, in the house she grew up in, having what she deemed a perfectly normal life, the next, she'd been knocked off her bicycle, lost the use of her legs, Russ had dumped her, and the man she viewed as her dad had died.

*Some life!*

At first it was a shock what had happened to her, damaged spine, wheelchair. It turned sad for a while, but anger made itself known, causing Lottie to fight back, take charge of her life, and make friends with her new chapter. She'd never been one to shy away from a challenge, seeing only solutions to problems. Always the natural problem-solver, she'd be the first to dive straight in and get things sorted.

Her whole world was back to that day waking in hospital. Lost. Scared. Lonely. Then she thought about her ex.

How strange it was to think they'd had a healthy relationship when it was obviously shallow. She wondered if she was as superficial back then. A lot about her had changed since her accident, so much so, she knew she'd never date someone like Russ again. She wasn't quite sure which personality type was a match now. Perhaps someone who liked art.

She stared out to sea, wishing she had her art equipment to help bring the peace she needed. Her favourite boat was at the end of the jetty. It never seemed to move, and she couldn't remember a time she saw anyone on board. It just sat there, alone. Like her. She felt the sudden urge to paint its picture, but with nothing on her but her phone, she turned and headed back to work.

A young man was dithering outside the Hub, so she approached to see if she could help.

'Erm,' he said, turning to her. He scratched the back of his neck and smiled nervously. 'Is this place the food bank?'

'Yes. I'm one of the volunteers — Lottie. Would you like a food parcel to take home? I can sort that for you.'

His sheepish expression told her everything she needed to know. Ever since the food bank started at the Happy to Help Hub, she'd seen that look time and time again.

'I don't need much,' he said, shifting from foot to foot. 'Just a few bits for my wife. She's pregnant, and I just lost my job. I've never been anywhere like this before. I'll find a way to pay you back.'

Words Lottie had heard before at the Hub. Often people felt the need to see the food parcels as some sort of loan, not accepting they needed help or feeling embarrassed to take any offered.

'You don't have to pay anyone back. We're here to help. Come inside.'

'I don't want to go in there, if I'm honest.'

'No one does, and they shouldn't have to either. We shouldn't be in a place where we need help, but hey, it is what it is. Sometimes we find ourselves in unwanted places.' She tapped her wheelchair. 'Come inside, and let's get you and your wife some food.'

A few seconds passed, then he nodded and stepped closer to the Hub.

Lottie thanked him for helping her with the door, then invited him over to the table to sit while she made him up a food parcel.

Alice was on duty. She introduced herself as she put the kettle on straight away, offering the young man a pastry, which he took, wrapped in a tissue from the box on the table, then shoved into the pocket of his cardigan.

'So,' said Lottie, putting a folded cardboard box together. 'What work do you normally do? We might be able to find you a job.'

It was clear he wasn't expecting that kind of help. 'Oh, erm, events, mostly. I was working over in Truro, but got laid off, then we had to move. Got a temporary place on the border of Port Berry, so here we are.'

'When is your wife due?' Lottie asked.

'Another three months, so I've got some time to find work before the baby arrives.'

She smiled at the hope brimming in his hazel eyes.

Alice brought him over a cup of tea. 'I've got a couple of numbers you can call.' She pointed over to the noticeboard behind her. 'There's one for a bit of labouring with a local builder named Shaun. He's very nice. You could call him, or the Les Powell Trust is expanding, and they're looking for workers to help with their charity. Might be worth you enquiring, seeing how you worked in events.'

The man beamed happily at the cards on the board. 'Oh, wow, thanks. Yeah, I'll definitely check out the charity place. I've worked for one before, and I've got references.'

'Make sure you mention the Hub,' said Alice. 'Our food bank here is part of that trust. The founder put the card up. He's already taken someone on from here.'

Lottie glanced her way. 'He has?'

'Yeah, didn't anyone tell you? Her name's Victoria. He helped change her life.' Alice turned to the man. 'He'll help you too. You watch.'

'Would it be okay if I called him now?' he asked.

'Sure,' replied Alice, shoving a plate of Hobnobs in front of him. 'Here, use the Hub's phone. Tell him Alice told you to call and that you're here now with me.'

The man removed the card from the noticeboard and took it over to the phone. 'Thank you so much.'

Lottie went out back, feeling the need to be away in case she heard Samuel's voice. As daft as she felt about that, it made her feel better to distance herself.

She started adding food items to the box on her lap as muffled voices came from the front. It was no good, she couldn't hide away forever. She had all she could carry, so headed back to the man at the table.

He certainly looked a lot better. A light glow filled his cheeks and his leg had stopped bouncing. Alice entered the back room to unload some donations that someone had just dropped off, and Lottie snaffled a biscuit while waiting for the call to end.

She wondered where Samuel was and hoped he didn't pop in while she was there. There was no way she could look him in the eye after what she'd said when they parted ways. She hadn't even been back to the Sunshine Centre, not wanting to see Hannah either.

Oh, what a big fat mess she'd made of everything. At least she was getting back on track with her volunteering, thanks to seeing this man outside. She offered a warm smile as he got off the phone.

'How did it go?' she asked.

'I've got a meeting with him tomorrow. I just need to print off my CV. Is there a library round here with a printer I could use?'

Alice poked her head around the back door and pointed at the window. 'Go to the Treasure Chest newsagent's along the way there. It's my family's shop. We've got a printer. Tell the woman behind the counter I sent you, and she won't charge you. It's all right, she's my mum.'

'Oh, Alice, you are a star.'

She beamed. 'We're all stars here at the Happy to Help Hub.' She giggled while splaying her arms. 'Goodness, that sounded corny.'

Lottie laughed, handing over the food parcel to the young man. 'See, aren't you glad I forced you inside now?'

'I honestly don't know what to say to you two. All I was expecting was a couple of tins of soup.'

Lottie gestured to the box. 'That's in there too.'

'Thank you so much, Lottie. I was two-seconds out from backing away and heading home empty-handed, then you came along.'

'Good timing, I say,' said Lottie.

Alice appeared again. 'No such thing, my nan says. It's fate. Meant to be and all that.'

Lottie followed the man to the door. 'Her nan's a psychic,' she whispered, adding a wink.

'Well, I don't care what it was,' said the young man. 'If it got me food and a job, I'm grateful.'

'Please let us know how you get on,' said Lottie, as he opened the door. 'We can always help find another job if this one doesn't work out.'

He tipped an imaginary hat as he smiled. 'Will do. And, once again, thanks so much. It really was a pleasure meeting you both.'

'You too. Ooh, wait, I still don't know your name.'

'Georgie. Georgie Watts.' He thanked her again, then left for the newsagent's.

Alice's laugh echoed from the back room. 'Fate,' she called. 'Nan says it's the angels at work.'

Lottie couldn't argue with that. She glanced up at the ceiling. Was George volunteering from the heavens? She wouldn't put it past him. Always one to help was George Watson.

'Huh!' She smiled to herself, said goodbye to Alice, then hurried off to talk to Spencer about the possibility of friendly ghosts.

# CHAPTER 19

*Samuel*

Samuel perused the church hall. It wasn't somewhere he'd usually host a work event, not that he'd hosted many for his company. Partying wasn't his scene, even more so when agoraphobia crept in. The social events he'd graced with his presence were mostly held in stately homes or fancy hotels. This was different. The volunteers for the Les Powell Trust wanted the more casual setting that All Saints Church provided to Port Berry.

The walls were bland and the high ceiling looked clean enough. It was imperative the toilets were wheelchair accessible. If not, he would have to hire portable lavatory units for outside.

'You all right in there, Samuel?' asked Robson, poking his head around the restroom's doorway. 'You've been staring at the loo for ages. You are allowed to use it, you know.'

'I was checking the hall had toilet access for wheelchairs.'

'Oh no. This place is old, mate. The one and only toilet they have got is small and, as you can see, basic.'

'I have those portable toilets in mind for outside, but the only ones I know are the ones they have on building sites. Do ones for wheelchairs exist?'

Robson pulled out his phone. 'Probably. They've got everything nowadays. Let's have a look.'

Samuel went back into the hall to see how much room there was on the stage set up at one end.

Spencer pointed up at the small windows lining one wall. 'I was just thinking, balloons would liven this place up.'

'And flowers, Spence,' called Sophie, counting stacked tables.

Samuel sat on the stage and shook his head at the Hub volunteers discussing ways to make the church hall pop. 'You know I can just hire an events team. I don't normally do this sort of thing by myself.'

Sophie smiled his way. 'You're not by yourself. You've got us, and trust me, parties are always better when you get involved yourself.'

Robson sat by his side, offering his phone. 'I found some wheelchair accessible portable loos. Look at this one, it's a bit fancy. All wood and shiny floors.'

'Ooh, let's see.' Sophie sandwiched Samuel, tilting her head towards the screen. 'That blue one looks like the Tardis. Lottie would love that.' She looked up at Samuel. 'Bit of a *Doctor Who* fan.'

He was too, but didn't feel the need to announce the fact. He glanced at the doorway for a second, wondering if she would make an appearance. She was in the church, talking to the vicar about wedding flowers or something. Spencer had told him she was working, but he was sure avoidance was top priority to Lottie right now.

It had been ages since Samuel laid eyes on her, and it had messed with his mind every day. Knowing she was so close was playing havoc with his concentration, but he was determined to gift the volunteers and workers of his charity with a party, as they deserved some payback for their kindness and time. He hoped Lottie didn't snub the function.

Zoning back in to Robson's conversation about portable loos, he told him to send over the link. The Tardis and the fancy wooden number were both getting hired.

Hannah entered the hall, with Felix in tow, and Samuel wasn't quite sure why they felt the need to turn up.

'Oh, this won't be a problem,' said Felix, scanning the area.

Samuel rolled back his shoulders as he approached Felix, making sure Hannah's love interest knew who was in charge. 'What won't be a problem?'

Felix had a warm, friendly smile, which only irritated Samuel more. It wasn't that he didn't like the man, it was just Felix was self-assured, totally in love with his little sister, and never seemed bothered by his dominating presence when he put it on full display, merely in an attempt to rattle the lad.

Hannah spoke first. 'I thought we'd help with party planning and prep. Felix helps run events at the Sunshine Centre, so he's an expert in the field.'

Samuel scoffed. 'It's a party, sis, not a military operation. Besides, if I wanted to use events staff, I have my own. We're being more relaxed about things here.'

Hannah knocked his elbow. 'The more the merrier. Come on, Felix. Let's see what Sophie has in mind, and we can work from there.'

There wasn't a chance to intervene, as Hannah marched her beloved away at the point Samuel opened his mouth to politely tell them both to bugger off.

With portable loos still owning his thoughts, he stepped out into the fresh warm air to assess the area that would house them. Standing with his hands on his hips, staring at a tree, a moment of reality hit hard. How had he become so uptight over the years? Could he even remember the person he used to be before his parents died? He'd promised himself he would loosen up. Not much progress in that area, he realized.

Samuel strained his brain, then pinched the bridge of his nose. His personality had taken a major hit. Perhaps it was something he could discuss with Jan during their next therapy session.

Once upon a time, life was about uni, hanging out with mates, and looking forward to the future. Thirty years old and all he had was emptiness and a mental issue that bugged the life out of him on a daily basis. He had to laugh. That or cry, and crying wasn't his style.

Muffled chatter interrupted his trance with the tree. He turned to see Lottie exiting the church with Father Stephen, and before he had time to think about his actions, he quickly hid behind the solid trunk, thankful the tree was huge.

*What the hell am I doing?*

The questioned lingered as Lottie moved over to the car park alone. She just sat there, doing nothing, going nowhere, and Samuel couldn't help but wonder what she was thinking. The normal thing would be to go say hello, but nothing felt normal when it came to her. Besides, he gathered she still wasn't talking to him, seeing how she'd made no attempt to contact him at all.

Samuel flung his head back, huffing silently at the grey sky. A thousand words filled his aching mind, but nothing stuck. There was one part of him that was motivated enough to make an appearance to the woman who blamed him for the death of her friend, but another that couldn't care less anymore.

Guilt weighed heavily on his shoulders as it was. The last thing he needed was someone adding to his baggage, thank you very much. His parents were gone and his sister had no legs because of him. The thought pumped adrenaline around his body, building sweat and palpitations.

Why the bloody hell should he take that kind of crap? It was about time she faced him and apologized. He deserved that much at least. She was the one in the wrong and should have sent him flowers, but did she?

'Nope,' he told the tree.

It was all too much. The way she got under his skin, tormented him, now hated him. Something had to give, and it was now or never. He would march over to her, demand an explanation, and let her know she couldn't treat him that way.

Samuel took a breath. He didn't have it in him to face her or demand anything from her. She had lost a friend who was more like a father. He knew how it felt. The pain his heart held for his deceased parents often worsened when least expected. What Lottie needed was love and care, not him and his needs.

He lowered his forehead against the bumpy bark, wishing life wasn't so complicated. All he wanted was peace, but it would seem that wasn't part of his journey. He just had no idea why.

Hannah's voice rang out, calling him from the doorway of the hall. His heart flipped, causing his stomach to curdle. Now Lottie would know he was hiding, or perhaps he could stay there and hide from his sister as well.

'Stop being an idiot,' he mumbled to himself. After a deep breath and a stern talking-to, he casually stepped out from his hiding place.

Lottie was nowhere to be seen, and Samuel wasn't entirely sure if he was relieved or not.

Hannah frowned. 'What are you doing over there?'

'Seeing where the portable toilets could go.'

She pointed at the grass to the side of the car park. 'There's good. I'll ask Felix.' She darted off before he could tell her there was no need to ask Felix anything.

Samuel's shoulders slumped. His one chance to talk to Lottie was gone, and now he probably wouldn't see her again until the party, and thanks to him being the host, there was a good chance she wouldn't show.

'Hello,' said a soft voice, startling him.

Samuel turned quickly to see Lottie, and just like that he lost his voice.

'I'm just waiting for Spencer to take me home.'

'I can drive you,' he said before thinking.

'That's okay. He won't be long.'

Samuel bobbed his head as he cleared his throat. 'I haven't seen you, erm, I . . .'

'I know. Wedding season. Busy.'

'Right.' He realized he was digging his shoe into the grass. He stopped, then met her eyes. 'I'm sorry about George.'

Her head dipped a touch. 'Thank you.' She glanced back up. 'I'm sorry I blamed you. I'm sorry I—'

'It's all right.'

'It was a terrible thing to say to someone.'

'You were upset.'

Her smile was small, soft. 'You sent me flowers.'

'I did.'

'Thank you.'

'Least I could do.'

Lottie's eyes held sorrow, and it took everything he had not to reach forward and give her a hug. She sniffed, straightened, then gestured at the hall. 'Party, eh?'

'The Trust is growing, so I thought it would be nice for everyone to mingle and relax for the evening.'

'Did you give Georgie a job in the end?'

'Ah, yes.'

'Is he helping with this event?'

'No. I thought he could skip this one, seeing how it's for the staff and volunteers. I thought I could just get on with it myself, but the volunteers from the Hub were determined to help arrange the party.'

Lottie's smile widened. 'They're like that.'

He glanced at the door to the hall. 'They're a good bunch.'

She twiddled her fingers on her lap. 'I would help, but weddings and that.'

He stepped forward. 'Will you be coming?'

'I was thinking about it.'

He offered her a warm smile. 'I'd like to see you there.'

'I wasn't sure if you hated me.'

Samuel frowned. 'I don't hate you. How could anyone hate you?' There was warmth in her eyes as they met his, and he was quite sure his heart just melted.

She went to speak, but Spencer called out.

'You ready, sis?'

'Coming,' she told him, then looked back at Samuel. 'I had Spencer give Hannah her tracksuit back.'

'I know.'

She touched her flowery cushion. 'Thanks for returning my things.'

They stared at each other for a moment, then Samuel dipped his head.

'Are you still training for your race?' he asked, relying on small talk to fill the silence.

'It's more a fun run kind of thing, but yes.'

Spencer called out again, gaining attention.

'I'd better get going,' she said, gesturing towards her brother.

He stepped to her side as she moved towards the car park. 'So, I'll see you at the party then.'

She stopped to face him. 'Yes.'

A voice in his head was yelling at him to ask to see her before then, perhaps not leave each other now. Anything, would be good, but he remained silent, concentrating on breathing properly instead.

'See you soon,' she said quietly, staying still for a moment.

'Look forward to it,' he managed, pretty sure he couldn't hold his cool much longer.

She smiled once more, then headed off towards Spencer.

Samuel inhaled deeply. Jeez, she made him nervous. He smiled inwardly, as she also made him happy.

# CHAPTER 20

*Lottie*

Twinkling fairy lights, silver, white, and pink balloons, and small posies of matching colours made the church hall a pretty sight, and Lottie felt a million dollars as she entered wearing a new dress bought especially for the occasion.

Spencer and the others had done a fine job decorating the premises, and it didn't go unnoticed that someone had been thoughtful enough to hire portable toilets for wheelchair users.

She felt a little bad that she hadn't got involved in the party preparations as well, but her brother had told her there were lots of hands on deck. Besides, she had so much to do, what with her food runs, fun run training, and trying to clear George's house. August had arrived, and wedding season was still going strong, so it wasn't as if she had much time.

Tonight was about clearing her mind from her daily chores, worries, and stress. All she wanted was to swirl in her chair to the music, tuck in to the tasty-looking buffet, and sip champagne till the bubbles tickled her nose, even though she wasn't much of a fan of the stuff.

Lottie brushed down her long shimmering pink gown, remembering the days she would dress up for beauty pageants. She always had a love of faffing about with hair and make-up and Disney princess dolls as a child. The closest she came to owning the look were the times she'd won Miss South-West Beauty Pageant, three years in a row, and was paraded on a throne around the streets upon a large sparkly mobile float. Winning that crown seemed like a thousand years ago, and representing her hometown as Miss Port Berry was fun while it lasted.

Life had changed, but Lottie's stubborn approach to life hadn't. She was damned if she'd let her accident rule. Legs or no legs, she was alive and ready to shine.

After snaffling way more mini sausage rolls than she'd thought possible to consume, Lottie downed a flute of Buck's Fizz, scoffed some ready salted crisps, then checked her teeth in the compact mirror she'd put in her clutch for such a situation.

While no one was paying her much attention, she used the mirror to have a quick sneaky peek at who else was at the party already.

Spencer was chatting to some blonde woman, and Sophie was on the dance floor with Matt. Lottie spied Jed talking to Luna over by the bar, and . . . whoops!

Lottie snapped her compact to a close and quickly stuffed it back where it came from. There was no way she was going to check out Mr Suave, even if the half a second glance at Samuel reminded her just how good that man could look.

'Oh, crumbs,' she mumbled, hoping he hadn't seen her snooping on the crowd, or worse, thought she was spying on him.

She hadn't stopped thinking about him since their chat outside the church. It was a relief to finally see him and speak, even if they didn't say much. Looking at him had been hard, as she could see she had hurt him.

He had been quite polite when speaking to her, and she'd wondered how he would have reacted had he known her thoughts kept drifting to his mouth throughout half the conversation. She laughed at herself, thinking it best to clear her head of how kissable his lips looked.

The fresh prawns looked good, so she decided to focus on the seafood platter instead. Sea Shanty Shack had supplied all the seafood, so she knew not to worry about levels of freshness, not when it came to Sophie's shop.

She laughed at the memory of Spencer throwing up one night due to food poisoning from prawns, or so he said. Rebecca scolded him for drinking too much but still sat with him by the loo, handing over a cool flannel and a glass of water. Funny thing, Spencer still ate seafood after that dreadful night but declined any tequila shots offered his way.

'Keep blaming it on the prawns, Spence,' Rebecca had mocked.

Lottie's thoughts were with her aunt, knowing how much she loved a party. She visualized Rebecca dancing the night away with George.

'You all right, chick?' asked Ginny, reaching over for the egg mayo sandwiches.

'Yes, but I didn't realize how hungry I was till I saw this lot.'

Ginny nodded. 'I know. It's a good spread, and the best part is, I didn't have to cook a thing.'

'It's nice to have a night off.'

'Yeah, it was good of Samuel to do this for us.'

Lottie was trying not to think about him. It was bad enough he might have caught her snooping at him through her mirror.

Ginny waved her over to a table and placed down two plates stacked with food. 'That should keep us going for a bit.'

'Ooh, lovely. When Sophie can tear herself away from Matt, I'm sure she'll want some.'

'Speaking of tearing yourself away, you do know you keep looking over at Samuel, right?'

'I'm not looking at him.'

Ginny laughed. 'You so are. Have you apologized to him yet?'

Just the thought made Lottie blush. 'I did. Everything is fine now.'

'Is that why you can't take your eyes off him?'

'I haven't been looking.'

'You fancy the pants off him.'

'I do not.'

Ginny patted her chest with one hand while stuffing a forkful of quiche in her mouth with the other. 'Worst thing ever is lying to yourself, chick,' she mumbled through her food.

'I'm not lying to anyone.' She totally was. He made her heart flutter whether she tried to ignore it or not.

Alice plonked herself in the chair next to Ginny. 'Ooh, I feel whacked out from dancing. I didn't realize I was so unfit.'

'Start jogging again every morning with Robson,' said Ginny, gesturing his way. 'You enjoy that in the summer.'

They all turned to look at him.

Robson showed his palm, then went back to talking to Samuel, who made eye contact with Lottie when her eyes gravitated his way without her consent.

It was getting ridiculous. She was a grown woman, and she could say hello to him if she wanted. But the night was dragging on and neither of them made any attempt to approach the other, even though many charged looks were exchanged, sending more and more fizz to Lottie's head.

She went outside to check out the portable toilets, thanking the thoughtful person who had invented them. The Tardis one smelled like fresh woodland pine and was easy to use and pleasantly clean, and she didn't need to use her disabled toilet key, as the doors were unlocked.

Back inside the hall, the party was in full swing, and half the buffet had disappeared. Within seconds of re-joining Ginny at their table, Lottie had locked eyes with Samuel again, and it was getting harder and harder to stay away from him. Enough was enough. It was time.

Lottie told her friends her plan, then turned her chair towards the bar, where most of the men had gathered. There were only two things to do. One, find a way to manoeuvre through the crowd, and two, speak to the man who made her heart skip beats. Both were a challenge.

As though reading her mind, Samuel indicated to an alcove by the stage where a small square hallway led to a side door that when unlocked allowed access to one of the church's back rooms.

With a push and a shove, a few feet trampled, and apologies left, right, and centre, Lottie made it to where Samuel was waiting.

They stared at each other as the music from the DJ pumped loudly around them. Being in the alcove next to the stage wasn't the best place for a conversation.

Lottie wanted to speak but just for a moment she found she was lost in his eyes. Softness was gazing back at her, filling her head with more fizz than the champagne. 'Hello,' she mouthed, knowing it was pointless to speak at a normal volume.

Samuel stepped closer and leaned down, his face so close to hers, and Lottie was sure he was going to kiss her, but his gaze slipped away along with his hand towards a large brown pot. He stood, revealing a key, then proceeded to unlock the arched door to the church.

Unsure but intrigued, Lottie followed him inside as he held the door wide for her before shutting off the music by closing them in. The muffled sounds were respite for her eardrums as she took in the musty scent of the mostly wooden room.

Tall black stands held cream pillar candles, and some oil paintings of flowers lined the back wall. There was no window, and the other door in the room was closed as well.

Lottie looked up, meeting amber eyes waiting for her. She felt the need to repeat herself in case he didn't have the ability to lip-read. 'Hello.'

'Hello,' he said softly, keeping eye contact. 'You look beautiful.' His gentle words silenced her thoughts, leaving her staring only at her dress.

Goosebumps erupted along with a slight pink blush to her cheeks.

'I've been wanting to tell you all night,' he added.

It was quite possible Lottie was alone with Prince Charming himself at a royal ball, as it certainly felt that way. His strong stance, confident eyes, and words filled with intention floored her completely. It wasn't how she'd expected their conversation to go.

She placed her attention on his dark-blue trousers and crisp white shirt. 'You look nice too,' was all she could manage.

'I missed you,' was his next jaw-dropping statement.

Perhaps the room would stop spinning if he averted his eyes, or maybe more alcohol was needed to be consumed to handle the charged atmosphere and dancing butterflies in her stomach.

At least he had the guts to say what was on his mind. Ginny was right, she had been lying to herself about her feelings towards Samuel. It would be so easy to show him how she felt, but surprisingly, it wasn't.

Samuel's gaze dropped to her mouth for a moment, and Lottie wasn't sure how much more her heart could take. Any more flutters and it might just take off.

The music had softened, taking the vibration in the floor with it. Everything seemed quieter now. Peaceful.

Samuel held out a hand. 'Would you like to dance?'

Lottie wasn't quite sure how to take that. 'In my chair?'

'Or in my arms. The choice is yours.'

She might have been on the floor before, but she was in the heavens now. 'You'll hold me?'

'If you're comfortable with that.'

She nodded, and Samuel carefully lifted her like a bride, and within moments she felt she was floating on cloud nine somewhere far, far away.

The soft music coming through the lump of a door was clear enough to hear that it was a love song playing. Something about new beginnings and acceptance, which seemed fitting.

The bottom of Lottie's dress flowed as Samuel swayed while holding her close. Not once during online dating did she imagine someone being so intimate with her. It was as though he held so much more than her body.

Their eyes were locked, and Lottie slipped away into the fairy tales she'd read as a child. No one had ever made her feel so special, so exclusive, so treasured. Her dress, his touch, the sweet melody was simply magical on each level in every realm. It didn't feel like their first dance. She was quite sure she'd been in his arms before.

'How you doing?' Samuel whispered, not taking his eyes off her.

'I feel like I'm in a dream,' she whispered.

'And are you happy there?'

She smiled to herself. 'I feel like I belong there.'

His lip twitched into the smallest smile. 'I think I belong there too.'

Lottie reached up, placing her fingertips lightly against the back of his neck, stroking his hairline. 'Do you feel I belong with you?'

'I just know something about you feels right.'

'Something about you feels familiar.'

'That's because we met on the road.'

Lottie burst out laughing, dropping her hand back to her chest. She took a breath and lowered her gaze. 'You can put me down now. Your arms must ache.'

'For your information, I work out. But if you want me to put you back in your chair, I will.'

'Not yet.'

'Then that's settled.'

The music seemed even quieter, and Samuel had stopped moving.

'Lottie?'

She glanced up. 'Hmm?'

'May I kiss you?'

No one had ever asked for her permission before. Was Samuel a genuine gentleman or was she really stuck in a dream?

'Yes,' Lottie replied quietly, leaning closer until their lips met. He felt so soft, so gentle, so perfect, and she was sure her heart had melted into a pool of slush.

It didn't take long for their kiss to heat or for Samuel to find a seat. He pulled her closer into his lap, and Lottie was completely his, ready for any and every step he wanted to take next.

The slight murmur that came from him had her grip tighten in his hair, and all thought of her dress creasing or her hair getting messed up went out the window. She wanted him to smudge her lip gloss and mess with her hair, even if they were in a church.

'Oh goodness, we're in a church,' she gasped, pulling away.

Samuel bit his bottom lip and grinned. 'We should go back to the party. I'm the host, after all.'

Lottie attempted to tidy herself as he placed her back into her wheelchair. 'Do I look okay?' she asked, wiping around her lips.

'You look as beautiful as ever.'

A fit of giggles rendered her useless for a moment. She pointed at his mouth. 'You have strawberry lips.'

He licked over them, then wiped away the sticky residue using the back of his hand. 'Better?'

'I prefer my lippy on you.'

'Oh, so do I.'

She laughed again, enjoying how easy everything felt with him. The party no longer mattered nor did much else. If it wasn't for the fact they were in a church, she wouldn't have stopped kissing him. 'I feel the need to apologize to Father Stephen.'

'He won't mind.'

'We behaved inappropriately.'

'We kissed in a church. It happens, especially on wedding days.'

'I felt we were heading for the wedding night.'

'Can be arranged.'

Lottie widened her eyes, and Samuel bent to his knees, kissing her cheek before peppering a few down her neck.

'Don't look so surprised, beautiful. If it wasn't for this party, I'd have you home already.'

'I want to go home now,' she whispered close to his ear.

He froze with his nose pressed against her cheek, then stood and straightened his shirt. 'I have guests. You can enjoy the night, then I'll take you home.'

Lottie flashed him a cheeky smile. 'Promise?'

Samuel rubbed a hand around the back of his neck as he breathed out a laugh. 'Oh, this is going to be one tough party to get through.'

'At least we're here together,' she said with meaning.

He gave her one last peck on the cheek before heading for the door. 'We can spend a lot of time together, if you want.'

Lottie smiled. 'I'd like that.'

# CHAPTER 21

*Samuel*

It wasn't until Samuel had reached Lottie's front door that he realized he had one big dilemma. If he slept with her, he'd want to stay over to hold her all night, but he hadn't spent a night away from home in years. He wasn't sure he was ready for that step. It was part of his plan, further down the road. One he kept pushing back. Now he wished he hadn't.

Lottie was staring at him, waiting for him to cross the threshold. 'Sam?'

Like Cinderella, he had to flee the scene at midnight without an explanation. What the hell was he going to say?

'I . . . I can't stay.'

She had every right to look confused. 'Why? Did I do something wrong?'

'Of course not.' He really didn't mean to snap, but her words cut deep. How could she think his irrational behaviour had anything to do with her? Even with her fringe, he could see her brow crinkle.

'What is wrong with you?'

'Nothing.' His moods were all over the place, and it was obvious she wasn't impressed with his blunt attitude.

'I'm tired. I'm going to bed.' And with that, she slammed the door on him.

It was no more than he deserved. She probably viewed him as some sort of player trying to mess with her mind. He would think that too if the shoe were on the other foot.

Samuel leaned on the wall, raking a hand through his hair. Agoraphobia had left him deflated on many occasion, but none quite like this. What was he supposed to do about having any sort of normal relationship if he couldn't even sleep over at his girlfriend's house?

*Girlfriend!*

He had to laugh. So close. Now what? It was too late to call Jan for advice, and he didn't have a best mate to ring to share his troubles with. Tossing back his head, he stared at the many stars twinkling, not that he needed them to remind him he'd been having a magical night up until now.

His parents could be up there, yelling advice, weeping for his wounded soul. Who knew what they would have to say about how his life turned out. Half the time, he didn't know what to say himself. He sure as hell didn't know what others would say.

So much told him to get off the wall and go home, but his legs weren't listening, and his heart had left home shortly after Lottie slammed the door.

'Oh, what a bloody mess,' he said through clenched teeth, hating himself. Hating everything.

A noise came from the door, gaining his attention. Lottie sat there, looking up at him, then motioned for him to come inside.

'I'll put the kettle on,' she said, heading for the kitchen.

Samuel followed, taking in the low cupboards and work-tops. He went to help, but she waved him to a chair, where he sat in silence, wondering why she had a microphone set up on the kitchen table. He started to twiddle with the stand, but then stopped when she glanced over.

'It's for when I do my kitchen table talks. I make videos for the Hub's website. People talk about their problems or what they've overcome, and it helps others. Well, I hope it does.'

Was a chat about agoraphobia due? Not if he could help it, but he did need to tell Lottie. She deserved the truth, no matter how awkward it was for him.

'I know there's something wrong, Sam. It's written all over your face.'

He happened to think he hid his feelings well, thank you very much. How had she sneaked under the radar to see what others couldn't? He always felt quite proud of the way he had the ability to function like a normal everyday person. Had he lost that too? Just when he thought his night couldn't get any worse.

Lottie placed two mugs of tea on the table, then leaned forward to hold his hand. 'Talk to me. I promise you your thoughts and feelings are in a safe place with me.'

The sweetness of her wording would stay with him forever, just like the taste of her mouth, but that wasn't a memory he could hold on to right now.

Samuel took a breath. 'I haven't spent a night away from home in a long time.' That seemed like a good start, if vague.

'Is this because of Hannah?'

'No. Felix is sleeping over at ours tonight, but it has nothing to do with either of them. It's just, well I'm . . . The thing is . . .' Words faded, so he sipped his tea, burning his tongue in the process.

'Take your time. It's all right, Sam.'

It was clear she was a lot better at this malarkey than him. *Oh, to hell with it.*

'I'm agoraphobic,' he blurted, not meeting her eyes.

'But you're out.'

Common misconception, he knew. 'It doesn't work that way. Well, obviously it does for some, but I'm not housebound. My invisible walls lay elsewhere.'

'Like where?'

'I'm currently confined to Cornwall, which isn't too bad. I'm going through exposure therapy, so I'm pushing on those walls I just mentioned and making my way closer to Devon at the moment. I just haven't got around to staying over anywhere to conquer the sleepover step of my disorder. I figured I could attempt it once I'd visited everywhere in Cornwall.' He breathed out a small laugh, not that he found anything funny. Saying *disorder* out loud made him feel like an idiot. He flopped his head into his hands on the table. 'Oh God. I sound so stupid.'

Lottie's gentle fingers were in his hair, lightly soothing his weary soul. 'Hey, don't beat yourself up. So you have a phobia, a mental illness, a disorder, whatever. It's not the end of the world. We humans are pretty good at adapting to our circumstances. You're in therapy, pushing your boundaries, and trying your best. That should be admired.'

'Why do you make everything sound so much better?' he asked, groaning onto the table.

Lottie sighed. 'Hey, everyone's got their demon. We just can't waste energy feeling sorry for ourselves or focusing on the problem. Solutions are needed, and that's what we have to gravitate towards. There's nothing to be ashamed of.'

Samuel raised his head. 'I hate talking about it. I am ashamed.'

'Should I be?'

'Should you be what?'

'Ashamed because my back got injured.'

'No, why would you say that?'

Lottie shook her head and tapped his arm. 'Why would you feel ashamed for your injured mind? You have a medical problem.'

'It's different.'

'It's not, Sam. And on the bright side, at least you can get help and fix your problem. I can't. Take yours as a win. Wait, people can be cured from agoraphobia, right?'

Samuel nodded. 'Yep, many have.'

'That's great. It shows it's doable.'

'Bloody hard.'

'But doable.'

'Do you always look on the bright side?'

Lottie shrugged. 'The other side sucks.'

Samuel laughed, releasing the tension building around the back of his neck. 'Look, Lottie, I didn't want to sleep with you, then leave. And I sure as heck didn't want to have this conversation, but here we are, and honestly, I don't know how to move forward.'

'You can use my home to practice.'

'What do you mean?'

'When you feel ready, you can try a sleepover. Stay in Spencer's room. He lives in the flat above our shop, but he still has a room here. You won't get any pressure or sex expectations from me, and—'

'Sex expectations?'

She shrugged and flashed a grin. 'I'm just setting ground rules. This won't be about us, Sam. This is your therapy. You come here, sleep, leave when you want. Try as many times as you like. It's got to be better than some standard hotel somewhere.'

'Actually, I had a rather posh hotel in mind. Thought I'd treat myself, seeing how I haven't had a holiday in years.'

'When was your last holiday?'

'The one I was coming back from with my parents when the accident happened.'

'Oh, sorry. Hannah told me about that.'

Samuel slumped back in his chair. 'Did she tell you it was my fault?'

'No. How was it your fault?'

'I was desperate for the loo and couldn't hold on, so Dad pulled onto a verge along the dual carriageway. I nipped up into some bushes, and as I took my first step back to the car, a lorry took it half way up the road.' He swallowed hard, wondering where all this disclosure was coming from.

Lottie moved closer, wrapping her hand around his forearm. 'Oh, Sam, that wasn't your fault. It was the lorry driver. What the hell was the driver doing?'

'Apparently he fell asleep.'

'I don't know what to say. You hear about these things but . . . Look, Sam, it wasn't your fault.'

He rubbed his tired eyes, making his skin below blotchy. 'It's a hard thing to live with.'

'I can imagine. But it's not your fault, you hear me. Don't do that to yourself.'

Samuel controlled his breathing and sipped some more tea, not really wanting it but needing something to shift the lump wedged in his throat. 'That's why I acted the way I did when I found you in my house. You were holding my therapy notebook that has my progress inside. I was mortified, thinking you'd seen it. I was going to explain, but then George's accident happened, and well . . .'

'I know I've already told you, but I promise you, I didn't snoop in your book.'

'I still feel so bad for the way I acted.'

'We're past that now.'

'Thank you for understanding. I'm not sure many would.'

Lottie glanced at the flowery clock on the wall. 'I'm a bit tired now, but tomorrow I'll find out everything I can about agoraphobia and see where I can help.'

'You don't have to do that.'

'I want to. I like helping people. In case you haven't noticed, I volunteer at the Happy to Help Hub. Bit of a clue there.' She smiled warmly. 'Everyone needs a helping hand from time to time. People rallied round me after my accident. I'm sure there's some way I can help you.'

Samuel was quite blown away, and not just by her can-do attitude. Her sweet words were full of meaning, but she didn't need to do or say anything. 'Just being around you makes me feel better.'

Lottie gave his hand a gentle tap. 'Do you want to stay here tonight or wait till you feel more prepared?'

He looked out to the hallway, deep in thought. Without his issue, he'd already be in her bed for the night, he knew, but his life wasn't that simple. Making a sleepover decision was just as annoyingly frustrating as all the other decisions he had to make, which involved things like travel, people, public transport, functions, relationships to name a few. Just the thought process alone was draining.

'I don't want to push you,' added Lottie when he hadn't replied.

'It's okay. You wouldn't be able to anyway. I can only do small steps. Jumping in the deep end could cause setbacks. Desensitization is about stages. This didn't happen to me overnight, so training my brain to reverse the process won't happen overnight. See, small steps.'

Lottie sighed. 'Strange how the mind works all by itself.'

'It's the dripping-tap effect. Drip, drip, drip, you don't notice till your sink is overflowing, by which time . . .'

'Yeah. There was a lady who came into the Hub last month. Told me she'd not long walked away from an abusive relationship. She mentioned something similar. Said it took her years to realize her mind had been conditioned by her ex. It's weird how we can be brain trained without noticing.'

'My condition crept up on me. Maybe it's some sort of survival mode we go into. With me, I started having panic attacks when I was out and about, and just like anytime you feel unwell, you go home, right?' He watched her nod. 'I kept running home on jelly legs I was sure wouldn't get me far but surprisingly always managed to get me home. The next thing I knew, I stopped going to these places I associated with the fear. Long story short, my world became a smaller place.'

'Like living in a bubble.'

'Exactly.'

'I'd hate it if I couldn't get out.'

'Honestly, I'm not too bad, as I'm one of those people who like being at home. I'm not sure if I've ever had the travel bug, but that's beside the point. If I do need or want to go somewhere, I should be able to just go. But it's such a chore, and I don't mean the packing. It's the overthinking. It's a bloody headache and so exhausting.'

She nodded. 'Whenever I catch myself overthinking, I tell myself to stop, and I change the subject, sometimes by singing.'

'You seem pretty well put together.'

Lottie laughed. 'My aunt raised me to be positive. I guess something stuck. Spencer says I'm a natural problem-solver.'

'I'm more the bury your head in the sand type.'

'Well, it would be boring if we were all the same.' She chinked his mug with her own and winked.

Samuel had a moment where he wanted to kiss her, but he also wanted to leave her alone. As much as he had fallen for her, he didn't want to burden her with his problems. The reason he'd stayed single for so long was so he wasn't a burden on anyone. Another dilemma added to his list was too much weight for his tired soul.

'What you thinking, Sam?'

'That I should leave now.'

She glanced at the clock again. 'It is late.'

He wanted to be honest with her. They'd come that far, and it was so easy to talk to her. 'I meant leave you alone. For good.'

'Oh, why would you think that? I felt a connection. I thought you did too. Are you getting cold feet?'

Samuel laughed to himself, thinking back to their time in the church. If there was ever a time to get cold feet, that was the place for it. 'No. I just don't want all my crap to enter your life. I like you too much. I feel torn now.'

'How about you let me worry about that? It's my choice, after all.'

'I know, but—'

'No buts, Sam. Let's not make this an issue. I don't see you making my wheelchair one.'

'That's because I don't see the chair, I just see you.'

She tapped her chest. 'And that's how I feel. Look, Sam, no one's perfect. Everyone's got something going on. So what if

151

you struggle to travel outside Cornwall, or if you have to spend time doing exposure therapy. I have to go the long way around sometimes because there are only stairs and no slopes on my journey.' She shrugged. 'We adapt, remember? We figure it out.'

'I love your brain, Lottie Jordan. I wish I could be as strong as you.'

'Strength comes in many shapes and sizes. I'd like to have your upper body strength.'

Holding her in his arms while they danced made him thank every ache and pain he'd ever gone through in the gym. Had he known she was in his future, he would have had more motivation to push on.

'I'd like to try a sleepover here.' He was having a now-or-never moment. Life was so much easier on the days where he felt able to take on the world. He'd make arrangements, cheer himself on, pump up the volume on the radio, and dance into the life he so desperately wanted. But when the time came to do the things he'd organized, he'd often crumble.

'Tonight?' she asked, holding more hope in her eyes than he had in his whole body.

Samuel nodded. 'I don't have my things, but, well . . .' He turned to the clock. 'It'll be morning in a few hours. I just have to get through the night, then I've taken the first step in staying away from home.'

Lottie moved her wheelchair closer. 'Okay. Let's get you settled in Spencer's room. You can wear his PJs, if you want. He's about the same size as you, only taller. There are spare toothbrushes in the bathroom, as Spence likes to buy packs of things. I don't know why. It's just his thing. Anyway, if at any time you want to go home, just lock up and pop the key through the letterbox. You don't need to wake me, unless you need me, of course. Otherwise, seriously, I'm someone who loves her sleep.'

'You had that all figured out pretty quickly.'

'Told you, natural problem-solver.'

'I bet you like jigsaw puzzles.'

'Love them. And just so you know, I can do a Rubik's Cube.'

'Now you're just showing off.'

Lottie led him to the stairs and moved into the stairlift. He walked up slowly, admiring her independence, positive mental attitude, and the ability to pretend she was wide awake when he knew she was ready for her bed.

Spencer's room had blue-and-white walls, white wooden flooring, and a view of the back garden. Lottie pointed out drawers and accessories and rattled off suggestions and upstairs floor plans, then left him alone while she went off to get washed and changed for bed.

Samuel stared at himself in the tall floor mirror along the side wall. Was he really going to do this? The whole night had been filled with one surprise after the other. If there was a time to go full throttle it might as well be now.

As soon as he heard Lottie go into her bedroom, he headed off to the bathroom to wash and brush his teeth. One of Spencer's tee shirts and his own boxer shorts would be okay to sleep in.

Samuel wondered if Lottie was already in bed. He approached her door, knocking lightly on the white framework. 'I just wanted to say goodnight.'

'Come in, I was just about to do the same thing. You've saved me the trip.'

He smiled at her flowery pink pyjamas. 'Very cute.'

Lottie flashed him one of her sweet smiles that he found so utterly adorable. 'You have nice legs, Mr Powell.'

Oh. He'd forgotten he was in his undies and a tee. There was no way he was going to blush. He bit his lip and grinned.

Lottie wiggled one finger, waving him closer to where she sat on her bed.

He bent his head and closed his eyes for a second while she kissed his cheek and said goodnight.

'I'll leave my door open all night,' she told him. 'I'm right here if you need me. Don't be a hero, Sam. If you need help, say so.'

He gave her a cheeky salute at the door, then said goodnight.

Spencer's double bed was comfy, and fresh sheets always made for a better sleep. However, Samuel wasn't sure if he'd be able to sleep. With wide eyes, he stared at the ceiling, almost waiting for some form of fear to kick in and chase him home. It was all so surreal. Could he really make it through the night?

He closed his eyes and took a deep breath. If nothing else, at least he would try, and if he had to do a moonlight flit, then so be it. Like Lottie had said, there was no need to feel ashamed.

The mantra helped him steady his breathing. One way or another his mind was getting the memo that he wasn't in any danger. It really needed to get a grip, and his demon needed to sod right off.

Samuel opened his eyes, taking a moment to gather his bearings. He turned his head to see an alarm clock on the bedside cabinet. 6 a.m.

*Oh my God!*

He'd fallen asleep. He did it. He spent the night away from home. Joy and admiration fizzled, waking him fully, encouraging him to dance, but then he noticed something else. Down at the bottom of the bed, on the other side to where he had just fist-bumped the air, was Lottie, sitting in her manual wheelchair, flopped over the quilt, sleeping peacefully.

How long she had been there was anyone's guess, but he was sure she would ache upon waking. He didn't want to disturb her, as she looked in a deep sleep, but he couldn't leave her like that. Smiling at having someone so wonderful in his life, he got up, carefully scooped her into his arms, placed her under the covers, moved her wheelchair to her side, then danced his way down the stairs to make a well-needed coffee in the kitchen, where he danced some more.

The last time he felt so elated was back in his uni days. The feeling was almost alien, it had been that long. He felt so incredibly blessed to be able to reunite with joy. Everything was magical, beautiful, and so, so bizarre. It was so much more than a win. Sleeping over at Lottie's, finding out she had watched over him at some point, and not having any fear, overwhelmed him to the point that when he finally found Lottie's coffee jar, water pricked his eyes.

Samuel glanced out the window at the early morning sky and mouthed, 'Thank you.' He had no idea who he was talking to but felt someone was listening, maybe even helping, because not only was he going from strength to strength, he had met someone filled with kindness, understanding, and the ability to take him on.

He quickly set about making her the best-ever breakfast in bed he could whip up before she woke. Lottie Jordan deserved everything and more, and he was going to make sure he could bring as much to the table as she already had. As early as it was into their relationship, he wanted them to be on equal ground, which meant he needed to up his game. There was no way he wanted to be the weakest link she had to constantly look out for. No, sir. Determination lifted him even higher than his sleepover had. He wanted to be someone his partner could be proud of, not a charity case in need of assistance. He silently prayed she wasn't going down that road with him.

Lottie was stirring by the time Samuel reached the bedroom with her breakfast. He placed the tray on the dressing table and sat by her side, smiling at how beautiful she looked. Gently, he pushed back part of her fringe, for no reason other than wanting to touch her face.

She opened her eyes and smiled up at him. 'You stayed all night, Sam.' The husky croak in her voice caused his smile to widen.

'I did.'

'How do you feel?'

'Everything's a bit surreal at the moment.'

She slipped her hand from beneath the quilt to lightly stroke his arm. 'I'm glad we got to wake together, sort of.'

They shared a warm look.

'Perhaps next time they'll be no sort of about it,' he said, placing his hand close to her hair once more.

Lottie curled her face into his palm. 'Perhaps what we wanted to do last night, we could do now.'

Samuel gazed at her for a moment. Her eyes were closed, her mouth raised in a teasing grin, and her cheek glued to his hand. 'You sure you don't just want breakfast.'

Lottie stared at him as she reached for his neck, pulling him closer. 'I'm sure.'

A hundred and one fireflies took flight in his stomach as he leaned over to meet her soft lips.

Lottie grabbed at his top, yanking it over his head, making him laugh.

'If you don't mind, I prefer to take my time with you,' he told her playfully.

Lottie grinned. 'If you lose the rest of your nightwear and climb into bed with me right this second, you can take as long as you like.'

'Good to know.' He nudged her nose with his own, then slowly peeled back the cover to reveal her body. 'And what about your nightwear?'

'That can go too.' She gave him a slow wink. 'If you think you can handle it.'

Samuel held back his laugh and hit her with his best sexy side smile. 'I think I can manage.'

# CHAPTER 22

*Lottie*

Seeing Samuel walk around all morning with the biggest smile warmed Lottie from head to toe. There was no doubt about it, she was going to do everything she could to help him with his battles, and on the days when he was worn through, she had already decided she would make him hot chocolate and simply sit by his side beneath the stars. That was definitely something she loved to do, so she was sure he could relax that way too.

She went home with him, as he needed to get changed, and she wanted to spend more time around him. He suggested lunch at his and told her she could do some artwork in his kitchen if she wanted.

The view from his kitchen window was to die for. So much so, she sat in front of the easel Samuel had set up for her and just stared dreamily out to sea.

There was so much to take in, Lottie didn't know where to start. She peered over at him, sitting at the table, typing away on his laptop, still looking happy.

'What's up?' he asked, not looking up from the screen.

'I'm overwhelmed.'

He laughed and got up to kiss her cheek. 'Just paint one thing.'

'I want to paint it all.'

'You can. You can come here whenever you like and paint.'

She gestured at his laptop. 'Don't tempt me. You'll never get any work done.'

'I'm just trying to draw up a business plan for Ginny. I want to see about using Harbour Light Café as another café, like mine. She closes at four, so I'm thinking perhaps the Hub could take over for a couple of hours a few times a week.'

'Sophie once mentioned that to her. I think Ginny wants to but has a lot on at the moment. She cares for her mum as well as runs that place, and she volunteers at the Hub. I do happen to know her one true love is baking cakes. She'd love a tearoom, but the fishermen would cause a mutiny if she changed the café. It's been there longer than the residents of Port Berry.'

'Hmm, well, I'm sure I could brainstorm with her. See what we can come up with. Meanwhile, I'm still hiring for the Trust. You got any plans to give up the flower shop?'

Lottie laughed. 'Never.'

'What would you normally be doing on a Sunday?'

'Training for my race, visiting my neighbours, with my cart filled to the brim with salad and anything else they might need. I have shopping lists they give me now.' She smiled, thinking how full-on the meals on wheels had got. It was a lot harder now George wasn't around to help. 'It's nice to have a day off and just paint.'

'I don't really do days off. I always find something to do.'

She nodded at the work he had set up before him. 'I noticed.'

'Well, I'm not going to just sit here and stare at you till lunchtime. I could, but I think I'm weird enough.'

'You're not weird. Anyway, when you invited me here for this, how could I refuse? In all honesty, I haven't been in the mood for much lately. I have George's house to clear, and the thought of the men from the second-hand shop coming to take away some of the furniture is disheartening.'

'You could leave it a while longer if you're not ready for that step.'

Lottie shook her head. George had left clear instructions about his belongings, and most of it was to be donated to charity. 'It's going to take some time, so I'm doing bits and pieces every so often. It's just sad. His whole life was wrapped up in his home, like everyone, I guess, and I've got to divvy it up and hand it over to strangers.'

'Yeah, it's strange. I remember doing all that with my parents' things.' He glanced over at the doorway. 'Hannah and I haven't got much of theirs.'

'I'm not sure I want to keep anything. I'd cry if something broke or got lost. I don't know. Not made up my mind yet.'

'He was good to you, wasn't he?'

There were no words to sum up just how wonderful George was. Not once did she take him for granted, always appreciating his presence in her life.

'He was the best, Sam. He was the dad we never had. Always there, never said no when we asked for help, and was full of advice and handy hints and tips for just about everything. If there was a shop where you could go to pick dads, I'd choose him. He really was the best. What were your parents like?'

Samuel scrunched his nose. 'Pretty boring. Ordinary. Not much to report. We had a nice family. No drama, food always available, Mum always there when we came home from school. Dad worked full-time, and she worked part-time. We had a two-week holiday every summer, and the best time at Christmas and birthdays. I guess we were a bit of a nuclear family.'

'My parents were more like the ones you see on the six o'clock news that put you off your dinner.'

'Oh, Lottie.'

She had to laugh, as she wasn't joking. 'I don't remember my parents, as I was a toddler when I went to live with my aunt, but I've heard all the stories. Read something in the paper. Googled the story once. Not my best idea. It's one thing to know, and another to see it in print.'

'I don't really know your story. I won't lie, I've heard bits and bobs but I didn't delve.'

'It's okay. It's old news back home, but when mentioned, a lot of people remember it. My parents were drug addicts, and during one of their highs, or maybe lows, not sure, they killed my little brother, Jordy. He was just a baby.'

'Oh my God, that's terrible.'

'Yeah, poor Jordy never stood a chance. They went to prison, and Spencer and I ended up in care until my aunt stepped in and took us under her wing. She adopted us in the end.'

'She sounds like a wonderful woman.'

'Aunt Rebecca was brilliant. I know I didn't have the best start, but between Rebecca and George, I had a fantastic childhood. Spencer was eight when it happened. He remembers things I don't, so he was more troubled than me. My aunt poured so much love into us, it helped my brother settle a bit.'

'Is he doing okay now?'

'It's not something he'll ever forget, but he's okay.'

'I'm so sorry about Jordy. For your past.'

'Thanks. It's hard to know what to say, isn't it?'

'You just don't realize how tough some kids have it.'

'Hey, don't feel sorry for us. Thanks to my aunt, life was good.'

Samuel pointed over to a framed picture of his parents, taken the year before they died. 'It's pot luck, isn't it?'

Lottie shrugged. 'I guess so.'

'Do you see your parents now?'

'No. We've never had any contact. Don't want any. We don't even know if they're alive, still inside, or what.'

The one time she'd mentioned them to Spencer, he'd shut her down so fast, her head was still spinning two days later. It was just a suggestion about finding out if they were still locked up, but Spencer hit the roof, and that was the end of that.

'I've always been grateful for my parents. They gave us a happy life.' Samuel stared at the window. 'You never know how others are living.'

'People are always shocked when they hear about my family, but it's old news to me. I don't feel any connection to that life. It's like it's someone else's story. All I know is growing up with my aunt and Spencer. I don't have any memories of Jordy.'

'Why did your parents call your little brother Jordy? Jordy Jordan?'

'They weren't exactly of sound mind, Sam. We preferred the names Rebecca called us . . . Oh!' Lottie slapped a hand to her mouth, shaking her head at herself.

Samuel's expression was filled with intrigue. 'What's your real name?'

Her shoulders slumped. It was too late to backtrack now. 'First time I've slipped up there.'

Samuel pulled his chair to her side. 'We bonded over my phobia, I think we can safely move on to your name.'

'Scarlott, spelled with an O instead of an E. That's where Lottie comes from, not Charlotte, as most people think. Rebecca started calling me Lottie, and when I was old enough, I changed it by deed poll.'

'And you don't like people knowing?'

She shook her head. 'It's not that. It's just not who I feel I am. I don't want any attachment to my birth parents, so I don't get into the story of my name. We never had our dad's last name. Jordan comes from my mum and Rebecca, so we stuck with that because of my aunt.'

'Did Spencer change his first name too?'

Lottie bit her lip. 'In his case, it was more about removing his first name, as Spencer is his middle name. Rebecca only called him Spencer, and when he was old enough, he got his name changed officially as well.'

'Now I'm even more intrigued.'

'If I tell you, I'll have to kill you, or rather, we'd have to leave town before Spencer kills us both.'

'Is it that bad?'

Lottie shrugged. 'Each to their own, I guess. Some might like it, but Spence cringes at the thought.'

'It's okay. You don't have to tell me.'

'I've told you everything else, so might as well. They named him Spaceman Spencer.'

'Oh, okay. I can see why he might find that a little awkward.'

Lottie reached over, grabbing his hand, which felt all levels of wonderful. 'Promise you'll take it to the grave.'

He kissed her knuckles and promised.

'Oh, Sam, life can be so strange, and isn't it odd how it can change so dramatically.'

'Yep. Everything that's happened to me I didn't see coming. Some people have dreams and goals, and they move towards them with ease or even a fight, but me, well, it all just happened and I didn't get a say in it.'

Lottie pulled him in for a hug. 'I didn't see you coming, but I'm glad I met you.'

'Does that mean you're going to give up the meet-and-greets outside Ginny's café?'

She moved back to assess the humour in his eyes. 'Are you mocking my choices, Mr Powell?'

He touched his collarbone. 'Moi?'

'Hmm. Well, let's see. I haven't been on a date with you yet, so I might keep my options open.'

'In that case, you, me, dinner tonight. Where do you fancy?'

'How about you cook for me.'

'Can be arranged.'

'Nothing too heavy though. I'll be training first thing. I need to get back into routine.' She watched his frown lines appear.

'Will you be on the road again?'

'No. Park. Robson's taking me all week. He likes to jog early, and I can fit in my sessions before work.'

'Are you working all week?'

'Yes, I've had far too much time off lately, and we're in wedding season. I have one shift at the Hub on Friday. I'll add you on the roster for then if you like.'

'Yes, sign me up.'

'Then, on Saturday, you can spend the night at mine again.'

'Aren't you organized.'

Lottie gave him a heated kiss before pulling away to gesture to the gorgeous view of the sea. 'Best get on with it.'

Samuel breathed out a quiet laugh. 'Oh, is that right?'

Before she had a chance to release a giggle, he was back on her lips, pushing all thoughts of landscape painting far from her mind.

Hannah clearing her throat interrupted the building passion, leaving Lottie pink in the cheeks and Samuel trying not to laugh.

'Well, well. This is a turn-up for the books,' said Hannah, grinning like the cat that got the cream. She nudged an equally smug Felix in the ribs. 'We'll just have our lunch somewhere else, eh, Fix?'

Felix nodded, taking her hand to leave.

'Come back.' Samuel waved them inside. 'You can still eat. I was about to make Lottie something anyway.'

'Are you sure? Only it didn't look that way.' Hannah hobbled inside, flopping to a chair.

'You okay?' asked Lottie.

Hannah rubbed her thighs as Felix made himself busy with the fridge. 'My thighs ache, that's all.' Her eyes widened with glee as she looked up at her brother. 'Ooh, have you shown Lottie the Terminator?'

Lottie laughed. 'The what?'

'He'll show you.' Hannah nodded at Samuel, who rolled his eyes in return.

'I had no plans to. I'm still trying to sell the flipping thing.'

'Give it to a recovery centre,' said Felix. 'I know one that would appreciate it.'

Samuel scoffed. 'Do you know how much that thing cost?'

Felix shrugged as Hannah laughed.

'What are we talking about?' asked Lottie.

Hannah folded her arms while directing her stubborn gaze at Samuel.

'Tell me, Sam,' Lottie pleaded.

'Yes, Sam, tell her,' said Hannah, gesturing towards the doorway.

Samuel huffed and shook his head. 'Fine, but you better have lunch ready for us by the time we come back.' He turned to Lottie and indicated for her to follow.

Lottie was thoroughly intrigued, even more so when he opened the door to the glass lift in the hallway. Inside smelled like furniture polish, and she could see her reflection in the shiny floor.

Samuel pressed the lowest button, and the lift started to move downwards, which wasn't where Lottie was expecting to go.

'You have a dungeon?' she joked.

Samuel winked, causing all sorts of fluttery creatures to take flight in her stomach.

The lift came to a stop, revealing a large space best suited to a warehouse conversion. Lights automatically came on the moment the glass door opened, and Lottie took in the exposed brick wall, lack of windows, and the many contraptions she was sure helped keep Samuel in shape.

She'd been to a few gyms in her time, but Samuel's basement looked like somewhere NASA astronauts might work out.

'Which one do you call the Terminator?' she asked, perusing the state-of-the-art equipment.

Samuel made his way to the far end of the room, and Lottie followed, glancing at the sheen on the wooden flooring.

Something resembling a high-tech wheelchair was what she was led to.

'What's the story with this?' she asked, poking a finger into the hard leather armrest.

'An impulse buy. Would you like me to show you what it does? Before you answer, it would require you to sit there.'

She tugged at one of the black straps. 'I'm not getting on that thing till you tell me what it does.'

Samuel lowered to a switch, then pressed something she couldn't see, which made part of the contraption rise up a touch. 'It'll bring you upright to a stand. It was for Hannah back when she refused to try prosthetic legs. I thought if she kept upright, she'd want to stay that way. It was one of the first things I bought when I made my money. Do you want to try it?'

The last time Lottie stood was the moment before she climbed onto her bicycle the day she got run over. Standing wasn't something she thought about, having accepted her wheels early on in her recovery.

'You can always test it out another day if you don't feel ready.'

'You're starting to sound like me.'

They shared a smile, and Samuel bent to kiss her cheek. And just like that, Lottie knew what she wanted to do.

'Strap me in, Sam.'

Sitting down wasn't so bad, but once the chair started to lift her, a slight wobble churned her gut.

Samuel stopped the elevation. 'You dizzy?'

'Not sure how I feel.'

'We'll do it bit by bit.'

'I feel like I'm at the dentist.' She breathed out a small laugh, then gave him the thumbs-up to raise her a little more.

On a scale of one to ten, the experience was quite possibly off the chart, as inch by inch, Lottie came to a stand. She swallowed hard, focusing on one brick in the wall slightly darker than its neighbours. She daren't close her eyes in case her head swirled and she threw up.

'Are you ready to turn? You can check yourself out in the mirror?' Samuel asked softly.

Was she ready to see that? She wasn't entirely sure she was ready for much right now, but she gave the smallest of nods. After all, she'd come this far.

'Oh my goodness.' Lottie couldn't control the tears escaping her eyes nor did she care to try. The sight before her may have had her resembling some sort of robot, but blimming heck, she was practically standing once more.

Samuel gently wiped away the dampness on her cheeks.

Lottie caught her breath and forced a smile. It was surreal and a touch overwhelming to see herself upright.

'It's a standing wheelchair. All very sci-fi,' said Samuel, pointing at the controls by her hand. 'You can get different ones. As you can see, this one is quite chunky at the sides. Do you want to try it out? Whizz around?' He splayed one arm out to the open space in front of them.

Did she dare go for it? That would be a hell to the yeah. Before Samuel got to finish his safety talk, Lottie was off, squealing with delight until she felt giddy again.

'Oh, Sam, it's like my legs work.'

He started to dance around her, making her laugh, especially when he began singing "A Whole New World" from Disney's *Aladdin*.

'How do you know that song?'

'Oh, please. Have you met my sister?'

Lottie laughed and tried to make the standing device dance along. She came to an abrupt halt, beckoning him closer.

He seemed to know exactly what she wanted. As he approached, he hit her with one of his sexy side smiles, then leaned in for a kiss.

So much of her wanted to say those three little words, but it felt too soon, and she didn't want to scare him off, even though she was sure they now had a bond stronger than glue.

Lottie kept quiet as Samuel stepped back.

'You ready for lunch yet?' he asked, stroking her arm.

She was ready for so much more than that but nodded.

Samuel helped her into her wheelchair, fussing over her cushion and back, making sure she wasn't in any pain.

'Hey, I'm fine,' she whispered close to his ear.

'At least now I know what to do with this thing,' he told her.

'What's that?'

'Give it to you.'

Lottie was gobsmacked for a moment. The standing wheelchair looked expensive. 'I can't afford that.'

Samuel smiled. 'I'm giving it to you, Lottie. Speak to your medical team first. Get some advice on—'

'Whoa! Back up. I can't accept. It's too much. Besides, Hannah might want to use it.' She knew that wasn't true. Hannah hardly used a wheelchair.

'Well, it's here if you change your mind. I'm not saying you have to swap your chair for this one. I'm just offering you another wheelchair, that's all.'

What a thought. She could just see herself zipping around the supermarket, reaching the higher shelves.

Samuel headed back to the lift. 'Being around Hannah has taught me not to interfere when it comes to people and their walking abilities. So I won't push the matter. Just know you are now the new owner of the wheelchair. It's up to you what you do with it.'

Lottie entered the lift, gazing over at the glass wall, her mind whirling with thoughts of Willy Wonka, ingenious inventions, glass elevators, and a recluse. Could this man be the most amazing person in the world or was she still in the kitchen staring out to sea, daydreaming?

'I've got some chocolate for after lunch,' he said quietly, eyes on the door.

Lottie smiled to herself. Perhaps she had won a golden ticket, just like Charlie Bucket.

# CHAPTER 23

*Samuel*

Samuel stared up at the fishing nets adorning the ceiling in the nautical-themed café owned by Ginny Dean. He felt the place had a friendly vibe and thought it would make a perfect evening-meal centre for the locals of Port Berry struggling to put dinner on the table or any lonely elderly people. He really needed to get some investors involved so started compiling a list in the notes section on his phone while waiting for Ginny to return from the kitchen.

As promised, Ginny brought with her four different slices of cake, as he'd agreed to be a food tester.

'I want to add more cake to the menu, but there's so much on offer at the moment, there's no room. The regulars don't want an updated menu. They just want café grub and this old place to look this way forever.' Ginny sighed as she plopped onto a chair opposite him.

'What's this green one?'

'Minty choc chip. Try some.'

Samuel didn't need asking twice. Scooping up a mouthful, he grinned. 'Mmm, very nice, but see if you can make the same taste without it looking fit for Halloween.'

Ginny flopped back. 'Ooh, good point. Can you see though? My cakes are good. I know they are, but my customers are only interested in bacon butties or pasties and chips. You're a businessman, what's your advice on shaking things up around here?'

'Hmm, well, not sure that's something I could help with. They say the customer's always right, and if you have a steady flow, perhaps it wouldn't be wise to change anything.'

'It's not that I don't like this place. It used to be my dream to own this café, but things change, and it's just that I'm happier baking cakes than frying eggs now.'

'Have you thought about selling?'

Ginny leaned closer. 'You interested?'

Samuel tried not to laugh. 'No. I'm looking for premises like the one I already have in Penzance. The Food Bank Café chain won't do takeovers that annoy the locals, and like you just said, this café means something to people around here. I'm not having them hate on me, thanks.'

'It's swamped in history. Been around forever. I wouldn't mind, but it's changed with the times every so often and no one's moaned about that, but apparently it's not ready for an update yet, so my customers tell me. They got the hump the time I removed omelettes from the menu. Hardly any were ordered, but did that matter? Nope. So, why do you want to use it to give out free evening meals? Aren't you looking for something a bit fancier around here?'

'No, I'm not putting a Food Bank Café in Port Berry. This is a small community, and I think we can work well with what you've already got around here. It shouldn't bother anyone if this place turns into something else come closing time, as I won't change anything. You close at four, and it's such a landmark, I think it would be praised.'

'Yeah, you might want to run that by Councillor Seabridge. I know I don't need his permission, but trust me, if you want something to be a success in Port Berry, you need him and his cronies on side. Do yourself a favour and go to the next council meeting and bring up the subject to get some feedback. Just duck if any flying crisps head your way.'

'Why do I get the feeling you're not joking?'

'I'm not. It happens from time to time, ask Sophie. We normally nominate her to face the council meetings. These things can get a little heated at times.'

'Thanks for the heads-up.'

'You're welcome.'

'So does that mean you're up for the challenge?'

Ginny shook her head. 'Not at the moment. But hopefully in a couple of months I might be able to sort a few things with you. I currently have personal commitments that take up my time, but meanwhile, you put the feelers out. See how the land lies.'

Samuel jotted down some notes before snaffling some mouth-watering lemon drizzle that surprised him by fizzing on his tongue.

'You're really into this charity malarkey,' added Ginny, grinning his way.

'My work pretty much takes care of itself, so I thought I'd turn my attention to the Trust. The Food Bank Café has been such a success, but in order for me to expand, I need way more staff than I currently employ.' He didn't want to talk about the financial side of things with her so skipped that part. The sooner he got more money rolling in, the better.

'Why don't you use the Hub to host a job event or fair or something like that?'

Samuel glanced out the window at the street. 'It's a bit small, but I like your idea.'

'I'll arrange a meeting with the volunteers. See what we can come up with.' She nodded out to the harbour. 'We have them in Robson's pub.'

'The Jolly Pirate. Why not?'

'Lottie will be there.'

Samuel held back his smile. 'I'm sure she will. You know, what with her being a volunteer.'

Ginny bit her bottom lip and clasped her hands together. 'You two look like you're getting close.'

'Is that right?' He wasn't about to give anything away. Lottie hadn't mentioned anything about announcing their relationship, so he wasn't going to be the one to tell her friends.

'We're having a pub quiz tomorrow night to raise funds for the Hub. Come along and join our team. There are some real competitors out there. You wait and see. It got a bit lively last time, all over a question about mountain climbers, would you believe? Anyway, spread the word. The more the merrier.'

Samuel took a mouthful of sample three, which tasted like a doughnut. 'It can be hard raising money, can't it?'

Ginny waggled a hand. 'Britain's a charitable country, and most of us know what it's like to struggle from time to time, so we tend to help each other more.' She placed her fingers to her lips. 'Oh, sorry, that wasn't a dig at you being rich. I know you are helpful too.'

'I wasn't always rich,' he said softly, turning his attention back to the cakes.

'Sorry. I don't really know too much about you. I meet so many people, I can't always keep up. Unlike Robson, I don't get much of a chance for a chinwag with the punters, as I'm usually rushing around.'

Samuel laughed, remembering how he was years ago. There were days when he didn't have time to eat. There were times when he couldn't afford to. He gazed over at a pirate story framed on the wall. Everyone had their backstory, but not many bothered to take notice. Wondering if Ginny had a backstory that led her to dress as though she lived in the 1940s, he complimented her on the red scarf holding back her bobbed dark hair.

She thanked him quickly, giving the impression compliments made her uncomfortable, then went back to work mode. 'I have another fundraising idea for the Hub, but we can share the money with the Food Bank Café, if you like.'

'What you got in mind?'

'Lottie's doing a wheelchair race soon, so it got me thinking. What if Port Berry held its own fun run? We can talk it over with the others at the meeting. I'm thinking, costumes, prams, getting some streets blocked off for the day.'

Samuel tapped the edge of the nearest plate to him. 'You have good ideas, Ginny. You could come work for the Les Powell Trust. Part of the events team, perhaps?'

'Oh, leave off. I've got enough going on.'

'At least help me with the job event. I know we're going to brainstorm at the meeting, but if I know you're already on board to help me with recruitment on the day, I'll feel less stressed.'

'Sure. I can do that.'

'I can pay you for your time.'

'Behave. I'm a helper. I'll not take your money. We're building something for Cornwall. I'm happy to be part of that.'

The people from the Hub really were the nicest he'd ever met, and with their help, he was certain their little part of the planet was going to receive as much love and care as possible.

'You know, Samuel Powell, you're a good man. I don't know how often you're told, but just know you are, and I hope you find your happiness, because you certainly deserve something good.' She patted his hand, then stood. 'I'll make us a cuppa.'

Samuel watched her disappear to the kitchen. He didn't do the things he did to find ways into heaven. He just wanted to feed the hungry because he knew all too well what it felt like.

He gazed over at the sea. In all his years of living right next door to Port Berry, he'd hardly ever spent time in the fishing village. He was so happy to be part of the community now. He'd kept his distance from people for so long, he'd forgotten what friendship looked like.

Sitting in the local café, making plans with Ginny, reminded him just how good connection could feel. So much about him felt alive again. He smiled to himself at his journey. It was slow and steady but he was heading in the right direction, and the smallest amount of pride crept into his heart.

# CHAPTER 24

*Lottie*

The Jolly Pirate was buzzing at quiz night, with way more people than usual. It was such a light, warm night, Robson had all the doors open and was hosting the event in the large front beer garden.

Lottie's team secured the table close to the sheltered grill area, which had just shut up shop for the evening.

The smell of onions and burgers still wafted in the air, taking away any alcohol scent, and the noise had simmered as the start of the quiz was five minutes away.

Lottie waved over at Hannah and Felix, part of the Sunshine Centre team. Samuel could have joined them, or even the Penzance Pirates, but he chose to sit by her side and be part of the Happy to Help Hub's team. She still hadn't told Spencer or her friends that she was dating Samuel, so she decided to show them instead.

Samuel glanced up from the paper and pens on the table to smile at her as she slipped her hand on top of his.

Their fingers entwined, and Ginny was the first to coo. Spencer raised his brow, and Sophie smiled. While Matt patted Samuel on the shoulder, Alice changed the subject by talking about the need for more crisps.

Robson tapped the microphone, gaining attention. He proceeded to remind everyone about the Hub's charity, pointing out Matt as a success story.

Matt raised a hand to everyone, then moved behind Sophie.

Sophie giggled. 'You're our most famous Hub story, Matt Rose. Let them all see the sparkle in those lovely blue eyes of yours.'

Matt blushed.

'Why are you so famous, Matt?' asked Samuel.

Lottie answered for him. 'He was our first guest, and Jed looked after him. Gave him a job, home, and spa day.'

Jed looked up at his name being mentioned. 'Nothing wrong with that.'

'I love a spa day, me,' said Ginny, smiling at Matt, who grinned.

Lottie leaned closer to Samuel, whispering in his ear. 'Matt was the first interview I did for the Hub's website. You should watch it, it's so good.'

He nodded and smiled.

'I could interview you,' she added, before he pulled back. Samuel lost his sparkle, so Lottie thought it best to move on from the subject. 'Could you pass my drink, please?'

He handed her a glass of pineapple juice along with a warm smile, easing her stomach, as she was sure she'd just upset him. Their hands were still linked, so that was a good sign. The last thing she wanted was to make him anxious. It was clear he was enjoying the evening, and she wished she hadn't been so stupid bringing his inner-battles to the front of his mind.

Samuel clinked her glass with his own, then winked when their eyes met. Maybe he could read her mind. It seemed like he didn't want her to feel bad for bringing up his issues during quiz night down the local boozer.

Robson announced the first question, and everyone huddled to confer, making sure neighbouring tables couldn't earwig and steal their answers.

Jed was adamant he was right, so they jotted down what he said and moved on to question two.

Lottie took a moment to look around the circle of love she had in her life. She loved Port Berry, and her friends even more. They were politely disagreeing about something, but she didn't care, knowing they would brush over any disputes they had about the quiz and go back to the close-knit community they were as soon as it was over.

Ginny had a crisp in her hair, and Alice kept batting away the pork scratchings her mum and nan tossed her way. Spencer was having an arm-wrestling match with Ginny to decide whose answer to write down, and Sophie was stealing kisses from Matt.

There was a moment where Lottie missed George. He would have been on Lizzie and Luna's table, joining in with their art of distraction methods. She visualized him sitting there, pint of bitter in hand and a cheeky glint in his eye.

Samuel lightly squeezed her hand, bringing her attention back to her own table. She smiled his way as he silently asked if she was okay. After a kiss on her knuckles, he got his head back in the game, and she thought it best to join in too, especially when no one seemed to know who Mr Gloop's son was.

The quiz came to an end and the papers were all handed in, and it didn't take long for Robson to announce the Penzance Pirates had won.

Lottie's table decided to get some food from the restaurant part of the pub, so Jed went off to place the order, and Spencer and Matt nipped to the loo. Samuel went over to talk to his sister, leaving Lottie behind with Sophie, Ginny, and Alice all staring her way.

'What?' she asked them, knowing full well what was on their minds.

Sophie started. 'When did this happen?' She wiggled a finger over at Samuel.

Lottie shrugged. 'We sort of had some chemistry before I accused him of killing George, then once that was cleared up, we kind of . . .' She linked her fingers up high.

'Are you his girlfriend now? Like officially?' asked Alice.

'I guess so.'

'What do you mean, you guess so?' said Ginny. 'You don't know?'

'I do. I am. We just haven't used any labels yet, that's all.'

Sophie muffled her squeal with her palm. 'How exciting.'

Ginny nodded. 'At least he's a lot better than that lot she dated outside my café. What a bunch of losers they were.'

'Cheers, Gin!' Lottie shook her head. 'In my defence, I weren't to know they'd take one look at my wheels and do a runner. It's on me though. I shouldn't have hid things about myself.'

Sophie gestured at Samuel. 'He's not bothered about your chair, Lott. That's good. One of the things Matt said he liked about me when we first met was that I saw him as a person, rather than as a recovering alcoholic.'

'It's important for people to feel seen,' said Ginny quietly.

Lottie leaned closer to her friends. 'Ooh, we should set Ginny up for online dating. It's about time she found someone lovely.'

Ginny frowned. 'After witnessing your experiences, I'll pass, thanks.'

'It wasn't all bad.'

'Didn't that Trey kid try to hook up with you?' Ginny gave her a pointed look.

Alice laughed. 'Did he?'

Lottie silently giggled at the young lad's cheek whenever she thought about it. 'Yep!'

'See, I don't need all that nonsense.' Ginny crossed her arms in a huff, as though sealing her decision firmly.

'I found it helped build my confidence, putting myself out there.' Lottie beamed. 'I know I can talk to anyone, but it was still a little boost.'

'Ginny can talk to anyone,' said Alice.

'Doesn't mean I want to.' Ginny laughed, then shook her head. 'Seriously, I'm fine. I like being single.'

Sophie nodded. 'I enjoyed my single time, up to a point. There were things I missed, and, no, not what you're thinking.

I mean simple things, like having someone to talk to after work, and holding hands. I'm a big fan of hand holding. I love Matt's hands.'

'I think it's nice to have company,' said Lottie, snatching a glance at Samuel, thinking she rather liked his big manly hands too.

'I've got you lot,' said Ginny. 'That's enough for anyone to deal with.'

Alice scoffed. 'Cheek!'

The women laughed and chinked their glasses together in the middle of the table.

Alice looked over at her grandmother. 'Nan reckons everyone has a soulmate.'

It warmed Lottie to think she might have found hers. Talking with Samuel certainly was easy, and being around him felt comfortable and familiar.

'Matt's mine,' said Sophie. 'I can feel it. When I'm with him, everything feels right. I guess it's hard to explain, as it's more of a feeling. I just know we belong together, and no matter what, we'll stick together.' She looked at Lottie. 'That's what you need in a partner. Someone who has your back, doesn't hide things from you, and treats you like a best mate. A real team player.'

'Basically, the opposite of my ex,' said Alice, sighing. 'He'd blame me for everything going wrong, never stood shoulder to shoulder with me, and often acted as though I was enemy number one. Not quite sure what I ever did to him, but the way he behaved, anyone would think he hated my guts.'

Ginny patted her arm. 'I'm just glad you got shot of him, Al. He was one of those energy-sucking narcissists, that's what he was. Jealous of you and your happy family. Wanted to drain the life from you. Well, good riddance to bad rubbish, I say.'

'Cheers to that,' said Sophie, raising her glass.

Lottie thought about her own ex. 'Russ only wanted a trophy girlfriend. It took me ages to see how shallow he was.'

'Really?' scoffed Ginny. 'I saw it in him straight away.'

'You never said.'

'I could hardly tell you while you were all loved up with the man. You wouldn't have listened.'

Now Lottie was wondering if there were things about Samuel her friends were keeping hidden. 'Do you like Samuel? And it really is time to be honest.' It wasn't the kind of question she'd ever hit her mates with before. Were they about to be brutal?

'I like him,' said Alice.

'Seems legit,' was Ginny's reply.

Sophie shrugged. 'He hasn't given me any reason not to like him, but it's about what you see, Lott. You know red flags now, so make sure you keep your eyes open for them.'

Lottie glanced at Samuel again. He was engaged in a conversation with Felix, which was amusing to witness, as she knew he was struggling to form a relationship with the man dating his little sister. She wondered what Spencer would say about her boyfriend choices. He never got on much with Russ. He was polite enough, but she would have preferred a bit of honesty.

'Ooh, how frustrating. I'm so over everyone's politeness. Right, that's it. From this moment forward, we must all agree, if we don't like the person our friend is dating, we have to say. If we can see something they can't, it has to be mentioned.' Lottie waited for them all to nod. 'We're sisters. We need to step up for each other.'

'Agreed,' said Ginny. 'Although that kind of honesty would probably cause arguments. No one listens to anyone when they're in love.'

'True,' said Alice.

'Wait,' said Sophie, momentarily looking perplexed. 'Does everyone like Matt?'

Alice laughed. 'What's not to like?'

'Of course we do,' said Lottie. 'I had a good feeling about him the first time I saw him. Ooh, it's a lot easier to pick up on good and bad vibes in someone else's bloke, isn't it?'

Ginny breathed out a quiet laugh. 'That's because love makes you an idiot.'

The women nodded in agreement as they laughed, then stopped when Matt joined them, swiftly followed by Samuel, who lightly kissed Lottie's cheek before sitting.

'I've got a surprise for you tomorrow,' he whispered to her.

Lottie studied his face as he joined in a conversation with Sophie and Matt. He was a good man, she was sure. He was just closed off to the world, except her. Somehow, he'd let her in, and even though she could see him smiling, she knew he was sad. But she figured everyone held some sadness within. Samuel's life was about to be filled to the brim with some good old-fashioned Port Berry love, and most of that would come from her, because she did love him. Already.

'Right, I was going to leave this to a Hub meeting, but we're here now, so let's talk about Samuel's job event for the Trust, then all things pram race,' said Ginny, interrupting Lottie's thoughts.

The lively group became even more animated as ideas were put firmly in place, and Lottie was so pleased Samuel joined in with the discussion. It was as though he'd always been part of their team. He was definitely part of hers.

# CHAPTER 25

*Samuel*

The sun was shining in all its glory over the tips of the dark, steady waves off the coast of Port Berry. Seagulls hovered in the salty air, swooping low whenever anything resembling food caught their beady eyes. *Hannah's Dream* sailed towards the horizon.

Nothing felt real to Samuel as he stood on deck, staring out to sea. Amazement ruled any emotion that tried to surface. Jelly legs didn't exist, heart palpitations had settled, and watching Lottie admire his yacht, washed away all worries.

It really was a surreal moment when Jed started the engine and Samuel felt the vessel move away from the safety of the harbour. Had Lottie not been there, he was sure he would have hurled his guts over the side. How did she have such an effect over his fears? He'd never felt so powerful before.

Lottie was on a sun lounger, smiling at everything. Her big white flower-shaped sunglasses did little to hide her sparkle. He knew her eyes were twinkling more than the sun upon the water.

Why Samuel had chosen a boat trip as a day out was still a mystery to him. Jed played a big part, talking up the tranquillity the sea offered. Unlike the old fisherman, Samuel wasn't as sure at first, but now, with no storm in sight, it was obvious Jed knew a thing or two when it came to finding peace.

'I love this, Sam,' called Lottie, waving from the other end of the deck. She looked every bit the yacht model, and way more suited to a life of luxury than him.

Over the years, Samuel had acquired some acquaintances born into the world of money, and they spent a lot of their time hanging out on superyachts and in country clubs. It had never been his cup of tea, but being on his own vessel was growing on him. More so because Lottie was there.

Jed saluted from the wheel, making Samuel laugh. There was something about the old man that was comforting. He seemed as though he had more stories than a library and knew more cures than a scientist. Whatever it was about him, he definitely made Samuel feel safe in his presence.

Samuel gazed back out at the open space and laughed to himself. He so wanted to jump in the air, fist-bump the sky, do a little jig, and scream out, 'I'm free.' Instead, he subtly swiped away the tear in the corner of his eye, sniffed, and straightened his posture.

Sometimes when he won a battle against his demon he felt overwhelmed. So much of his life had been taken from him, so the small wins meant more than he could ever express to anyone.

Jan understood. His therapy sessions with her were going well, and he appreciated the time spent going over his notes with someone who knew how anxiety associated agoraphobia worked.

'Sam.'

He turned to see Lottie wave him over. 'You okay?' he asked, approaching.

She tugged him to the cream lounger at her side. 'This is brilliant, isn't it?'

He nodded. 'Yeah. We'll have to get more use out of her, eh? Hannah and Felix want to go out next time. I just wanted it to be us today.' He pointed upwards. 'And Jed.'

Lottie laughed, then pulled on a wide brim floppy hat.

Samuel couldn't resist. He slipped under the sunhat to kiss her cheek. 'How is it possible to be so bloody gorgeous?'

'I get it from my aunt. Funny isn't it how you can look like other members of your family rather than your parents.'

'I look like my dad. Hannah looks more like Mum.'

'It's really uncanny, but Spencer is the spitting image of a great-grandfather of ours. I've seen the one and only picture of the man, and I swear, it's like Spencer time-travelled or something.'

'My mum believed people had previous lives.'

Lottie snuggled her hand in his, warming his heart along with his fingers. 'I hope I met you in one of mine.'

'Yeah? I hope I met you in all of mine.'

They shared a smile, and Samuel relaxed back on the lounger, dropping his sunglasses from his head to sit on the bridge of his nose.

'Maybe that's why we get on so easily. Think about it, it didn't take long before we were talking like friends.'

'Yeah, but it didn't last.'

'Neither did our falling out.'

Samuel shrugged. 'There was something familiar about you.'

'See. We met in a previous life.'

'I hope my parents meet each other again in their next life,' he added softly.

'I'm sure they will, and they'll have another wonderful life together.'

He smiled at her sweetness. If only he could know for sure if there were more lives to come. One thing he was sure of, if it was true, he'd fight tooth and nail to find her again.

The boat stopped, and Samuel stood to see they weren't as far away from land as he first thought, which was settling. If push came to shove, he was sure he'd be able to swim back. Survival mode wasn't needed, and he quickly reminded himself to not look for escape plans. Taking a breath, he made a mental note of how he was feeling, how long he was calm for, then sat back down, took a sip of cold refreshing water, then completely forgot he was worried just a second ago.

Lottie sipped on pineapple juice and smiled. 'I feel really rich.'

'Gets you like that, doesn't it?' said Jed, appearing from inside. He looked at Samuel. 'I'm going to do a bit of fishing the other end, out your way, so don't mind me, and after lunch, I'll teach you how to steer this beauty. You game, son?'

Samuel much preferred being in the driver's seat when it came to anything. Not only did it help occupy his mind, having full control, but settled his nerves. 'Aye, aye, Captain.'

Jed croaked out a laugh, then went to go about his own day.

'Hey, I wouldn't mind trying some fishing,' said Lottie.

Jed nodded as he turned to Samuel. 'What do you reckon, son? I brought a couple of rods.'

Seeing how Lottie had lowered her sunglasses and was beaming those pretty sea-blue eyes she possessed, how could he say no?

Before long, Jed had them both set up along port side, rod in hand, and instructions loud and clear, and when Lottie's rod bent, moving her plastic seat forward, Samuel's heart did a loop-de-loop. She laughed, then cheered as Jed helped her reel in her first catch of the day.

Samuel had felt stress and fear many times, but thinking Lottie was about to go swimming with the fish took his adrenaline to a whole other dimension. 'This deck chair's not very sturdy,' he said, frowning at her seat.

'It's fine, Sam,' she said, glancing at him. 'Take a picture,' she added, beaming with pride at Jed.

He did as he was asked, then jolted when his own rod moved. Excitement and panic put him in a frenzy as he tried way too fast to reel in his catch. Jed stood by his side, calming him with advice and a gentle pat on the back.

Even though Samuel was fishing, he was still amazed he caught anything. Lottie took his picture, then decided she wanted to change her beach dress, as the white one covering her pink bikini had some slime on where the fish had rested before it was put back in the sea.

Jed took over the rods as Lottie asked Samuel if he wouldn't mind carrying her to the bathroom, as there wasn't much room for her wheelchair to move inside.

He didn't mind at all and gently placed her in a chair by the sink.

Lottie turned the taps on and washed her hands first. 'It's posh in here, isn't it?'

Samuel took in the white and chrome features that hadn't been touched since installation, with the exception of the odd clean. 'I was going to sell this soon.'

'Oh, what are you thinking now?'

'You love it, so—'

'Hey, this isn't about me. If you don't want a yacht, then sell.'

'I'm enjoying owning it now, and, yes, it does matter to me if you want to keep something.'

'But it's yours.'

'I'd like to think of it as ours now.'

Lottie grinned as she whipped off her dress. 'I'm glad I bought more beachwear.'

'You just wanted a photo shoot in as many outfits as possible.'

'What's wrong with that? For all I knew, this could've been my one and only chance to be on board a luxury yacht.'

Samuel took her clothing and placed it into a stripy bag while she took a flannel and some shower gel to her arms. 'Well, it won't be. I'm keeping it now, or *her*, as Jed says. Anyway, you can come on here anytime you like.'

Lottie looked up through her lashes, flashing him a cheeky smile. 'As soon as you're confident enough to take this out without Jed, I want us to make love on deck, under the stars.'

Samuel swallowed hard, trying hard to hold back from making love in the bathroom. 'I'm definitely keeping it now.'

Lottie kissed him. 'Or we could do stuff now, right here or in that bedroom next door,' she mumbled on his lips.

'We could,' he agreed, peppering kisses along her jaw, then down her neck. Groaning, he moved back. 'Nope, can't do it. Not with Jed around.' He waggled his eyebrows. 'Wait till we're moored back at the harbour and he's left.'

Lottie laughed and pulled him down to wash his arms. 'One of my favourite things about you is—'

'My charm?'

She nudged his wrist. 'Your hands.'

'You like my hands?'

'I like all of you, and I especially like the lunch you brought. I feel famished after all that fishing.'

'I thought you were going overboard at one point.'

Lottie laughed. 'I know. Your face. It was epic.'

'It was not.'

'Anyway, don't you know, I'm also a mermaid.'

'Is that right?'

'Yep. You should have seen me with my tail. We put on a pirate show for the tourists. I thought we were raising money to help the Hub. But it turned out the fundraiser was to get my electric chair.'

'You can dress as a mermaid for the pram race day, then I'll get to see your tail.'

'Ooh, were you thinking of pushing me?'

'Did you want to take part in the race?'

Lottie nodded, giving him a look that said *of course*.

'I've seen those pram races before, Lottie. You could fall out.'

Lottie huffed. 'I'll be fine. Anyway, Spencer is going to push me, and trust me, he'll be way more careful than you.'

'You might be the death of me, you know that?'

Lottie shrugged. 'My aunt used to say that about Spencer. Hey, if you are going to race, you could team up with Matt. I know Sophie doesn't want to run.'

'Okay, I'll talk to him later. When Ginny brought this up at the pub, I wasn't expecting everyone to jump straight in and set it up there and then on the spot.'

'That's what we're like around here.' She giggled, pointing at the door. 'Or is Port Berry over there?'

'You lot certainly make this world a better place.'

'There are lots of helpers in this world. You're one of them. Don't forget that.'

Even though he had started his own trust and was now expanding his charity, he didn't feel like one of life's helpers. He was just putting his money to good use.

'You make everything feel better for me, Lottie.'

She smiled warmly, drying his hands with a small blue towel. 'You're your own hero. Don't give away that credit.'

'But when I'm with you, I feel as though I could climb mountains.'

'We'll add that to our to-do list.'

There was something else he wanted to add to their to-do list, but it was far too soon for him to whip out a diamond ring. The last thing he wanted was to start declaring his undying love and scare her off. Something magical was happening, and there was no way he was going to do anything to jeopardize what they had. Lottie Jordan was his blessing, and there wasn't anything in the world strong enough to tear him away from her now.

'Speaking of the pram race, I've got my wheelchair race next week.' Lottie smiled softly. 'I know you haven't ventured that far yet, so if you don't feel you can make it, I've arranged with Ginny to record the race for you. You can even watch it live through her phone if you like. Either way, please don't let this stress you. I know you'll be with me in my heart.'

Reality smashed him back to earth. Lottie's race was just over the border. He had to try to get to that part of Devon. He just had to.

Irritation automatically filled him. Most days he was fine with his condition because it didn't affect anything on a day-to-day basis, but now it was like a great big thorn in his side, making itself well and truly known.

Telling himself to focus on the dilemma later when alone, he kissed Lottie's head before carrying her back to her chair for a spot of lunch on deck, hoping the sea air would once again clear his mind and ease his weary soul.

# CHAPTER 26

*Lottie*

Lottie had never felt so excited as she readied herself at the starting line. When she first thought about doing the race, she didn't realize how much it would mean to her. There was a buzz in the air and so many people cheering on the participants, bringing the warm, cloudy day to life. All around her were racing wheelchairs, causing her to take mental notes on who had what. She just hoped her entry-level chair was good enough, because she hadn't put too much thought into it when choosing one, not seeing racing in her future, more keeping fit.

It looked like half of Port Berry had turned up, but she couldn't see Samuel anywhere, not that she was expecting to. She knew how challenging the trip to Tavistock would be for him, as it was in Devon.

Signs held high had Lottie's name painted in bright bold colours, and lots of noise was coming from the direction of her group of friends, who looked way more excited than her.

Lottie had to remain focused, stop thinking about Samuel, and get her head in the game. There was little chance she'd win, what with it being her first time, but it wasn't her goal anyway. As long as she completed the course, she'd be happy.

It only seemed like five minutes ago she was telling George about signing up, and he'd told her he'd watch. Little did either of them know what was down the road.

The klaxon started the race, jolting her out of her daydream, and she was off, pacing herself, like an online tutorial had taught her. She had been pleased to find so much helpful advice on the internet, and as a newbie on the scene, she wanted to absorb it all.

She silently thanked whoever invented rubber padded gloves, as what a help they were each time she gripped the rubber push rims as she made her way around the track the owner of the land had created.

Lottie found out that the owner was also in a wheelchair and had built the track for his own personal use, but he came up with the idea of a fun race day for charity after a club he'd joined needed more funding. She hoped to return the following year and many more to come.

Cheers and encouragement ran the length of the course, and it didn't die down by her third and final lap. The music coming from the small band on the veranda of the main house livened the tired racers up no end, not to mention the crowds, as they danced along to the upbeat tunes.

Lottie's shoulders were burning and her wrists ached, but there was no way she was stopping, not that there was any shame in it. She bypassed those who'd slowed and the ones taking a breather. Positive mental attitude and sheer bloody determination were keeping her going.

The padding George had added to the seat made her feel he was with her, which helped to ease the journey somewhat as she headed towards the finish line, heart pumping and excitement building.

*Come on, come on.*

Her mantra moved her on, blocking out the noise of the crowd, as she edged closer and closer to the end. And with every last ounce of energy she had, she crossed the line, coming to a breathless stop.

'I did it. I completed the race,' she mumbled to herself.

Spencer ran at her, draping a small white sheet over her shoulders, with the words *our champion* written on it in big red letters. Someone else placed a multicoloured ribbon attached to a silver medal around her neck, and Ginny offered a bottle of water.

There were pats on the back, cheers of delight, so many congratulations flying around, and Lottie felt overwhelmed and overjoyed. Her head swirled, her body chilled, and her angels in the sky made her feel she had made them proud.

Spencer kissed her cheek as he removed her helmet, then wiped back her damp fringe. 'That was brilliant, sis.'

She touched the medal, happy she had received one for participating, then glanced up to thank her friends for their endless support. She stopped when she locked eyes with Samuel. Another swirl of adrenaline hit as he gave a slight wave with a bunch of flowers.

Life couldn't be more perfect. She'd accomplished what she set out to do, and now Samuel had made it across the border to Devon.

He bent to tell her how proud he was of her, kissing her lips while placing the small posy in her hand.

'Sam, you're here,' was all she could manage.

His smile was wider than hers. 'I've been practising all week,' he whispered in her ear. 'I wanted to surprise you.'

She could do no more than wrap her arms around him, holding him tightly. The morning was special now on so many more levels.

'Come on, you two,' said Spencer. 'Lottie needs to get changed, and we all need some lunch.'

'I second that,' said Sophie. 'But let's get some pictures first.'

As Lottie posed for everyone's cameras, Robson and Matt let off confetti bombs, making her raise her head to laugh at the falling colourful paper pieces raining over her. She lifted her medal in one hand and her flowers in the other and cheered for herself while secretly cheering for Samuel as well.

The owner of the land had a couple of huge barn conversions that were doubling up as changing rooms for the day, so Lottie headed over with Alice, who was her designated helper for the event, as decided by Alice.

As soon as they were done, it was back in the cars and off to Polperro, where Samuel had booked them all in at a restaurant one of his work associates owned.

Lottie left her electric wheelchair with Spencer, as she wanted to sit by Samuel's side for the drive. The more she looked at him, the more she knew she never wanted to not be by his side.

'I'm so proud of you, Lottie.'

'I'm prouder of you.'

'Ah, this is your day, not mine.'

'We're a team, Sam. Each day belongs to us both now. The good, the bad, and the damn right ugly.'

He laughed, reaching one hand over to rest in hers.

Lottie glanced out the window. 'Everyone's ahead of us. You don't have to drive this slowly, you know.' She smiled as his focus briefly slipped to her.

'I've got precious cargo on board.'

'Speaking of which, did I make that posy back there?' She gestured to the back seat where she'd placed her flowers.

Samuel grinned. 'Well, I could hardly buy them from your competitors.'

'I like your style.'

'And I like how you completed that race without stopping. I swear, I've never met anyone more determined than you.'

'Try looking in the mirror. You didn't get to be where you are today by sitting on your backside twiddling your thumbs or crying in the corner.'

'I can see this is going to be a journey where we swap compliments.'

Lottie raised their linked hands so she could kiss his knuckles. 'Not a bad start to our relationship.'

'Here's to us, and all that money you raised today for the Trust.'

Lottie grinned. 'Ooh, it's shaping up to be a good day.'

'With you, my talented girlfriend, it's shaping up to be a good life.'

All the butterflies inside her did a little hop, skip, and jump at the word *girlfriend*. She squeezed his hand lightly and settled back, looking forward to their lunch, and their future.

# CHAPTER 27

*Samuel*

The volunteers for the Hub had set up a stall for market day at Old Market Square in Port Berry, using the busy Saturday as a good opportunity to draw some interest to the Les Powell Trust. Samuel had job roles on offer in many areas from admin to chefs for the food bank cafés he was about to build.

He got off the phone to an investor as Alice signed up another volunteer at their pop-up booth. So far, funding had been secured by generous private donors and new premises secured over in St Ives.

Robson sat at the back of the stall, chatting online to applicants, gaining info and setting up interviews, and Victoria was walking around Anchorage Park with her kids, handing out flyers to anyone interested.

Samuel's most recent employee, Georgie, was busy advertising the Trust with Samuel's senior member of staff, Cathy, and PA, Anita, over in St Ives. His most trusted volunteer at the Food Bank Café, Kaz, was announcing all openings over at the main headquarters in Penzance, and Hannah and Felix were spreading the word at the Sunshine Centre.

With so many roles to fill and people crying out for work, Samuel was sure he'd have a full team by lunch. He'd arranged earlier in the week for the local jobcentre to get involved, explaining his long-term plans and conditions, and Jed and Luna were staffing the Hub, letting anyone passing by know of their big one-day event.

Looking around at the packed market, Samuel was blown away by the support of the community. Councillor Seabridge was shaking hands with all and sundry, telling all how Port Berry was everyone's friend. His booming voice carrying over the crowd, no matter where he stood.

For so many years Samuel had kept his circle small, closing himself away from the world and life in general. It wasn't lost on him how much had changed in his day-to-day, and each time he glanced over at Lottie — in the process of holding court with a group of teenagers — he felt more vulnerable than he'd ever had.

There was something empowering about being included into the heart of the close-knit society of Port Berry, but with friends now feeling like family, Samuel had more to care about, and he wasn't entirely sure about that part.

Hannah had occupied his time for so long, it was strange to see her fly the nest. If it wasn't for the Food Bank Café, he was sure he wouldn't feel needed at all. There was no way Lottie needed anyone, so he couldn't even include her.

It certainly felt good helping others, and he sure as hell would have jumped at the chance of one of the jobs he was offering, way back when he had little to nothing.

Samuel smiled at a passing lady who removed one of the leaflets from his hands while he was daydreaming. Snapping back to reality, he told himself to stop letting negative thoughts slip in, especially as he had nothing to worry about. Life was good. He was happy. Hannah was even happier, and soon he'd have a fully functioning trust helping the whole of Cornwall.

'It's going well, isn't it?' said Ginny, handing out mini cupcakes to entice people over.

Samuel quickly snaffled a banana one as he nodded. 'Hopefully, I'll have a full team by next week. Lottie put herself forward for the role of interviewer because of her kitchen table interviews. I told her it's not the same thing.'

Ginny laughed. 'In her defence, those Hub interviews she does are really good. Matt's one is my favourite. Hey, you should do one with her.'

'Why?' Samuel recoiled as Ginny frowned at the snap in his tone. He didn't mean to bite her head off, but just for a second, he thought Lottie had told someone about his personal issues. 'Sorry. I . . .' His voice trailed off because he didn't know what to add.

'It's all right. I get it. You're feeling a bit of the pressure of the day, that's all.' She glanced at the fluffy white clouds in the sky. 'This heatwave isn't helping. Makes everyone a bit short at times.'

'Oh no, that's not it. I don't know. I just . . .' He couldn't tell her about his problem. It always felt so crazy to him so he wasn't sure what anyone else would make of it.

'I was only thinking of your rags-to-riches story. It could inspire folk.'

Of course that's what she meant. He really needed to get a grip. 'I guess. I'll think about it.'

Ginny was side-eyeing him. Perhaps it was time he spoke about his disorder. Jan was always telling him that speaking out helps break down the stigma.

He scratched his eyebrow and smiled softly at her. She was a nice lady, who he always found easy to talk to. It was a big step but one needed, he felt. 'I have a mental health condition, and I thought Lottie had told you and that's what you expected me to do an interview about.'

Ginny chewed her bottom lip for a moment, either assessing what he said or him. 'Everyone's got problems, Sam. Not always easy to talk about, I know.' She lowered her head, then snapped it back up as though hit with a second wind. 'Still, we get on as best we can, right?'

He nodded and smiled, sensing she had her own troubles. 'I'm not good at talking about it. It's anxiety associated agoraphobia, and it's just all messed up. I don't know. It's hard to explain. Not like other phobias. I don't know why I'm even talking about it now.'

'No rulebook that says you have to talk about it at all, but just so you're aware, you mentioning your mental health to me is a great start in your healing.'

'You think?'

Ginny nodded. 'Yeah. Big time. When you keep things bottled up, well, let's just say you suffer more. Talking is underrated, like walking for your health. But it's huge, Sam. Getting crap off your chest, finding people in the same boat, breaking down walls, it all counts. The more people speak out, the more we learn, the better we all cope with each other, and the best part is, we see there's no such thing as normal.'

Samuel breathed out a laugh. 'Yeah, I definitely don't feel normal, even on my best days.'

'Welcome to the club.'

'I honestly don't know why I told you about myself.'

Ginny shrugged, holding her tray of cupcakes out to a passer-by, who swiped one away. 'I guess you're ready to move forward in your journey.'

He watched her waltz off into the crowd, leaving him behind to mull over her statement. Perhaps he was ready to try more than crossing borders and expanding his charity. Maybe his whole personality was due an upgrade, and Port Berry was showing him it was time.

Lottie waved, then went back to offering jobs to anyone who'd listen.

Robson called him to the back of the stand, pointing at the laptop while grinning. 'Who knew there were that many chefs out of work. Look, we've got loads lined up. I can get my head chef at the pub to interview them if you like. He'll know what to look for.'

'I was going to use the interviewer I have, but they could do the chef interviews together. That'll be helpful. Victoria is helping with interviews for admin staff, and Georgie is on events, so we're good there.'

Robson sat back in his foldaway chair, stretching his arms behind his head. 'It's coming together fast, isn't it?'

'Yeah. I've never held a job event before.'

'I went to a careers day back when I was a teenager. Didn't think I was going to take over my uncle's pub at that time. Come to think of it, I kind of fell into the job.'

'Do you still like it?'

'Yeah, it's okay. Keeps me sane.' Robson sat forward. 'I like my routine.'

'I'm a big fan of routine as well.'

'After my wife died, I needed it more than ever, because I just crumbled at first.'

Samuel knew about Robson's wife, Leah, dying of cancer, as Lottie had told him. She was so young. His heart went out to the man. They had their whole life ahead of them, then tragedy struck. He knew all too well what that was like.

'I'm sorry about your wife.'

Robson's piercing blue eyes shined his way. 'No worries, mate. People never know what to say. Makes you realize just how precious life is though, eh?'

'Yep.'

'It's one of the reasons I like helping people.' Robson shrugged. 'Life can be so hard. You just don't know who's suffering with what out there — that's why it's important to be kind. Little did we know that we'd go on to have a food bank after starting the Hub.' He splayed his arms. 'And now look. It's all happening in Port Berry.'

Samuel nodded, mostly to himself. It really was happening, and like Robson had pointed out, it was because of change. The people of Port Berry weren't the only ones to change the way things were. He was doing that too.

Lottie gained his attention, stopping at his side. 'I don't think I've ever talked so much in such a short time before.'

'Come on, let's go over to the tea stall and get you a drink.' He asked Robson and Alice what they wanted, but they both had bottles of cool drinks, so he took a timeout with Lottie.

There wasn't much of a queue for hot drinks, so they were at the front in no time.

'Let's sit by the pond for five minutes, Sam.'

Samuel waved over at Victoria in the near distance, still drumming up interest, as he followed Lottie into the park to sit at the end of a wooden bench.

'A bit more peaceful over here,' said Lottie, taking her tea from him.

Samuel stared at the ducks mooching by the water's edge. 'You had enough today? I can take you home.'

'No, I'm fine. Besides, I can't leave our new girl alone on the flower stall all day, and Spencer won't be out of the shop till closing. I won't lie, I'm glad he's taken on staff to help out this summer.' She indicated over to the church steeple poking up through some trees further away. 'I feel like I haven't stopped going up there, what with all the weddings on.'

Samuel grinned. 'I wonder if anyone else has ever had a quick snog in the back room.'

Lottie spat her tea. 'Oh, goodness, don't make me laugh.'

'What you got planned for tomorrow? You want another trip to church?'

'Funny. In all seriousness, I'm clearing out George's, with Spencer. We've got people coming to take away the last of his furniture.'

He held her hand and settled back on the uncomfortable bench, sharing a moment of companionable silence until Lottie spoke, startling him.

'I love you, Sam,' she said softly.

It was so unexpected, it rendered him speechless, and by the time words managed to form, Lottie had tossed her takeaway cup into the bin and told him it was time to head back.

Walking back over to the busy cobbled square didn't seem the right time to declare the strength of his love, so he decided he'd go all out by creating a romantic dinner on

Sunday night, as he figured she wouldn't feel like cooking after another day of house clearance.

Yes, that seemed like the best plan. He would make it super special, and he could talk to her about spending more nights together, as he wanted so badly to start living with her already. He wanted everything with her. A slight skip entered his step as he made his way through the market. Change really was in the air, and it felt good. She loved him. She actually loved him, and by the time tomorrow night was over, she was going to know just how high he held her. He couldn't wait.

# CHAPTER 28

*Lottie*

It didn't matter if it was the kettle or an old rolled newspaper Lottie removed from George's home, it was still hard. Those were his things, and it felt so many levels of wrong to go through them, deciding what to bin.

Out front, Spencer helped two delivery men load their van with bedroom furniture — off to the Use Again Centre, as instructed by George's will. Nothing of George's was to be tossed in the bin if it could help someone, and the local centre worked closely with tenants on benefits struggling to furnish their homes.

Lottie sat at the kitchen table, sorting through the boxes of paperwork Spencer had brought from upstairs. The neat piles of receipts, bank statements, and extended warranties showed just how efficient George had been, and it made life a lot easier for her.

She took a deep breath, staring over at black bags filled to the brim with clothing, bedding, and towels. It made her think about her own home. Should she have a clear out? There was so much in the loft that could go. Half the things in her home weren't used, and suddenly, being a minimalist seemed like a better option. At least no one would have to spend weeks sorting her bits and pieces after her death.

Muffled sounds came from the front garden as furniture continued to be loaded, catching her attention, or rather, helping to take her mind off her unwanted task.

Her thoughts drifted to Spencer's flat above the flower shop. Not much was up there, and he didn't seem to care. It was decided, once George's home was sorted, she would rake through her own place and give it a thorough spring clean, even if it was the end of summer.

Lottie removed a large pile of manila envelopes from another box, placing them on the table. 'Oh, George.' Life just didn't seem fair.

Even after her accident, she never adopted the war mentality of life's too short so let's do anything and everything and not think about the consequences. Perhaps she was too busy focusing on powering through, not allowing her new circumstances to get the better of her. She couldn't be sure. But now, George's death had triggered something, and she was glad she had jumped in with Samuel, not wanting to waste any time.

Time was ticking on, and there was still so much paperwork to sort before lunch. Spencer was getting on with his day, sticking to the schedule, working hard. The least she could do was stop dithering and lighten the load.

With another long sigh out the way, Lottie lifted a square-shaped book that looked handmade, judging by the string-threaded spine and velvety material. It seemed out of place in among the paperwork.

When she was little, George had taught her how to make books using cardboard and a hole punch. A whole bunch of memories came flooding back, catching her breath.

'You all right in here, Lott?' asked Spencer, poking his head around the doorframe.

'Hmm? Oh, yeah, getting there. You?'

Spencer nodded, thumbing over his shoulder. 'Just about to load the last bed.'

Lottie gave herself an internal shake as her brother went back to work. Today was the day the boxes were getting done.

Smiling at Spencer's muffled swear word as he tripped up, or down, the stairs, she couldn't be sure, she opened the quaint book on the table.

Inside was a photograph of George and Rebecca with another man and woman she didn't know. They all looked to be mid-twenties.

A couple of letters, folded once, sat in the second page, one addressed to George, the other for Rebecca. She recognized her aunt's handwriting scribbled on one side of the fold and automatically brushed her fingertip over the blue ink.

Lottie's hand twitched, desperate to read what her aunt had written to George, but at the same time feeling beyond nosey; this wasn't his bills she was gawping at.

It was all too much. The mystery of why her aunt had written to the man next door when she could have just spoken to him over the garden fence was all a bit too odd.

The letters could be tossed in the shredder, then George's private business would remain his own.

'Bugger that!'

Lottie opened the letter her aunt had written, gave it a quick glance, looked up as though someone might come along any second and scold her for snooping, then read it properly.

'What?'

Nothing about what Rebecca was saying to George made sense. She certainly had the hump, that much was obvious and explained why they weren't speaking face to face.

In all the years Lottie lived next door to George, she'd only ever seen her aunt and him act friendly towards each other. She'd never known them to fall out. George was always around with his big smile and helping hands.

Lottie eyed the other letter, thinking perhaps she should have read that one first. It was definitely intriguing, whatever had happened between them.

Before reading what George had to say, Lottie scanned the top and bottom for a date, but neither letter told her when their dispute had taken place.

'Right, George, let's get to the bottom of this.'

Lottie took a breath to stop herself from speed-reading, as she wanted to absorb George's words. His handwriting was neater than her aunt's, giving the impression he had taken his time, unlike Rebecca's scribble, which Lottie knew only happened when Rebecca was in a hurry, usually jotting down the shopping list while halfway out the door.

George's letter was a little longer than the reply he'd received from Rebecca, who had basically told him to mind his own business. Reading over his words, Lottie could see why her aunt had snapped.

'Oh my . . .' She quickly looked at the kitchen doorway. 'Spence!' she yelled.

The front door slammed and hurried footsteps followed. Spencer dashed into the room, eyes wide and concern obvious.

'What's wrong? You okay?'

Lottie had no words. She shook her head as she waved him to the seat by her side.

'You in pain, Lott?'

'No, I'm fine. It's just . . .' She held the letter aloft.

'What's that?'

Lottie glanced at the door. 'Have they gone?'

'Yeah. It's just us. What's wrong?'

'I've found out something that I'll never be able to un-find.'

Spencer frowned. 'What are you on about?'

Lottie offered him the letter. 'George wrote this to Rebecca. I'm guessing when we were kids.'

'Okay. What does it say that's got you in a tizz?'

'George is basically having a go at her for sleeping with a man.'

'Oh. Wait, are you telling me George and Rebecca had a thing going on, then she cheated on him?'

Lottie shook her head. 'No. Rebecca was sleeping with a married man, and George had the hump about that.' She waved the other letter. 'Rebecca told him to mind his own business.'

'So they weren't together?'

'He loved her, Spence. He tells her at the end of his letter. Obviously didn't make any difference, seeing how we never saw them romantically involved.'

'Wow! I wonder if that's why he never had a relationship. All those years, he loved Rebecca.'

Lottie's shoulders slumped. 'Do you think that's why he became our substitute dad? He did it for her, not us.'

Spencer reached out for her hand, giving it a gentle squeeze. 'No, don't think that way. He loved us all. Come on, Lott, anyone could see that. All I remember is him and Rebecca showing us love. They kind of tag-teamed us.'

Lottie breathed out a small laugh. 'They did make a good team. Oh, Spence, what a shame Rebecca couldn't love him back.'

He pointed at the letters. 'She never had a relationship all the time she had us. Maybe she never stopped loving the married man.'

'Oh goodness, Spence, that's the worst part. Look who she was seeing.'

Spencer peered at the line Lottie held her fingertip to. 'Please don't tell me it was Councillor Seabridge, because I swear I'll . . . Who's Les Powell? Name rings a bell.'

'Les Powell, from the Les Powell Trust. Samuel's dad.' Lottie swallowed hard, wishing it said another name.

Spencer met her eyes. 'Might be another Les Powell.'

'What are the odds? Rebecca was here in Port Berry. Les Powell was right next door in Penzance.'

'We can't jump to conclusions, Lott.'

'What conclusions? It's all here and black and white, well, blue ink. You don't have to be part of the Scooby Doo gang to figure this out.'

Spencer shrugged. 'It could still be another . . .' He glanced at the photograph on the handmade book. 'Oh, look how young George looks, and . . . Whoa! That's definitely Samuel's dad. He looks just like him.'

She hadn't paid much attention to the other couple in the picture when she'd first looked, only homing in on the two people she loved. 'Flipping heck.'

'So what, they had an affair. George found out, told her off about it, but they didn't fall out forever. We grew up with the man. Whatever happened back then didn't roll over into our lives. It's not a big deal.'

'Not a big deal? Are you kidding me? Samuel thinks he grew up in some Christmas advert two-point-four family where the sun always shone and everything was magical. What's he going to think now?'

'Why does he need to know?'

'Wouldn't you want to know?'

Spencer shook his head as he leaned back in the chair. 'I don't want to know anything about our parents.'

'I meant if he held all the cards and didn't tell us about Rebecca.'

'It hasn't ruined our family, Lott, but it might just upset him.'

Lottie sighed, not knowing what to do for the best. Having inside info on the Powells made her feel as though she were keeping a secret from Samuel, and that was no way to have a relationship. How could she not tell him?

'Don't stress it, Lottie.'

'I wish I didn't know about any of this, but I can't hide it from Samuel now that I know.'

'It probably happened before he was even born. Leave it alone, is my advice.'

'But what if it didn't?'

'It's in the past.'

'Do you think Rebecca ended things because she took us on? Maybe that was the reason. I wonder if we hadn't been her priority she'd have ended up with Les Powell.'

'No point going down the ifs and ands road.' Spencer pulled the book closer to him and turned the page. 'Looks like George wrote a love poem. Unrequited love, eh!'

Lottie glanced at the cream card stuck on the page. 'He was quite creative, wasn't he?'

'Stupid in love with Rebecca more like.'

'I think it's sweet. I just wish she had chosen George instead of Les.'

'She did, in a way.'

'She chose us, Spence.'

'And look how it all turned out. We got a happy family, and so did Samuel. So, Lottie, leave it alone.' He flicked through the pages, showing no signs of interest in reading George's notes, then got up to leave. 'I'm just popping next door to make us some lunch. Won't be long. Get this lot sorted so we can move on to the next task.'

Lottie pulled George's precious book back towards her as soon as Spencer left. She wanted to read his short diary entries, even if Spencer didn't, and she was glad she did, as they confirmed what she thought. Rebecca was the one to end the affair, and it was because she had taken custody of her niece and nephew.

'Oh, what a mess.'

How on earth was she going to tell Samuel? Would Hannah want to know? Maybe telling her would be the easier option. She shook her head. She couldn't do that. What would Samuel say then? It would just make matters worse.

'Oh, George. Why land this on me?'

She didn't really want to blame him for keeping evidence that she wished she hadn't witnessed. It was in her hands now, and she had to come to terms with the fact that Samuel might not take the news so well.

Flipping the pages back to the poem, she smiled at George's love for her aunt. It was heartbreaking he never got the girl, but at least he still helped her when needed and maybe they did have the occasional secret rendezvous. No one could be sure. George certainly didn't tell if they did have a canoodle behind the garden shed.

Lottie wanted to believe they cared for each other on a deeper level, as it made her past sweeter, especially the thought of Rebecca not pining away for a man she couldn't have. It felt nice to think her aunt led a happy life, single or with George. She so wished she could talk to her.

'Les blimming Powell, of all men. Oh, Rebecca, what a small world it is.' Lottie shook her head, then leaned over to silently read the poem.

*If I could travel to every port and see each pretty maid,*
*I'd feel your heart within me, and their faces would just fade.*
*If storms beached me on golden sands and I was all alone,*
*I'd think of your hand in mine, and you would bring me home.*
*When I see the stars so high, and the waves are where I stand,*
*I steady with the thought of you, being my wife and I your man.*
*If only you could hold my heart and feel the beats are simply yours,*
*You'd know you are my north star, my love, all the oceans and the shores.*

## CHAPTER 29

*Samuel*

Dinner was going to be perfect, but as Samuel perused his kitchen table and surrounding area he wondered if he'd gone overboard with the mush.

There were more red and pink roses than Lottie had in her flower shop, and the petals adorning the white tablecloth might be a bit much. The pink and white balloon arch could be pushing it, and the heart-shaped plates now seemed corny.

Samuel questioned his romance skills. It didn't look like that in his head. Perhaps if he hadn't paid someone else to do the job for him, he could have brought it to an end halfway through.

He stepped out to the hallway, following the line of rose petals all the way to his street door. The broom sprung to mind. Surely he couldn't let Lottie see the lovefest disaster, and what was that smell?

Samuel followed the sickly scent to find a pink diffuser bottle over by the wide hall mirror. On closer inspection, he knew it was a likely candidate for the bin.

'Oh my God!'

Heading back to the kitchen to lob the offender, Samuel grabbed a large paper love heart, as that could disappear as well.

He'd only made a cold chicken salad for their dinner, wanting something light to go with the heavy declaration of love he planned to hit her with, and she was due any minute. If he was going to lose some of the display, he'd better hurry. But what should go and what should stay? What would she like and what would she hate?

Samuel was fast hating it all. A sneeze was on its way, thanks to numerous blooms, and the streamers hanging from the ceiling had already come loose. He tugged one of the trails, hard, releasing half the presentation, but there was no way he was going to fetch a ladder to repair the damage.

A few bits and pieces ended up squashed in the bin, but there was still so much cheese, literally, as he eyed the platter of heart-shaped chunks side by side with plain crackers and olives he didn't even like.

'Oh, what was I thinking? She'll think I'm going to propose.' He went to fetch the vacuum cleaner, but the main gate gained attention.

Lottie had arrived.

Within one minute of her saying goodbye to Spencer and thanking him for dropping her off, her lips quirked at the decorated floor in the hallway.

'Nice touch, Romeo.'

Samuel's cheeks heated. Wait till she saw the kitchen. He thought about bypassing the room and heading to the back garden via another route, but he'd come this far so swallowed hard and waved her forward.

Lottie's face was a picture when she saw how much love had thrown up in the kitchen. He just couldn't figure out what kind of picture it was. Her eyes were wide, her lips parted, and one finger was slowly circling the air.

'Erm, I was going to—'

'I thought we were just having dinner, Sam.'

He nodded. 'We are. I wanted to be romantic, that's all.'

'Well, it's certainly . . . something.'

Samuel joined her at the table, watching her twiddle with a tiny bottle, shaped like a pair of lips that had bubbles inside. Who knew? Not him. First time he'd noticed the thing.

Lottie opened it and started to blow bubbles into his face, laughing at the same time. 'Not had these with dinner before.'

'Honestly, I don't know where half this stuff came from.'

'Did Hannah decorate?'

Samuel lowered his head sheepishly. 'No. I might have hired someone.'

Lottie laughed. 'Might have?'

Samuel had little else to say on the matter. He shrugged and went to fetch their dinner from the fridge, hoping he didn't spot any other surprises inside.

Pink champagne chilled, but with everything around them, he felt foolish offering some.

'Water?' he asked.

'Yes, please,' she replied.

Samuel sat by her side and leaned over to kiss her lips, smiling on her warm skin. Right there and then he could have told her he loved her, but he'd gone to a lot of trouble so wanted to get at least that part right.

'Hmm,' said Lottie, tucking in. 'I love your potato salad.'

'Mum's recipe.'

Lottie choked, cleared her throat, then sipped some water.

'You okay, Lottie?'

'Uh-huh.'

Something didn't seem right, and he was sure it wasn't the food, as she always appreciated anything he made for her. Life sure was easy with someone unfussy.

Samuel carried on eating, glancing up every so often to see if Lottie's expression had changed at all. It was hard to work out, as there was a combo of seriousness and nerves written all over her face, and he pondered over the idea that she might be worried he was going to bend to one knee at any given moment.

'Sorry about all this.' He circled a finger in the air.

She looked over at the balloon arch and smiled, but it was weak. 'I like it. It's funny.'

'I wasn't trying to . . . Well, I wasn't . . . It's just. I guess the hired help got the wrong idea about my idea.'

'What would you have done?'

He nodded at the table. 'One candle would suffice.'

Lottie leaned forward and blew out the other three. 'Better?'

If only it was that simple. Something was bugging her and she needed to spit it out before dessert, because there was no way he could stomach chocolate mousse and strawberries if she was about to dump him or something.

Samuel lowered his cutlery and took a mouthful of water, all the while studying her.

'You keep staring at me, Sam. Have you got something on your mind?'

He did, up until the part where the atmosphere changed, igniting a whole heap of questions.

'I was thinking the same thing, Lottie. You seem . . . off.'

She put her fork down, and he saw her swallow. 'I want to talk to you about something.'

He wished he hadn't eaten now. Something churned and it didn't exactly feel pleasant. 'Should I be worried?' Stupid question, seeing how he was way more worried than worried could be.

Lottie drew breath, then met his eyes, adding the smallest of smiles. 'I discovered something today, and I wasn't sure what to do with it, as it involves you.'

Samuel's eyebrows lifted. 'Oh?' Now he was intrigued more than anything else.

'I don't want us to keep secrets from—'

'I have no secrets from you.'

Lottie bit her bottom lip. 'I don't have any from you. Until now.'

The churning was back. What on earth could she say to settle the rattling beneath his skin? He really needed her to spit it out and calm him, but all he felt coming was a storm.

'Tell me,' he said bluntly, not meaning to sound so demanding, but he felt sick.

'I've rehearsed this in my head, but I still don't know how to tell you, Sam. So . . . I'm just going to—'

'Lottie, please!'

She took a breath, giving a slight nod. 'It's about your parents.'

That wasn't what he was expecting. 'Sorry, what?'

'I found something out about your dad.'

'So, this isn't about us?'

Lottie shook her head. 'No, but now I know, I figured it would be about us if I kept it from you.'

'You're not making any sense.'

'I was going through George's personal items, and I came across this.' She pulled a photograph out of her bag and handed it over.

Samuel looked at the picture of his parents when they were in their early-to-mid-twenties. 'George knew my parents?'

'Yes. That's him next to your dad. So, that is your dad then?'

'Uh-huh.'

'That's my aunt Rebecca.'

'With my mum.' He looked up and smiled. 'Small world.'

'Not always a happy one though.'

Samuel glanced back at the photo. 'Why do you say that?' If there were any clues in the picture, they weren't showing. He looked directly at Lottie.

'Your dad and my aunt were sleeping together behind your mum's back.'

It sounded like that was what she said, but it couldn't have been. Somehow he'd misheard, because never in a zillion years would his father do that to the love of his life. Something wasn't adding up, and he was starting to boil up.

'Do me a favour, Lottie, and just explain that crap you just shovelled at me.'

Lottie sipped her water, then pulled out two letters. 'George and Rebecca weren't on talking terms because of the affair, so he stuck this through her letterbox, and the other one is her reply. Les Powell is the name mentioned as my aunt's . . . erm, lover, for want of a better word.'

Samuel snatched them out of her hand, earning himself a frown in the process. 'You probably read it wrong.'

'I did not.'

He ignored her snap. There was no room for anything except his dad and the misunderstanding. 'My parents loved each other very much,' he told her while speed-reading.

'I'm sure they did, Sam, but sometimes these things happen.'

He snapped his head up. 'Not when you love someone. I would never . . . ' He let the words hang and went back to reading the lies.

'I'm so sorry.'

His eyes were fixed on each and every word slandering his father's name.

'I . . . I . . .' Lottie stopped talking.

'This could be another Les Powell.' He lifted the letter along with his glare. 'Did you stop to think about that before you tried to ruin my family?'

Lottie pointed at the photograph. 'They were together,' she said quietly.

'So were my parents,' he said loudly, standing abruptly.

'I didn't tell you to upset you, Sam. I just couldn't keep it from you.'

Samuel clenched his fists. 'These are lies you're bringing to me. Your aunt's fantasies, no doubt. Wanted what she couldn't have so made up stories. Probably tried to ruin their relationship. No doubt she lied to George to make him jealous or something. I bet she—'

'Don't you dare say another word about my aunt. Rebecca was the kindest, loveliest woman to walk this planet, and I'll not have you tarnish her name. People make mistakes, and she wasn't the only one in the affair.'

Samuel's arm shot out to the door. 'I want you to leave.'

'Gladly.'

He stepped out the way as Lottie headed for the street door. 'And take your lies with you.' He scrunched up the letters and tossed them her way, but they landed on the floor to her side, and Lottie, try as she might, couldn't bend far enough to reach them. He sprinted forward and placed them into her lap, getting his arm pushed away for his trouble.

Lottie stopped close to the ramp outside. 'I didn't want to have secrets between us, that's why I told you, but had I known you would react so spitefully, I'd never have told you.'

Samuel slapped his chest as Lottie reached for her phone. 'Oh, I'm the spiteful one, am I?'

'All I did was tell you the truth.' She turned her head. 'Hello, Spence. Can you come get me, please? Now.' She slammed her phone back into her bag and headed towards the main gates. 'I'm not listening to you put the sole blame on my aunt.'

Following her, Samuel continued to rant. Of all the things she had to come out and say, she said that. 'Get a kick out of destroying other people's families, do you?'

Lottie held nothing but contempt in her eyes as she spun round to face him. 'Your dad had the affair, not me, and Rebecca was the one who ended it when she took on two kids that weren't her own.' Lottie slapped her chest. 'That's how wonderful she was. She walked away from your dad to raise us instead, and you know what, even if she didn't take us on, I'm so glad she didn't end up with someone who treated her as a hobby.'

'Your aunt's a bloody liar.'

Lottie's mouth opened but then closed again. She went to the side gate and waited for it to open before heading out to the pavement.

Samuel's heart was racing, his hands shaking, and he couldn't understand why Lottie was being so cold. What did she know about his parents? Nothing, that's what. He grew up surrounded by love. They were happy. Weren't they?

'Argh!' he screamed, clutching the back of his neck while marching around in circles. He stopped, turning to the gate.

'They're my parents, Lottie. Mine. What right have you got to rip my memories to shreds?'

If she replied, he didn't hear, as he turned his back on her, stomping back to his house, but then he stopped, not wanting to leave Lottie alone, so he headed back to the side gate.

'Go away, Sam.'

'I will, once Spencer arrives.'

'I don't need babysitting.'

Samuel had no idea why he slumped to the driveway like a protestor refusing to move for traffic, but there he was, cross-legged and uncomfortable.

Lottie huffed. 'All I did was tell you what I found out today. Don't you think you could have handled it better?'

Samuel scoffed. 'Are you kidding me?'

'Do you know what, don't speak to me. I'm taking a leaf out of my aunt's book and saying goodbye to Mr Powell.'

'Is that supposed to be funny?'

'Do you see me laughing?'

Samuel sat in uncomfortable silence, exploring all the possibilities that what he had been told could be true. He shook his head at his thoughts. He lived with his parents. They were happy. If his dad didn't love his mum, he would have left her, not lived happily ever after. It didn't make sense.

'You're wrong, you know,' he said quietly.

'My aunt wasn't a liar, so you'd better not say that again.'

'I wasn't going to say anything about her,' he mumbled to himself, feeling exhausted on every level.

Adrenaline levels eased and logic crept back, forcing Samuel to take a good hard look at the two people he'd always worshipped, even more so since their death. He sniffed away the driveway dust, swiping back his hair. There was only one thing worse than the current news, and that was the row he'd just had with the woman he claimed to love.

*I shouldn't have spoken to her like that.*

It mattered now. Every snap, each harsh word, the darkness in his tone. The shock had turned to anger so quickly, he didn't see it coming, then he blamed her. Maybe he was too immature to handle serious subjects. He was pretty sure he was a grown man, but sitting on his drive, sulking, all he felt like was a complete loser. He needed to speak to Hannah. Hear her thoughts about Lottie's findings, but there was someone else he needed to speak to first. He creaked to a stand.

'Lottie.'

'Go away.'

'I'm sorry for biting your head off but—'

'Don't care.'

'I still can't get my head around—' He stopped as Spencer pulled up.

'Everything okay?' asked Spencer, looking straight at Samuel.

'Open the door, Spence. I want to go home.'

Spencer did as he was asked, lowering the ramp for Lottie to enter as Samuel approached the vehicle. 'She told you about your dad, didn't she?'

Samuel nodded as Lottie got into the car.

'Told her it wouldn't end well.' Spencer strapped her in, then closed the door.

Samuel went to the window. 'Lottie, talk to me.'

Lottie lowered her head.

His mouth gaped as he watched them drive away. Everything hurt way more than his thumping head, and now he had to tell his little sister that their parents' love life was tarnished.

# CHAPTER 30

*Lottie*

The pram race was due to start in half-hour, and the participants were all eager to go, chatting away happily out front of the Jolly Pirate. Everyone was in fancy dress and the happy atmosphere cheered Lottie up no end.

Ever since her argument with Samuel the week before, she hadn't been able to smile from the inside. All her friends knew what had happened, and Spencer wasn't talking about it.

Why Rebecca's private business had suddenly become Lottie's was all down to George, and she only blamed herself for poking her nose in. She couldn't help but have the hump because her aunt's love choices had now affected her own.

Each night Lottie fell asleep with thoughts of Samuel, and he was the first thing to spring to mind on waking. It really was quite irritating, not to mention heartbreaking. She missed him so much.

She really had sprung the affair on him. Was it any wonder he had been all over the place?

Lottie couldn't keep going over it in her head. She had her own life to worry about, which right now included winning the pram race with her brother. They had been messing about like that since they were kids. They had it in the bag, she was sure.

Robson was on the microphone, giving instructions, and Sophie was waving people forward to the start line, which was where Jed stood in the middle of the closed-off road.

Lottie adjusted her mermaid costume as Spencer placed her into a large, old-fashioned, grey-and-chrome pram. She sank as deep as possible, faffing with the small padding either side of her hips.

'I hope you're sure about this, sis. There's still time to back out.'

'No way, Spence. Stop being a baby.' She laughed. 'Hey, do you remember when we used to do this down Berry Hill?'

'Yeah, Rebecca would come after us, flapping her hands like Kermit the Frog.'

'I wonder if she's watching now?'

Spencer looked at the overcast sky. 'Probably.'

Lottie always felt a warm and snuggly feeling whenever she thought about her aunt watching over her. She'd had many thoughts about Samuel's family since they fell out, and she came to realize that it didn't matter what kind of family anyone had, as long as they loved each other. Rebecca, George, and Spencer made her family the best, and she wished she could have a family of her own one day, where each member loved one another too.

Samuel hadn't contacted her at all, which to be fair was what she had asked for.

Ever since she was a little girl she wanted to fall in love and live happily ever after, and she thought she stood a chance with Samuel, but her dreams didn't contain immaturity, and they certainly had no room for anyone who wasn't a team player. Problems would come up in their relationship, that was a given, but if he was going to turn on her instead of work with her to sort said problems, then he wasn't the one for her after all. It didn't stop her missing him though.

She glanced up at her big brother, dressed like a clown. He was definitely a team player and would make someone a great husband, if only he wasn't so afraid of commitment. She really wished Spencer would fall in love and settle down. It would do him the world of good.

Ginny bounced over, dressed like a nurse from the 1940s. 'Georgie said he's got a bungee cord in the boot of his car. I was thinking we could tie you down with it.'

'No, thanks. I wish everyone would stop worrying. It's like you're putting the mockers on me.'

Ginny patted her shoulder. 'Ooh, no. I wish you all the luck out there. I've got Alice pushing me, so I'm the only one who should worry. We all know how clumsy she can be.'

Lottie knew Matt was supposed to be pushed by Samuel, but she hadn't seen him around. 'Who's pushing Matt?'

Ginny scanned the crowds. 'Sam. I can't see him, but he was here a minute ago.'

It wasn't just the pram that felt uncomfortable now. Lottie's guts churned. A mixture of excitement for the race and nerves rattling in case she saw Samuel, made the worst cocktail.

Alice came over, dressed in her mum's handmade creation that was supposed to be an orange octopus but looked more like a battered cod.

Spencer flapped one of her arms. 'I think you've lost one, Al.'

'I think I lost more than that when I put this thing on.'

Lottie laughed, gazing down at her long shiny green fishtail flopped over the end of the pram. 'At least you're not a prawn like Sophie. I have no idea where she managed to find that costume.'

Alice glanced over the road. 'She's advertising her shop. Haven't you seen what's written on her back? Sea Shanty Shack.' She tried to check out her own back. 'Did Mum put anything on me for the Treasure Chest?'

Spencer spun her around in a circle while laughing. 'Nope. You're all alien octopus.'

Alice slapped his arm, then waddled off to Ginny and their multicoloured pram.

'Right,' said Spencer, tapping Lottie's shoulder. 'Let's get over to the start line.'

Lottie grabbed the sides of the pram as it began to move bumpily through the beer garden. 'Goodness, this is a bit springy.'

Jed was standing at the front, holding a large Jolly Roger flag and sporting the Captain Birdseye look.

Robson's voice was loud but not always clear, as the crowd was noisy and raring to go.

There were quite a few prams squashed together, balloons tied to most, and glitter, confetti, and streamers splayed all over the road. Competitors playfully nudged each other, but no one knocked Lottie's pram, which made her feel left out a bit. She hated being treated like china but understood where they were coming from.

Samuel and Matt caught her eye as they joined the huddle, and she pretended not to see them, letting her peripheral vision do all the work. Her lip quirked at their bride and groom outfits, then dropped as the thought of never marrying Samuel loomed. He looked good in a top hat.

'You ready, sis?'

Lottie jumped out of her daydream about Samuel as Spencer touched her shoulder. Nodding, she straightened herself, gripped the sides, and took a breath. With a bit of luck not only would the residents of Port Berry raise a shedload of money for the Happy to Help Hub, but she'd beat Samuel in the race as well.

Robson read out the course one more time, then told everyone to get ready before letting off the klaxon that sounded like a damaged foghorn.

And they were off.

Lottie squealed with excitement as Spencer took the first turn, heading along Harbour End Road at full speed ahead. She wasn't mindful of the others racing alongside her, because she was far too busy concentrating on leaning the same way as Spencer when needed.

People lined the pavements, cheering and clapping for their friends and family members, and just as the front line made it to the bottom of Berry Hill, Lottie visualized Rebecca and George standing there, waving and applauding their effort.

Pride overshadowed all else, including Samuel and Matt overtaking them at the turn.

'I saw them, Spence,' Lottie called. 'Rebecca and George were waving, and Rebecca said move your bloody arse.'

Spencer burst out laughing, then upped his pace.

Lottie lifted her arms as the race hit the back roads, leaving the harbour behind. 'Woo-hoo!' she cheered, clapping for good measure.

'Hold on, Lott.'

Just as she went to grip the sides of the pram, Spencer made a sharp turn, nudged the low curb with a wheel, dipped into a drain, and tumbled to the narrow pavement to his right. The pram flipped, Lottie went flying, and Spencer shot up to sprint to her side.

'Ow!' Lottie cried.

Spencer fought with her fishtail, the ruffles around his neck, then her mane of a pink wig. 'Is it your back?'

'No, it's my arm.'

'Oh God, is that your bone? I'm going to throw up.'

Even though she had been warned, she looked at her arm anyway to see the mentioned bone, then she also wanted to hurl.

'Do something, Spence.'

'We're going to the hospital. Hold on.' He picked up the pram, then her, got a shove for his trouble, as he knocked her bad arm, making her cry out, placed her back in the seat, then limped in his big clown shoes all the way back to Berry Hill to get the car.

# CHAPTER 31

*Samuel*

Samuel and Matt cheered as they made it over the finish line. A small crowd gathered around them, patting their shoulders and helping Matt out of his cramped position, all tangled in white lace and taffeta.

'Oh, I need a back massage after that,' said Matt, rubbing his lower spine.

Sophie nudged her way through the masses to swing her arms around Matt's neck and pepper his cheek with kisses.

Samuel wished he had Lottie wrapped around him. He perused the prams coming in behind him, hoping to catch a glimpse of her. She'd ignored him all morning, he was sure. Not that he made any attempt to speak to her. What could he say anyway? 'You make one hell of a sexy mermaid. Sorry I called your aunt a liar.'

Earlier in the week, he'd had a therapy session with Jan, which only made him feel worse, as Jan had pointed out how he needed to start learning how to work with a partner. She pointed out, quite bluntly, that when problems appeared, he should join forces with Lottie to solve them, not turn his frustrations on to her. It made sense. Jan always made sense. He never should have blamed Lottie for telling him something that was hard to hear. All she had done was not keep a secret from him.

Samuel watched Matt disappear into the hustle and bustle, taking the pram and most of the public with him. He seemed to be well liked, and Samuel wondered what the locals thought of him, especially as he was an outsider to them. Not that he cared. Oh, who was he kidding? He had started to care very much. Port Berry had grown on him, and he wanted nothing more than to fit in, especially with Lottie and her friends. Matt made it work, so he could too. He hoped.

'I can be a team player,' he mumbled to himself, walking over to the pier to stare out to sea.

The race was a breeze and a blast, and Samuel had returned to the start delivering Matt in one piece. As far as he was concerned, that showed good team player qualities.

He sat down, dangling his legs over the edge, and thought back to the first time Lottie was in his home. Grimacing, he wished he could turn back time as his notebook flashed though his weary mind.

Jan had told him he'd been working by himself for so long, he'd forgotten how to work with others, but he didn't agree, reminding her he had Hannah. As far as he could see, Hannah was his team mate just as much as Lottie was Spencer's, but Jan had explained the difference. Lottie had Rebecca to parent her, so Spencer still held the position of brother. Whereas Hannah had no guardian, just her big brother. Without seeing it happen, Samuel became a single parent, fighting the world alone.

He watched the calm waves rolling his way and wondered what it would be like to sail around the world. How surreal it would be if he could actually take on such a task.

Breathing out a quiet laugh, Samuel shook his head at himself. At his life. What had he morphed into? How had trauma caused such an odd condition?

At least Hannah was happy, and it was time he loosened the reins. He decided to tell her he was going to move out and let her have the house. Felix was there every day with her, so they could perhaps build a life together without him in the way. It made sense for Hannah to stay, as it was adapted for her needs. He could live anywhere. Perhaps his boat, like Jed.

The boats bobbing in the near distance encouraged the thought.

'How hard can it be?'

Music started blaring from the pub at the same time as the smell of onions and sizzling sausages wafted over to the pier.

Samuel's stomach rumbled. He decided he'd have lunch with his Port Berry friends, who he was pleased were still talking to him even though he'd fallen out with Lottie, then he'd find Hannah and tell her his idea. At least he'd be able to make one person happy, although he was pretty sure Matt appreciated him for completing the race with him in one piece.

The day was shaping up nicely. The run had certainly cleared away a few cobwebs, and Matt was so easy to get along with, it made the race so much more fun than he'd anticipated.

Samuel smiled at the sky, watching the gulls swoop closer to the food at the pub. He stood, stretching his arms and rolling his shoulders. 'Time to change my life once more,' he whispered into the warm breeze. 'And this time, I'm going to stay on track.'

It wasn't just his sister he wanted a conversation with, he desperately needed to talk to Lottie as well. She deserved the biggest apology and so much more.

Samuel made his way back to the pub, wanting to drown his sorrows but knowing that wasn't the best option. He had work to do, for himself and for the sake of those he cared for deeply.

Hannah was in the food queue, and the scent from the grill made Samuel want to eat first. He figured he could join his sister and Felix, then hit them with the news.

'Hey, sis.'

Hannah tugged his arm. 'I want to talk to you now the pram race is over. Come over here.' She moved him to one side. 'I was going to tell you last night but you went to bed early, so I thought I'd let you enjoy the race, then talk. I looked through Mum's diaries to see if I could find anything about this affair business. And I did. It's all true, Sam.'

He sighed quietly. 'I figured it was.'

'Mum was heartbroken, but she forgave him in the end.' She smiled softly. 'I know it's sad, for all of us, but they gave us a good life. We had a happy home, Sam.'

'We did.'

'I called Lottie last night and told her what I'd found.'

'I need to speak to—'

Matt nudged his arm. 'Mate, have you heard? Lottie's in hospital.'

The flushed cheeks Samuel had acquired from the race evaporated immediately. 'What?'

'She fell out the pram. She's . . .'

Samuel didn't hear the rest of Matt's sentence, because he was running again, this time to his car, parked a few streets away due to all the road closures for the race.

With a pounding heart, light head, and shaky hands, he drove to the hospital, with little thought for anything but Lottie. Every bad assumption hit him, one after the other. He couldn't lose her. He just couldn't. She didn't even know how much he loved her.

Samuel beat himself up all the way to A & E, trying hard to remain calm and not bite anyone's head off, as the hospital staff were so slow in informing him of Lottie's whereabouts.

A blue curtain was wrapped around a cubicle, and Samuel took a deep breath before tugging the material to one side to see if Lottie was there. Third time lucky. The last thing he needed was another patient telling him to sod off. It wasn't his fault the wrong cubicle was pointed out to him. He was just following directions.

Lottie was asleep on the bed. Her arm in a cast, and Samuel was sure his heart left his body. He quickly grabbed her hand, avoiding her bad arm, and kissed her knuckles, but she didn't stir.

'Lottie?' he whispered, moving her fringe back.

She remained asleep.

Samuel felt sick. Quickly, he looked around for a medical chart, not that he'd understand any of it, but he had to know if she was in a coma or something. Surely there would be something around the bed that would at least tell him that much, but no.

Flopping to the blue armchair by the bed, Samuel hit himself in the forehead with his palm. What had he done? How had he messed up so badly? The love of his life was unconscious in hospital and there was nothing he could do to fix any of it.

Samuel scraped the chair closer to the bed so he could hold Lottie's hand. He thought about what doctors he could bring over to the hospital to help, as the ones around him clearly had no clue, seeing how they'd just left her alone. At least she wasn't hooked up to any breathing apparatus. She didn't even have a drip. That must be a good sign. He didn't know. He couldn't think straight.

'I'm so sorry, Lottie,' he murmured on the back of her hand. 'I love you so much. Please don't leave me. You're the best thing that's ever happened to me. I don't want a life you're not in. Please wake up. Please.'

# CHAPTER 32

*Lottie*

Spencer said he was off to get them some lunch, which Lottie was really looking forward to, even if it was hospital food. She felt totally drained just from all the sitting around waiting. Some food was just what the doctor ordered, then she would be signed out and ready to go home.

Lottie yawned, feeling the effects of the pain medication. Maybe a catnap would help. No one would mind, surely. She was lying on a hospital bed, after all. Patients were expected to sleep half the day. She closed her eyes.

Samuel entered her dream, talking about love and regrets or something. His voice was muffled at first, then someone turned up the volume.

She wasn't dreaming at all. Samuel was there at her bedside, holding her hand, opening his soul. Everything was a bit blurry at first, but after a few blinks, her vision cleared. He looked so sweet with his head buried in her palm, she had to smile. She closed her eyes, absorbing his presence for a moment.

'I had plans for us, Lottie. I wanted everything with you,' he said softly, melting her heart.

His soft tones and gentle kisses on her hand relaxed her more than the medication.

'You need to wake up so I can tell you how much I love you.'

*I love you too, Sam.*

'I had therapy in the week with Jan. She pointed out where I go wrong and has shown me some techniques on how not to react before thinking. See, Lottie, I'm learning how to play nicely with others.'

She tried not to smile at the laughter in his voice. There was no way of knowing if he was looking at her.

'I've come up with an idea. I'm going to move. Let Hannah and Felix have the house, and—'

Lottie's head shot off the pillow, making Samuel jump. 'You can't move away.'

There was about five different expressions that rolled through his amber eyes within the space of two seconds. She was sure the spin would land on anger, but he leaned over, cupped her face, then kissed her hard, making her even more light-headed than she was when she woke.

His eyes shone as he sat back down and held her hand, which she took as a good sign.

'Please don't move away, Sam,' she whispered, her throat dry and her heart thumping.

Sam's lips curled ever so slightly. 'I'm agoraphobic. It's a given I won't go far.'

She forgot that part, but still. 'Where will you go?'

'I don't have any immediate plans. I haven't spoken to Hannah yet. How are you?' He finally broke eye contact to glance at her cast.

'I broke my arm,' she replied.

'So I see. Anything else?'

'A few bruises. Nothing much.'

'And where's Spencer?'

'He went to get us some lunch. I think I fell asleep.'

'You think?' His lips twitched.

Lottie tried to shrug but found it difficult with one arm in a sling and Samuel owning the other.

'Hmm,' he muttered.

It was a tough battle, but Lottie's smile won the war. She couldn't hold back any longer. 'So, you love me, eh?'

There was a glimmer of amusement staring back at her. 'Hmm.'

Her grin was so wide, her cheeks ached. 'Well, I am adorable.'

'Is that right?'

Lottie dropped her smile, knowing they needed to talk. 'Sam—'

'It doesn't matter. I just want you to know how sorry I am for the way I behaved. It was childish, uncalled for, and damn right rude.'

'You had a shock.'

'Don't stick up for me.'

'I'm sorry for the way I behaved too.'

Samuel kissed the back of her hand.

'Did Hannah tell you she called me last night?' added Lottie.

Samuel nodded. 'She told me she apologized on my behalf, which I was annoyed about, as I can speak for myself. She also mentioned she'd told you about my mum's diary.'

'At least it confirms everything for you.'

'Yes.' Samuel lightly squeezed her hand. 'My mum had written a diary since she was sixteen. Hannah knew where to look for evidence.'

'Yes. Hannah said your mum had written about her heartbreak. Your dad had confessed.'

Samuel lowered his head. 'I'm sorry for how I reacted. I'll never argue with you again.'

'I doubt that's true. If we plan to spend a lifetime together, I reckon we'll have loads of disagreements and—'

'You plan to spend your life with me?'

Lottie offered a warm smile. 'We love each other, don't we?'

'Yes, but—'

'No buts. We're different, you and me, so it might take time learning how to connect in some places.'

Samuel lifted his brow as he grinned. 'I think we got the gist of connection.'

Warmth filled her at the memories of the nights he'd spent in her bed. He really was getting the hang of things staying away from home. 'Not that. You know what I mean.'

'I do, but I want you to know I don't plan on us arguing our way through life.' He tapped his chest. 'When life throws us lemons, I won't be the one squirting them in your eye. I'm a team player now. We'll make lemonade together.'

Lottie bit her lip as she laughed at the visualization of him squirting a lemon at her. 'We all have a lot to learn when it comes to partnering up with someone. When Spencer and I took over the flower shop, we bickered no end, and we've always worked pretty well with each other, but the pressure was on, we were grieving for our aunt, and we took our frustrations out on each other for the first couple of months. Then George stepped in and sorted us out, bringing us back to the team we'd always been.

'You're right, we all have a lot to learn, and I'm glad I know about my dad. If nothing else, it's kind of made me feel better about always striving to be as perfect as I believed him to be. I fought long and hard to make them proud of how I was handling things, especially with Hannah.'

'She speaks so highly of you. You've obviously done a great job raising her.'

Samuel nodded. 'Jan mentioned that. Told me I'd become Hannah's dad.'

'I guess you are, in a way, and she's lucky to have you. You stepped up, did everything you could for her, and you made sure she was happy. She is definitely a bubbly character.'

'I felt a little lost when she told me she loved Felix.'

'It doesn't mean she no longer needs you in her life.'

'I know. I'm just not good with change.'

'Oh, I think you've done a great job. Look at your life. You quit uni when your parents died, got more than one job, looked after your sister, made yourself a millionaire, you're fighting demons, and me sometimes, and you go to therapy.'

Samuel shrugged. 'Just trying to get by. Aren't we all?'

'I'm proud of you, Sam,' she whispered, moving his hand to her mouth.

'You make me want to try harder. I look at you and everything you've been through, and I wish I had half your guts and positive mental attitude. You're amazing, Lottie. You're inspirational.'

They shared a smile and a kiss.

'What are we going to do, Sam?'

'About?'

'Us.'

'Tell me what you see when you look at your future.'

Lottie chewed her bottom lip for a moment. 'A happy family, a prosperous business, and knocking down the wall between my house and George's so I can make it into one, as I can't bear the thought of anyone else living in his home. What do you see?'

'Hmm, me making waves over in Devon before conquering the rest of England, and, what else? Ah, yes, you.'

'Would you consider making some waves in Port Berry?'

'As long as you're there.'

'I'll be there.'

'Then that's where I'll move to, and when we're ready, you can make some room in that big house of yours for me. Sound like a plan.'

'Best plan ever.'

'You know, Miss Jordan, I think I'm going to enjoy building a life with you.'

Lottie flashed him her cheeky smile. 'It's the mermaid costume, isn't it?'

'It's certainly something.'

'You could come home with me, stay till my arm gets better, see how we get on living together. That's another plan.' She watched him smile.

'I like that plan.'

'See, we've made a good start.'

Samuel nodded. 'And we'll have one of those happily ever after jobs as well.'

'We've already got one, Sam. When you think about it, we both created good lives for ourselves after everything went belly-up. We're fighters, you and me, and together we'll be unstoppable.'

'You should write self-help books.'

'Perhaps that'll be my next task.'

'Perhaps your next task should be kissing me.'

Lottie happily obliged. 'I love you, Sam,' she mumbled on his lips.

'I love you too. Now, let's get you back in your hot wheels and get out of here. I really hate the smell of these places.'

'I have to wait for the doctor or nurse or someone to say I can go.'

Samuel went to stand, but Lottie tugged him back. 'Don't go. Spencer will be back in a minute. He can find out. Stay and talk to me.'

'What do you want to talk about?'

'Where's your top hat? You can't get married without it.'

'I'd get married butt naked if it meant I could marry you.'

Lottie laughed. 'That's got to be the strangest proposal ever.'

Samuel frowned. 'That wasn't my proposal.'

'You can't take it back now. So, where's your hat?'

'Lost it during the race, but at least I'm still in one piece.'

'It can be quite dangerous all this fundraising malarkey, can't it?'

Samuel gently stroked the top of her sling. 'You can say that again.'

'At least we raised loads for the Hub, and we're sharing some with the Food Bank Café.'

'And on behalf of the Les Powell Trust, I thank you.'

'You're welcome. Now, what fundraiser should we do next?'

'How about one where we sponsor you to stay in bed.'

Lottie squeezed his hand. 'You and me in bed all day. I could get on board with that.'

'Ever since I met you, you've been zooming along the road, racing around a track, meeting strangers from online dating, and now flying out of prams. I swear, you'll be the death of me, Lottie Jordan.'

'Perhaps I could make some more paintings to sell, just to give your poor old heart a rest.'

'I'd appreciate that.'

'Only if you do something for me.'

'Ah, a negotiation. I like your style. What do you want?'

'I want you to talk about agoraphobia on a video for the Hub's website. I honestly believe it makes things worse for people when they hide their conditions.'

'Jan said the same sort of thing. Well, just so you know, I made an executive decision today while staring out to sea. I'm moving on to the next level of my life, so you've got yourself a deal.'

'Oh, Sam, are you really ready to open up about this? I know what I just said, but I don't want to put pressure on you.'

He nodded and kissed her hand. 'I'm ready. It's time I moved forward with this. You can document my journey if you like. Maybe it'll inspire someone else to push on their invisible walls.'

'I love it. You're amazing, you know that.'

Samuel twiddled his cravat. 'I'm getting there.'

'Oh, Sam, we really are moving forward, aren't we?'

'Yep.'

'Let's make a pact.'

'About what?'

Lottie grinned. 'To love and respect each other forever.'

'Do you want to spit shake on that?'

'No. A nod and a kiss is fine.'

Samuel nodded, then kissed her lips, melting her heart once more.

Lottie snuggled her face into his hand as it came up to lightly brush over her cheek, closing her eyes for a moment. All was well in the world again, even if she was lying in hospital with a broken arm.

She could hear George telling her to enjoy the love she'd found, and she could see Rebecca agreeing. Whatever kind of relationship they had, they proved that partnerships came in all shapes and sizes, and Lottie figured if they could make a happy family without romance added into the mix, then she could achieve anything.

'You know, Lottie,' said Samuel softly. 'I might not ever be able to show you the world.'

Lottie smiled. 'That's okay, Sam. Now you're moving to Port Berry, I have everything I need at home.'

## THE END

# ACKNOWLEDGEMENTS

This story is dedicated to everyone on a healing journey. You are powerful, resilient, problem-solving masters who know how to survive the deepest, darkest pits of hell. Remember that next time you doubt your strength.

\* \* \*

Huge thanks goes out to the Choc Lit/Joffe Books team for their help, support, and encouragement for the Port Berry series and my author journey. Much appreciated.

\* \* \*

I'm also sending a cheer to my readers who are a constant support to my author journey. I want you all to know that I'm so completely and utterly grateful to each and every one of you.

\* \* \*

As always, sending lots of love and light your way. Keep reading. It's good for the soul.

# THE CHOC LIT STORY

Established in 2009, Choc Lit is an independent, award-winning publisher dedicated to creating a delicious selection of quality women's fiction.

We have won 18 awards, including Publisher of the Year and the Romantic Novel of the Year, and have been shortlisted for countless others. In 2023, we were shortlisted for Publisher of the Year by the Romantic Novelists' Association.

All our novels are selected by genuine readers. We are proud to publish talented first-time authors, as well as established writers whose books we love introducing to a new generation of readers.

In 2023, we became a Joffe Books company. Best known for publishing a wide range of commercial fiction, Joffe Books has its roots in women's fiction. Today it is one of the largest independent publishers in the UK.

We love to hear from you, so please email us about absolutely anything bookish at choc-lit@joffebooks.com

If you want to hear about all our bargain new releases, join our mailing list: www.choc-lit.com